THE GYPSY TALISMAN

THE GYPSY TALISMAN

A Victorian Romantic Suspense Novel

Evelyn Roberts Brooks

iUniverse, Inc.
New York Lincoln Shanghai

The Gypsy Talisman
A Victorian Romantic Suspense Novel

iUniverse books may be ordered through booksellers or by contacting:

iUniverse
2021 Pine Lake Road, Suite 100
Lincoln, NE 68512
www.iuniverse.com
1-800-Authors (1-800-288-4677)

This is a work of fiction. All of the characters, names, incidents, organizations and dialogue in this novel are either the products of the author's imagination or are used fictitiously.

ISBN-13: 978-0-595-40279-3 (pbk)
ISBN-13: 978-0-595-84653-5 (ebk)
ISBN-10: 0-595-40279-8 (pbk)
ISBN-10: 0-595-84653-X (ebk)

Printed in the United States of America

In memory of
my dear parents
Jean Kirtley and Carl Roberts
(1913-2001)   (1911-1992)
who taught me a love of books

CHAPTER 1

The strange and tragic events at Kenwick Manor in the spring of 1861 actually had their origin in a precipitous decision I had made six weeks earlier. In the interim was a period of deceptive calm which gave no premonition of what was to come. Circumstances in my life had changed, leaving me not only orphaned by widowed.

Thinking back, I recall that after I returned from Easter services, the rest of the day passed without fanfare in my black-wreathed London home near Hyde Park. Being nineteen years of age and relatively sheltered from life for all that I was a town woman, I was unaware of the danger in tempting Providence by wishing for more excitement.

Perhaps I would not have been so annoyed at the enforced lack of gaiety had I known how soon my life would drastically change, or had I been grieving my husband's death in a more conventional sense. Widowhood did affect me, of course, but primarily by its repercussions: Edward Horton Whitney had left several unwelcome surprises for his young bride when he died nearly a year earlier in a hunting accident.

Since my attendance at social engagements in this stage of half-mourning was only acceptable if the occasion were serious, involving the immediate family, I had to forego spring parties and rides in the park with the other young people in my circle. In any case, I had always been too much of a bluestocking to have many close friends, and now I would not want them to suspect my current circumstances. I could not countenance their censure or curiosity.

Longing for a diversion of some kind, I put on an old party dress which still fit my slender frame, and had tea with Ellen Armstrong, my maid-of-all-work.

We ate in the back parlor, one of the few rooms in the tall house that was still habitable.

Ellen was more of a taskmaster than a servant, having been my childhood governess. She pursed her lips in disapproval at my pink gown and the matching ribbons in my unruly chestnut-brown curls. "You are being both obstinate and unreasonable," she said. Short and sturdy, her fair hair greying at the temples, Ellen was a Quaker who believed in gender equality and coeducation. However, she also had a firm grasp on what was proper for a young widow of quality, and was determined to keep me on the straight and reverential path.

I was restless that day, and paced the floor, my heels clacking loudly on the bare wood, the carpets having been sold months ago. The crinoline cage beneath my skirts swayed gently as I walked past shelves empty of any and all valuable curios or silver pieces. Bitterness washed over me. Not only was my financial situation perilous but my life was utterly dull.

"I am so tired of this hypocrisy!" I snatched a sandwich from the tray. "There's no one in the house but you and Dora to see that I am not strictly following the rules about what colour gown I may wear and which engagements it is proper for me to accept. Even if a caller should deign to arrive, which will never happen again because I'm a social pariah, surely everyone has guessed that I married for duty, not love. Papa thought Mr. Whitney was a good choice to continue the family trade. If Papa were still alive—"

"Your father would disapprove."

"Yes, he would cringe to see the mockery of my life and to see his house being gobbled alive by creditors!" Sobered by the reality of my predicament, I poured another cup of tea and sat heavily, sinking into a foul mood that even a party dress could not elevate.

Ellen cut into my dreary thoughts. "What will you do when there is nothing left to sell?"

Events had so ordered it that after my husband died, debtors had flocked to my door like vultures. Little by little, in one miserable wave of discovery after another, I had learned the extent of the financial ruin Edward had wrought from the dowry I brought to the marriage. It didn't seem possible that anything else could go wrong. Then I found out Edward had not only mortgaged my family home, but had also signed over to a gambling house the jewelry business established by my grandfather.

For nearly a year, I had been able to maintain a *facade* of normalcy by letting go all servants but Ellen and Dora the cook, and by discreetly selling whatever in the house would fetch a decent price, from silver candlesticks to gilt-painted antique chairs to gold-threaded ball gowns.

I was determined to hold onto my family home, one way or another. The first necessity was to secure enough funds to ease my debt, and the second was to ensure a continued livelihood to support myself and my household. The only sensible course for a young lady in my position was to procure a rich husband. Once that fateful idea seized me, I was filled with elation. The veil of uncertainty over my future suddenly lifted. I decided that as soon as my year of mourning was over, in only three more weeks, I would begin the hunt for a man in earnest.

I glanced up from my ruminations and plotting, to find Ellen eyeing me speculatively. "What?" I asked with a practiced air of innocence. "What is it, Ellen?"

"I will find out eventually."

"Perhaps."

She looked at me in indignation. "You've never been able to keep a secret from me."

"There's no secret about it," I said, enjoying the rare chance to tantalize her. "Your loyalty is going to be rewarded soon."

One on another, the days passed with no significant change in my fortune. A fortnight later, Ellen came into my bedroom with the morning mail as I was breakfasting on a meager meal of leftovers from supper. I picked the gristle from my teeth. "Anything of interest?"

"More bills," she replied.

"I suppose it is time to sell that Vermeer painting which was such a favourite of my mother's." I sighed and wiped my mouth with yesterday's napkin. Even laundry had become too expensive and I ran the house with the strictest economy.

Ellen threw open the shutters and let in the noise of the street below. I heard a familiar voice outside, talking to the chandler about the quality of his beeswax and wicks. It was the voice of my neighbor Wilhelmina Jersey, a cheerful, rotund woman in her mid-thirties. I thought for a moment of her situation, reflecting that I had never known her to be out of mourning. Both she and her husband came from large families, and it seemed that just as the months gave way to a time when half-mourning colours would be permissible in her wardrobe, the death of an in-law or uncle would send her back to black.

When my husband died so suddenly, I was at a loss. Wilhelmina had bustled in and taken me under her wing. Escorting me to a mourning warehouse where she was a valued customer, she procured the best prices for me and unraveled my confusion over all that was necessary to purchase for my husband's funeral.

Everyone who learned of Edward's death felt sorry for me because I was only eighteen at the time. No doubt they assumed I had been left well-provided for, and would continue with a life basically unchanged, at least in the financial sense.

I was determined that there would be no whiff of scandal about me, but with each passing day, my situation became more desperate. If my parents had only lived! But my older brother Miles had been one of the twenty-two-thousand British soldiers killed during the Crimean War when I was still a schoolgirl, and after his death my parents were shattered souls. My mother perished of a broken heart within months of the tragic news. The doctor said it was influenza, but even though I was only twelve at the time, I knew better. She died of grief for her beloved son, and thereafter my father became a shell of his former exuberant and expansive self. He aged greatly and walked in a stooped manner, like a rheumatic old man.

Earlier, when I was about ten years of age, my mother had hired Ellen to be my governess. After my mother's death, Ellen indulged me by letting my studies drift away from geography and mathematics, and toward literature. We would spend the days reading amiably together, then discussing the plight of Jane Eyre or Oliver Twist. I silently compared my grief to theirs, and drew strength from the stories. It was only later that it occurred to me Ellen had tried in her own quiet way to heal my sorrow by selecting those very books on purpose.

I grew up in this tall house with my father and a full staff of servants. As the years passed, Ellen taught me how to oversee an orderly household, how to manage a staff and be mistress of a tranquil home. I carefully left the bedrooms of my mother and my brother untouched, in veneration of their lives. At times, particularly in the early days when their deaths were still fresh wounds, I would enter their rooms and breathe in slowly of the silent stale air, as if I could somehow communicate with them. For a few moments, I would feel comforted by old memories of happier times.

When I was seventeen, my father became seriously ill with consumption and began putting his affairs in order. He seemed oddly contented, as if he had already denounced this life for the next and would not loiter in this realm much longer. I would hold his hand and stroke his cheek, and we would talk of Mother and Miles, and the tears would spill down our cheeks. In the midst of bittersweet sorrow, however, it was necessary to be practical and thus his speech turned to plans for my future welfare.

My heart filled with trepidation. If I had been fortunate to be born a boy, my father would have simply turned the house and the family business over to me, with perhaps an older mentor and also a solicitor to help with legal matters until I came of age. However, being a mere female, I needed a protector no matter how much I railed inwardly against society's stricture. I cried on Ellen's shoulder that it was unfair, and though she empathized, she knew I could not change the rules overnight. Time and again she would remind me that the day would come when women would have equal footing with their brothers, but that time was not today.

I think that enduring so much loss while still young affects one's outlook, and makes one more willing to tramp behind the banner of Duty rather than drift after the dreams of a capricious or lackadaisical heart. Perhaps it makes life simpler when the choice is limited to one of responsibility. After the deaths of my only sibling and then my mother, at times I would be overcome by melancholia, even in the midst of an ordinary task such as shopping for ribbons or writing out the week's menus for Dora.

It was in such a sad and distracted mood that I heard my father's rambling description of a widower he had met before his illness, by the name of Edward Whitney. Papa's account of this stranger, who was past the impetuosity of youth but not yet in his dotage, was interspersed with racking coughs of the consumption soon to take his life. When my father rasped out the word 'wedding,' I dutifully nodded my acquiescence.

Thus with only a slight movement of my head, I became betrothed to a supercilious man aged forty-two whom I privately loathed upon our first meeting. But I took comfort from the knowledge that it pleased my father and so, with little ado, I found myself hastily married to a businessman whose first wife had died some ten years earlier.

At parties during our brief engagement, rumours drifted towards me that Edward had an unsavory past involving other women, and even an illegitimate child from his youth, 'a son' someone whispered, but no one presented facts and it was too late in any case. I had no power to refuse the marriage. Feeling only that it was my filial duty to fulfill my father's dying wish, I became Mrs. Edward Whitney.

If only I had been born a male, my fortune would have been different. As Ellen would point out, quoting the founder of her religion, George Fox: "Art thou a child of Light, and hast thou walked in the Light, and what thou speakest, is it inwardly from God?" Whenever I railed against my oppressive fate in being Mrs. Whitney, she would quietly tell me to cease saying 'if only' so often. She would remind me firmly that if I walked in the Light, all would be well for me.

Since I continued living in the home of my childhood, and Ellen remained as my personal maid, I let myself drift into a fantasy in which I was the despondent princess held captive by a cold cruel man and destined to know only sorrow. In fact, Edward was rarely home, and my days and nights were lonely. Other girls in my set were still unmarried and I was suddenly outside their circle of activities. They envied my marital status. I was outside the circle of the married women in the neighborhood as well, since they were busy doting on their children and entertaining their husband's friends and performing charitable works. Thus subtly outcast from both groups, I had little to fill the hours each day but reading, and moping.

Edward frequently came in after midnight, smelling of liquor and cigars. Eager for company of any sort, having listened keenly for his arrival, I'd rush out in my dressing gown, and pepper him with questions about the play he'd gone to see or the people he'd met with, and beg him to take me the next time. With barely a mumbled greeting, he'd brush me aside to go to his own room, where he would sleep until noon the following day, depleted by the excesses of his dissolute life. I took some comfort in the knowledge that my father had died without knowing what kind of husband he had pressed upon me.

My heart yearned for the sweet romance I sighed over in novels and in my dreams. I prayed that soon Prince Charming would storm the path to my town house door and rescue me. In a sense, when Edward's death came after only a few months of marriage, it had seemed to be the first part of the fairy tale coming true. Now it was up to me to find my elusive Prince Charming, and find him fast.

After opening the other draperies, Ellen took the breakfast tray from me, and I took the mail from her. After glancing over the bills, I'd have gladly kept the tray.

"I don't know where all these expenses come from," I said. "I haven't entertained since Mr. Whitney's funeral lunch. I haven't bought new clothes. I'm living on air!"

Ellen looked apologetic. "Dora and I do have to eat."

"I'm not admonishing you. Even Dora has lost weight and if my cook is not getting enough to eat, it is certain no one else is."

"You must do what thousands of other women in your situation do, indeed what I had to do, to keep a watertight roof over my head and adequate money in my purse to save for the day when I can no longer be of service."

I automatically hushed her, having told her countless times that I would never turn her out in the street. There was no point in repeating the circular argument we'd had too many times, about my refusal to become a companion or governess. I'd insulted her on one occasion by blurting that it would be degrading to work in someone else's home, too late wishing to undo the sting I had caused by my unthinking words.

Since Edward's debts had come to light, I had spent innumerable hours brooding over my fate. I had no particular talents to recommend me for work. I was not an excellent musician whom one might hire to teach piano. My painting was indifferent, my French and German only passable, my embroidery even worse. Who would hire someone with no skills? I reread *Vanity Fair*, hoping for inspiration, but realized that I was not even pretty or alluring enough to be a courtesan. I had been raised to be a wife, mother and chatelaine of a fashionable household.

If I were a man, I could simply brush off my coat, polish my boots, march up to a banker or merchant and begin an apprenticeship or clerkship of some sort. My options as a genteel woman were severely limited. The idea of being a governess to sniveling brats or a companion to a cranky old lady filled me with horror. No matter how I examined and turned the problem to search for new solutions, my best choice was to remarry.

Now I looked over the mail and circulars. "Wait, here's something." I sat up straighter and slit open a letter whose feminine handwriting was dear to me.

"Does it have money in it?" she asked with a dark glance at the missive.

"No."

"Then I am not interested." She turned away to lay out my clothes.

"Why, Ellen! Don't be so down-in-the-mouth. It is <u>better</u> than money." I leapt from the bed with more energy than I'd felt in weeks and began dressing in the dark green gown trimmed in black which she had selected from the meager choice remaining in my once overflowing wardrobe. I had been counting the weeks til I could come out of mourning, but today I had errands to do and I dared not start gossip by appearing in bright colours prematurely.

"Who is the letter from?" she asked, helping with the buttons. "Your fairy godmother?"

"Excellent deduction, Ellen. You would make a superb detective. It's from my _real_ godmother, Mrs. Goodwin. My godfather's sixtieth birthday is to be celebrated with a country ball next month. There will be eligible men there. And I'm going!"

At that time, I was heedless of all the unfortunate events set in motion by the arrival of that simple invitation, or rather, by my acceptance of it.

Still in my bare feet, I dashed to the writing table in my sitting room and quickly penned acceptance to the invitation. Since the desk's chair had been sold, I wrote standing up, and hopped from one foot to the other on the cold uncarpeted floor, regretting the loss of the fine Aubusson which had also found its way to an auctioneer's coffers.

Calling out to Ellen, I urged her to quickly post my letter. "And then hurry back so we can plan my wardrobe for the visit to Kenwick Manor. We'll buy ribbons and trim for some of my old gowns. I will be out of these widows weeds just in time to snare a rich husband!"

CHAPTER 2

I left London with Ellen Armstrong settled across from me in the shiny blue and black wagonette I'd kept to maintain appearances, despite the expense. The horses sported fresh plumes and polished harnesses. The hired groom was decked out in a new uniform. Everything from my shoes to my newly trimmed hat had been calculated to give an impression that my station in life had not changed other than becoming a widow. I must conceal the fact that my finances were in a shambles.

Even my godmother could not be trusted with the truth. Gloria Goodwin was a delightful hostess but a notorious gossip, always certain that she was helping matters by her meddling. I'd never catch a wealthy husband if the magpies jabbered about my intentions. My motives would be embarrassingly clear and would repulse any suitors I might acquire. I would already be competing in the marketplace with unmarried debutantes in virginal white gowns.

We were to *rendezvous* with Miss Claire Lewis at The Hare and Hounds in Twelveoaks. There we would rest the horses and partake of lunch before continuing the journey to Kenwick Manor in the heart of Kent. The region was known as England's Garden, and the profusion of early spring flowers all around us filled my heart with hope for a new beginning.

Passing a village with steep cobbled lanes, in the distance I could see the imposing towers of an ancient castle otherwise hidden from the road by wooded dales and blooming gorse. It seemed we had stepped back into another century after the modernity of bustling London, and I felt more than ever like I was living in a fairy tale where at any moment I would come across ogres or fairies… or perhaps even Prince Charming.

Ellen's several attempts to engage me in conversation were met with little response on my part. I was face to face with a new anxiety, and my thoughts kept returning to a disturbing letter I had received two days earlier. It was from a Wilfred Jennings, a man who apparently had loaned Edward large sums of money on more than one occasion, not all of which had been remitted.

I took the letter from my reticle. It was wrinkled and worn from my constant re-reading, as if somehow another look would change the message. It still said the same thing: Mr. Jennings demanded two thousand pounds, and would wait no longer than thirty days to obtain it. According to the letter, he had been gracious enough, as he put it, to wait for my period of mourning to end. If he did not receive the money by the deadline, he planned to make the debt publicly known. I knew if that happened, other debtors I had placated with a payment or two would no longer feel a compunction to remain silent. I would be ruined.

I passed the letter across to Ellen, who quickly read it with a frown and returned it to me. We shared a look of apprehension. At once I regretted showing it to her. She was in my employ and I should spare her needless worry.

"Never mind," I told her with a vestige of my old optimism as I put the letter away. "I wish we would get there faster. Our troubles will soon be over. I'll take care of you." But later, that brave prediction came back to taunt me.

The groom urged the horses to pick up speed, backing his command with a whip crack as if he, too, were anxious to reach the inn and refreshment. The light carriage surged ahead, bouncing and jostling over the dusty highway.

Each clip-clop of the hooves brought me closer to what I had begun to consider my Judgment Day. If I were found deserving at the ball, I would soon be married, pay-off the mounting debts, salvage the family jewel trade, and of course, live happily ever after. My other alternatives were far too wretched to consider.

The old timber and stone inn was dark and musty inside. After my eyes adjusted to the shadows, I noticed Claire Lewis slumped on a bench in a corner. She was a plain young woman, unmarried, about twenty-two years of age, with no distinguishing beauty or personality. I caught myself thinking how unattractive she made herself with such unflattering clothes, hairstyle and down-turned mouth, but then felt a moment's pang for my uncharitable thoughts.

Claire Lewis was an acquaintance for whom I'd garnered an invitation to my godparents' ball. She did not live in London, so we had arranged to meet *en route* to the country manor. When I corresponded with Claire about the trip, I did not reveal to her the state of my finances. We were not close enough for such a confession, and in fact she was not really a friend of mine, but someone Edward had known before I met him. He invited her now and then to dinner parties at our house. I formed the impression that she was the daughter of someone he knew, but I had never been clear on the association. However, I must have met her people at some time in the past, because something about her face was familiar to me.

There were no other guests. The table in front of Claire was bare, so I assumed she had just arrived. I was glad we had not kept her waiting overlong. Turning to Ellen, I asked her to locate the innkeeper and have a meal sent in for Miss Lewis and me. In a whisper, I reminded her to order the least expensive food. Ellen noticed a candle stub stuck in a wax puddle on a tin plate. She lit the candle and placed it in front of Claire. The girl shrank back from the light.

After Ellen left, I sat across from Claire. Noticing she was still shying from the light, I slid the candle aside. I became aware of a sour smell around her, as if she had recently been ill. I noticed that her drab brown hair had come loose from its pins and was in need of combing, and her traveling clothes were none too tidy.

"How are you, Claire?"

She shrugged listlessly in reply.

"Would you mind if I open a window? I haven't seen you since the—" I stopped short.

"His funeral." She looked away. "Do as you please," she added indifferently.

I noticed that she tried to keep the light from her eyes as I threw open the shutters, disturbing cobwebs and raising a cloud of sooty dust. Sunlight streamed through the broken panes, revealing the untidiness of the inn. It looked as though it hadn't been swept out in weeks, or even months. I wondered why the proprietor did not connect the filth with the lack of a clientele. From prior trips to my godparents' country home since childhood, I remembered stopping at this inn, and in my memory it was a sparkling place filled with warmth, good company and good cheer.

"I fear for the quality of food we'll receive," I said. "Hopefully the cook isn't as haphazard as the servant."

Claire made a visible effort to rouse herself. "The owner was cursed by a gypsy after her horse died here."

"Who told you that?"

"I know these things. So people stopped coming. If you don't like it, why don't we leave? I am not hungry."

Her lack of consideration was irritating but I tried to keep my tone pleasant. After all, she was my guest, and there was no need to let her anger me. "My horses need rest. I am hungry, and so are my maid and the coachman."

I took off my chocolate brown linen traveling cloak and its matching bonnet, and laid them gingerly on the bench. My dress was yellow dimity, with brown trim. Taking my seat again opposite Claire, I was startled to hear her suck in her breath noisily.

"You are supposed to be in mourning." Her face and neck were flushed and her hazel eyes seemed constricted even though the light was still dim.

I noticed how gaunt she seemed. Perhaps her stomach upset was a chronic illness.

"I know you were a friend of Edward's," I said, "but a full year has passed and—"

She cut in, outraged, "So you've mourned long enough." Leaning forward intently, she went on maliciously, "You were glad when he died, weren't you?"

"What a ridiculous statement."

Claire kept darting malevolent glances at me, as though the subject she'd raised was of great consequence to her. She mopped her brow with a crumpled handkerchief, seeming feverish or upset. I couldn't fathom why she would be so interested in my reaction to my husband's death.

I had never questioned her relationship with my husband, as his actions toward her had never inspired jealous thoughts. Now my mind began spinning with curiosity. But she was still looking at me. Her posture made me uneasy, and for some reason I found myself squirming under her probing gaze as if she read my thoughts and condemned me for them.

With a small sigh, I told myself it wouldn't hurt to confide in her. We were friends, after all, and would be spending a week together. It would be more pleasant to pass the time amicably. Indeed, I was beginning to feel guilty for not telling her about my financial difficulties or my goal this weekend at the house party. Her curiosity, though somewhat morbid, was surely harmless.

"Shall I be frank?" I asked her.

"By all means."

"I was not 'happy' over Edward's death. That would be monstrous, no matter what the circumstances of our marriage. But after the shock, I came to see that a door had opened for me, a door of freedom to a better life. You see—"

She cut me off with a gesture. "Poor Loretta! How rude of him to be shot by a fellow hunter and cause you such problems. He was killed and all you think of is your happiness." With the back of her hand she wiped spittle from her chin, then to my further disgust cleaned her hand against her sleeve instead of using the napkin on the table.

I tried to recall if I'd ever seen Claire act this way, but I had spent so little time with her, and always with others around. She was little more than a stranger, and now I found myself deeply regretting the invitation I had extended to her out of pity.

Before I could reply, a young lad entered the dining hall with a heavy tray. This he awkwardly placed on the table and unloaded steaming bowls of soup and a golden shepherd's pie.

"Ellen managed this," I murmured to myself, knowing she must have bullied the cook into giving us better fare than most would be served. "This looks delicious," I commented to the lad, who smiled shyly.

He placed cutlery by my plate, but when he moved to do the same for Claire, he knocked a dish with his elbow. Soup slopped onto the rough tabletop and splashed Claire's dress.

"You clumsy oaf!" She raised a hand to strike him.

I quickly leaned across the table and caught her by the wrist to halt the intended blow. The boy glanced at me, sweat beading on his brow. "Clean it up, please," I told him gently, handing him my napkin.

Too shaken to do more than nod, he hastily mopped up the spill on the table and then loped off to the kitchen.

"You're hurting me," Claire whined.

I realized I hadn't let go of her. I didn't loosen my grasp yet. "I will send you home from my godparents if you repeat such ill-bred behavior in the coming days. Promise to act like a lady."

She gave a surly nod. "I promise."

I let go of her.

Claire started to say something, but swallowed her words, swiped at the splotches on her dress and then began eating desultorily.

I wondered what Claire would say if she knew about the debts Edward had left. Watching her pick at her food, and glance at me occasionally with sullen hostility, I was grateful that I had held my tongue and not confided in her. When the dishes were removed, I finally ended the strained silence between us.

"Why are you acting so oddly today?" I asked. "And why are accusing me of thinking only of myself? You can't possibly know what my marriage was like—"

"I didn't accuse you of anything." She glared hard at me. Seeming unaware of it, she raked her fingers up and down her throat, leaving white streaks that turned red before fading.

"But that's what you are thinking, is it not? That I hated Edward Whitney, while you…" I paused as sudden memories flashed through my mind of her clasping Edward's arm, and gazing up at him adoringly. "While you worshiped him." I sat back in my chair, stunned by the idea. "You were in love with my husband. No wonder you've always resented me—"

"You are a fool." Claire scraped her chair back, snatched up her cloak and hurried out to the courtyard.

CHAPTER 3

The wagonette swung onto the long U-shaped drive leading to the massive double doors of Kenwick Manor, the stately home of my godparents, Peter and Gloria Goodwin.

Claire had slept throughout the journey, and it was difficult to wake her now. With a bleary look on her face, she surveyed the estate. "It is so... beautiful.... "

We stepped down from the wagonette, and I linked arms with Claire to approach the front entry. I felt that if the coming visit was to be enjoyable, I would need to mend the rift between us and show by my munificence that all was forgiven. Even though we had started the trip by quarreling, nothing was going to mar the first party I had been to in a full year.

On either side of the tall carved doors, blooming red roses exuded a heavenly scent. Hovering honeybees buzzed a cheerful welcome. The manicured lawn contributed its own aromas of clover and freshly cut grass.

I felt buoyed by a sudden feeling of excitement, and a certainty that my fortunes were about to reverse. I had always been close to my godparents and maintained a regular correspondence with Mrs. Goodwin, so I was looking forward to seeing them.

My excitement must have communicated itself to Claire. She suddenly laughed gaily. "I have never seen a place so wonderful! I never want to leave."

A playful breeze sent our hooped skirts swaying and bobbing. Two footmen appeared from the house and Ellen directed the removal of our baggage. From around the side of the house, my godmother's two black-and-tan terriers suddenly appeared, barking joyously and then turning circles in front of me and leaping to be petted. I bent to greet them, wishing I had thought to bring scraps of pie crust from lunch. They seemed disappointed I had no treats, and I laughed at their antics as they jumped around, vying for my attention.

All at once, I felt marvelously alive, for the first time in months. For the moment, I was able to push aside my cares and woes, and simply indulge all my senses. I was young, I was happy, the whole future was ahead of me, shining brightly.

I hummed a spontaneous tune, the type a splendid afternoon so readily inspires. I had an exhilarating feeling that nothing could go wrong for me, that I would not only have an amicable visit with my godparents, but that I would find an acceptable way out of my financial difficulties.

Inside the manor, Claire and I followed one of the maids up the grand staircase and then we forked to the left at the landing and continued up to the first floor. The maid stopped outside a door adjacent to the stairway, flung it open and stepped aside. "Mrs. Whitney," she said, "This is your friend's room. Do you wish to go to yours now?"

"My usual room?"

She nodded, pointing to the end of the hall.

"You may go now," I replied. "It is not necessary for you to wait."

With a swift curtsey, the girl departed. I entered the spacious front room where Claire was looking around with joy at the blue and cream decor, the matched set of Regency furniture with paw feet and gold-leaf trim, and the magnificent garden view out the wide windows.

Claire's mood was suddenly euphoric. She interlaced her fingers behind her back and rocked on her heels like a schoolgirl. "I want to meet your godparents now! Take me to them," she commanded.

Just then two servants arrived with our baggage. I directed them to take mine to my room after bringing Claire's into hers. "Why don't you get settled, Claire, and freshen from our dusty travels? I'll do the same and meet you back here in half an hour."

But after I left her, I took a moment to wander the familiar halls, and so Ellen was already unpacking my things when I walked into the corner apartment I had used at Kenwick since childhood.

"It's like a homecoming, isn't it, Ellen?" I looked around the familiar room, feeling a sense of peace wash over me that I hadn't felt since before my marriage, when my father was still alive.

On the western wall of my bedroom, red striped draperies were tied back with heavy gold tassels. Afternoon sunshine brightened the room with a rosy glow. I pushed a window open and inhaled the fresh country air, so invigorating to me after the confinement of my London rooms.

I couldn't help twirling about as I used to do as a girl, suddenly feeling the burdens slip from my shoulders. "I could almost forget my problems."

"You've become much too serious of late, worrying about money."

Her tenderness surprised me. As if to make sure I didn't think it was to be an ongoing laxity, she briskly set about putting the room in order. I held back a laugh. Ellen had a tender heart she hid beneath her gruffness, but I would not be the one to embarrass her by pointing it out after nearly ten years together.

"I have to worry," I told her blithely. "There's no one else to do it for me." Sudden tears filled my eyes and I brushed them away impatiently.

"You have more than most young ladies—"

"You think I'm crying? Don't be silly, Ellen! I got some dust in my eye, that is all." We shared a look, and I relented. "I was remembering the days when I used to come here with my parents and brother. We had happy times together. I can picture myself on a horse, sitting in front of Miles in the saddle, laughing as we rode with his arms around me to keep me safe." I quickly struck a nonchalant pose, before I became overwhelmed by bittersweet memories. "Older brothers and parents are a wonderful convenience. They do all the worrying that needs to be done. All a child has to do is enjoy herself and be as boisterous and carefree as she likes."

I crossed the room and looked out at the vacant driveway below, half-expecting to see my father's grand old laundau roll up the gravel path.

"It was just a touch of nostalgia, Ellen. I was wishing for a knight in shining armor to charge to my rescue."

"Like in those fairy tales you always loved."

Watching her put my dresses in the wardrobe where some of my old frocks remained from prior visits, I sat at the walnut dressing table to splash on *eau de toilette* and smooth my coiffure.

A bouquet of spring flowers was crammed into a tall burnished copper urn by the mirror, no doubt ordered by my godmother as a special welcome. Impulsively, I snapped a yellow rose from its stem and tucked it behind one ear. "And they all lived happily ever after," I told Ellen flippantly.

I crossed my fingers and made a silent wish that it would be so.

CHAPTER 4

I found my godmother downstairs in the drawing room, directing an exasperated maid in the placement of silver baskets filled with sweets and nuts. Seeing me, Mrs. Goodwin abandoned her task and rushed to take my hands in hers. We hugged. It was so good to see her, I felt happier all at once, as if my worries were not as serious as they had seemed when I was alone.

I introduced Claire Lewis to her, and my godmother dismissed the maid, who scarcely concealed her relief as she hurried from the room. From past experience, I surmised that my godmother had been typically indecisive and exhausting to work with. Although everyone loved Gloria for her generous spirit and kind heart, she could be tiresome. She always wanted every detail perfect but frequently wavered in choosing one option over another, anxious to have no cause for a guest's complaint or discomfort.

The little terriers danced around my godmother's legs and she gave them a few shelled nuts from one of the baskets. Now her sharp blue eyes focused on Claire and gave her a quick study. I wondered what her impression of the young woman was.

When I had stopped by Claire's room a little earlier, her door had been ajar. My hand was raised to knock, when I noticed her put a cork in a small bottle, furtively hide it behind a cushion, then take it out, and glance around anxiously before deciding to put it inside a shoe in the wardrobe.

I shrank back, lest she see me spying. My heart beat rapidly. I couldn't think what the bottle might contain. When I judged it safe, I called out her name. She came out in the hall to join me, seeming much more gay than earlier. I put the matter of the bottle out of my mind and took her by the hand to go in search of my godparents. We had found Mrs. Goodwin first.

"I'm glad Loretta asked to bring you, Miss Lewis," Mrs. Goodwin said now. "It's nice you two are such good friends." Without waiting for a reply from either of us, my godmother rushed on in her breathless manner, asking if our journey had been comfortable and if our accommodations here were satisfactory. We answered in the affirmative, and she launched into details about the birthday celebration to be held Saturday night.

During this, Claire wandered around the large room, surveying everything with a dreamy air. She seemed bright and happy, a singular contrast to the sullen girl I had lunched with earlier. All the while, she picked things up here and there, but put them back down in any old place as if she couldn't be bothered to notice that she had kept walking while holding the item. She ran her hands lightly across chair backs and fingered the fringe on the velvet draperies at the french doors.

Reading the consternation on Mrs. Goodwin's face, I called to Claire to rejoin us. She was examining an antique silver Stuart candlestick and returned to us, idly dropping the antique candlestick on a chair in passing. I quickly picked the candlestick up and set it on a table, exchanging a confused look with my godmother. She shrugged in response, both of us puzzled by Claire's strange behavior. It almost seemed she was walking in her sleep.

I recalled suddenly that Edward had mentioned to me Claire's family was of uncertain means, and the girl's life had been one of vicissitudes from fortune to darned stockings and back again, as her mother's situation changed erratically over the course of Claire's life. Apparently, there had not been a father on the scene, and the mother had remarried only to die shortly afterwards, leaving Claire to be raised by a reluctant stepfather. Without a mother to propel her forward in society, Claire had languished with no suitors. I could not imagine her flirting with a man and making herself pleasant, but perhaps after she had a chance to rest from the journey here, I would discover her more favorable qualities.

My godmother engaged Claire in a discussion of the party, and Claire happily told her about the ball gown she had brought for tomorrow night's affair, and how excited she was about the chance to meet young men of good families. She seemed overly gay, but I was to come to know these moods of hers during the ensuing days.

Uneasily, I recalled a time when Edward had been talking alone with Claire in a corner after one of our dinner parties, and I had come upon them unexpectedly. Claire's head had shot up and she looked at me with startled guilt. At the time, I had assured myself their *tête-à-tête* was innocent, but now I couldn't help wondering if Claire's outrage about Edward's death lay in the fact that they had been *paramours*. Perhaps he had even given her lavish gifts, and she was angry when they stopped with his death.

With all this running through my mind, I managed to interject a comment now and then about the upcoming party and ask about the other guests who would be staying at the Manor over the next few days. I also decided privately that I would have a long talk with Claire before nightfall, and remind her to behave properly. She could chase after all the men she wanted, in her quest for a match, so long as she did not embarrass me with sullen outbursts… and so long as she did not interfere with my own plans to find a husband.

Watching Claire's face as she chattered with Mrs. Goodwin, I deeply regretted having brought Claire with me. I couldn't forget the strange way she had treated me at the inn, but I consoled myself that there would be other people around us, and I would not have to spend overmuch time with Claire alone. And, I was relieved to note, she was speaking and acting more normally now than earlier. Perhaps the bottle she was so careful of contained a restorative or elixir to calm her nerves.

I filtered out my thoughts and rejoined the conversation just as my godmother told us that of the thirteen house guests she was expecting, we were the first to arrive.

"Thirteen," Claire repeated, blanching. "You invited others first, twelve it must have been, then Loretta asked to bring me, so I am the thirteenth. It's bad luck! Something awful will happen to me here." She glanced around wildly, as if expecting a demon to appear.

"Stop it!" I grasped Claire's hands in mine and gave her a little shake. "You're scaring my godmother with your silly superstitions. Nothing is going to happen to you, and I don't want to hear you speak of it again."

Later, I went alone to my godfather's library on the ground floor to find something to read until dinner. Scanning the titles of books in matching mahogany breakfront bookcases, I noted several familiar works and a few new ones that sounded interesting. There were also shelves near the desk, overflowing with well-thumbed volumes. Many of these were reference books and monographs, for which I had little use since I was seeking something non-taxing. My mind was already overworked in trying to ignore my problems and pretend to be carefree.

I sank into an overstuffed chair and flipped through the contents of a brass revolving magazine rack. I saw American publications such as *Godey's Lady's*

Book and *Harper's Monthly.* The new magazine from Berlin, *Der Bazar*, was of little interest since I do not read German well enough. In *Punch* I found satirical cartoons mocking the enormous crinolines in fashion, and I had to admit the satire was not that broad. It was indeed awkward to pass through doorways and complete everyday tasks men take for granted, all in the name of beauty and style.

In *The Englishwoman's Domestic Magazine*, I found an article on etiquette which I put aside to show Claire Lewis. Perhaps it would be a tactful *entrée* to a conversation on how to deport herself this week.

And for me, I settled on a copy of *The Queen*, a new publication I had been wanting to see but had not been able to afford since my budget no longer allowed the luxury of newspapers and periodicals.

Thus armed with reading material, I propelled myself from the chair and started toward the door which I had shut earlier to block the noise of hammers coming from the ballroom.

The knob turned in my hand, but from the other side. Someone was trying to come in. Inexplicably, prickles ran up my back and my knees trembled. Claire's superstitions had made me alert to the supernatural. But taking control of my nerves, I stood back and let the door swing open silently on its well-oiled hinges.

Serena Harmon swept into the room, looking as if she'd just stepped out of one of the magazines I'd been perusing, her red hair perfectly coifed, her gown the latest style, her jewels glimmering in the light from the mullioned windows. She was some ten years my senior, of average height, about my own size, although her waist was thicker than I recalled. There was a sassy look in her brilliant green eyes, and her upturned nose had a perpetually snooty attitude which complemented her personality. And yet, I knew that many considered her a beauty and she was much sought-after in society.

"Why, little Loretta Whitney," she said in that strident tone which had always set my teeth on edge, "imagine finding you here, in a library of all places." She glanced at the magazines in my arms. "But you didn't bother with even a novel? Surely your brain could stretch to encompass more than a mere article or two? Or are you just going to look at the pretty pictures?"

My back stiffened.

Mrs. Goodwin had failed to warn me that the Harmons were among her guests, but I should have anticipated it. Serena's husband was a nephew of my godfather, and it was only my bad luck that they were no longer living in Italy.

I could see she was waiting for my response to her barb. "Your voice, Serena. It sounds strange. Have you got a cold, my dear?"

I knew that Serena was vain about her low, husky voice. She entertained friends at home by singing popular ballads and contemporary songs to her own accompaniment on the piano. When she wasn't singing, Serena Harmon's tongue was as sharp and biting as her sardonic mind. I had been the victim of its lashings on countless occasions.

She glared at me. Since she didn't have a comment, I went on, in a parody of her condescending tone. "You're so amusing, Serena darling. These magazines are a frivolous pastime until we dine. I have been in mourning the past year, and it suits me to see what the world has to offer as diversion now that I am re-entering society."

With pleasure, I noted how her jaw set as she looked me over. The sparring ritual had commenced.

"So long as a pursuit of diversion doesn't convey you along foolish paths," she said.

"Don't concern yourself with me."

"But I am concerned, Loretta. A motherless girl needs guidance." Withdrawing a lace-edged handkerchief from a pocket of her *tan d'or* silk moire gown, she dabbed at her eyes as if pity for me had brought an onslaught of tears. "A mother would warn you, but since you haven't one, and since your godmother is, let us be honest, too capricious to give useful advice, I must act the role."

"What advice are you so anxious to give?"

The redhead suddenly wagged a finger in my face. "Stay away from my husband this weekend. Do you hear me? If I see you so much as asking him the time of day, I'll—"

"You'll what? Don't be ridiculous, Serena. If I didn't speak with him, everyone would notice and what would the gossips make of that? You do care what people say, don't you?" I boldly stepped closer to her. I could feel her heated breath on my cheek. The rose cologne she always wore wafted toward me. "They would start whispering, 'Look how that Loretta Whitney and Thomas Harmon pretend to avoid each other. There must be something between them. After all, his wife isn't getting any younger!'"

Her eyes narrowed. "Stay away from my husband," she repeated. "Or you'll be very sorry." With that, she sailed from the room, slamming the door behind her.

Confrontations with Serena Harmon always sent my heart racing nervously. She brought out the wicked impulses in me and I said things I later wished to retract, but it seemed there was no other way to handle her. I had to meet her on her own ground and use the same weapons she did or she would stomp over me like a doormat.

Since I had turned fifteen, Serena had begun accusing me of trying to steal her husband, and nothing ever convinced her that I found the idea ludicrous. But clearly Serena saw nothing innocent about my old friendship with my godfather's nephew, Thomas Harmon, especially now that I was widowed and back in circulation.

After I returned to my room to change for dinner, I crossed the hall to my godmother's dressing room. It was decorated in hues of green from delicate mint to rich jade. The lamps were lit and a fire glowed in the grate. It was an inviting room, and I had spent many hours here in conversation with Gloria over the years.

She sat at her dressing table, smoothing her hair with a tortoiseshell comb. She caught my eye in the mirror as I entered. "Come in, dear."

I sat on a small stool near her. The dressing table was over-run with ruby glass scent bottles, mother-of-pearl boxes for powders and creams, silver curling irons, and an untidy pile of gloves and hairpins. I idly straightened the mess as she chatted about the coming ball. She fretted that it might not be a success despite all her efforts. I had my own worries, and sighed to myself more than once, but tried to hide my mood from her.

When she finished her *toilette*, my godmother changed her tone. "I'm worried about you, Loretta."

I gave a little start. "You needn't—"

"You have never been able to fool me, child. You are upset about something. I know it cannot be grief for Edward Whitney, so don't insult me with that excuse. Even your letters have been different the past months, secretive somehow. You told me three times about a new cake recipe that I hadn't even asked for. Clearly the sign of someone searching for something to write when the truth cannot be told." She looked at me and held my gaze. "Don't say it's my imagination."

Those words were on the tip of my tongue. I didn't know what else to say.

"It's not like you to be so withdrawn, at least not with me. You've always confided in me. Won't you do so now, dear? I think something is troubling you. Can't I help?" Her kind face and bright eyes were filled with concern, but I didn't dare trust her with my secret.

"I had a headache from the travel today," I said easily, patting her arm.

She shook her head. "I know you haven't had an opportunity to talk to me this afternoon. Your young friend was always there—"

"But I have nothing to confide, Gloria dear." I kept up my protestations of fatigue, omitting an observation that she was too scatterbrained to trust with vital secrets. It was one thing to tell her as a young girl that I was dreaming of love, marriage and a family, but quite another to reveal my financial straits. She might remember too late that she was not to talk about it. And Serena Harmon would relish the opportunity to snipe at me over something new.

Abruptly, she said, "You don't like Claire Lewis, do you? I wonder why you invited her."

"I only meant to show the girl some fun." I didn't feel like admitting that I had invited Claire so my own efforts to find a husband might not be so noticeable. I would be able to pass off my interest in asking about various and sundry gentlemen by making it seem I was hoping to find a match for my friend, an unmarried girl whose advancing age I would not mention. It was common knowledge that if you hadn't found a husband by twenty-five, you were unlikely to do so, since men were naturally interested in younger women who would produce a large family.

"My dear girl," Mrs. Goodwin chided, "you no doubt think that I am too wrapped up in myself and my little problems to notice what is happening around me. But I don't miss much. These old eyes are still sharp. And my hearing ain't half bad either. You hate to let anyone know anything about you that might give them the upper hand. I've told you more than once that your pride is going to be your downfall. It wouldn't hurt to swallow it once in a while."

An embarrassed flush crept up my cheeks. I avoided her searching eyes, mumbling that she was wrong. But in fact, she was right to say I had never given her credit for being perceptive. I'd always thought of her as superficial and frivolous. Taking a deep breath, I decided to confide in her, and so I told her I had some financial difficulties, without going into much detail.

"Is that all?" She laughed in relief. "Ask Peter for a loan!"

I couldn't help smiling. She made it seem so simple. We talked a while longer and I confessed I had run into Serena Harmon, with the usual results. My godmother counseled that I avoid being alone with Mr. Harmon, and stay away from Serena. "When someone is that jealous," she concluded, "there is neither reason nor rhyme to it, and you'd be better off steering clear of both of them."

I promised compliance, and induced her to put my problems from her mind, but I felt a great comfort from her advice. It appeared I had misjudged her. Perhaps it was a habit I had unwittingly cultivated, and I had also mis-judged Claire Lewis. I decided I would take pains to get to know the young woman better at dinner, and befriend her.

CHAPTER 5

Gloria and I had been too long in talking, and were the last to join the buffet line at the old Georgian sideboard. Some of the other house guests had arrived during the afternoon and were chattering among themselves. I greeted them, then filled a plate from the tempting array of dishes. I found a place next to my patrician, silver-haired godfather, Peter Goodwin, at the long dining table.

I couldn't help but notice Claire Lewis consorting with Serena Harmon as if they were old friends. Turning away from them, I spoke with my godfather about his birthday ball and how excited his wife was about the celebration. After talking with Gloria, I had decided to swallow my pride as she'd suggested, and ask my godfather for a loan, at least enough to pay Wilfred Jennings the two thousand pounds he said was long overdue, and thus silence his public announcement of my debts.

Just as I was about to broach the topic, Mr. Goodwin said, for my ears only, "I'm afraid this will be the last grand cotillion we have for a long while."

"Whatever do you mean? You're not ill, are you?"

Although Gloria had told me he was in poor health, he now reassured me that his health was fairly good. "Nothing to complain about, I suppose. But I've suffered some setbacks recently. Too late to cancel all this—" he waved a fork at the party— "and your godmother wouldn't have believed me anyway. You know what she's like," he added with affection. "She thinks I am made of money." He went on to explain further details about his monetary setbacks.

My dilemma was ironical. I had planned to pour my financial woes on his sympathetic shoulder, and instead my godfather was telling me of his own troubles. It would have been embarrassing if I had spoken sooner. Now there was a tight knot where my stomach should be.

I had entertained hopes of easily solving at least one of my problems, but now I would have to return to my original plan of finding a husband to take on all my debts. With my plate still full, I laid down my fork and tried to decide how to proceed. My thoughts were in a turmoil and I reflected, not for the first time, that I should never have married Edward Whitney, no matter how good a match my father had thought him to be.

Mr. Goodwin commented on my lack of appetite. To avoid any searching questions, I resumed eating.

"Mind you," he said, "we're not headed for the poor house."

"I'm very glad to hear that." I cared deeply for my godparents and would be distressed to see them in any difficulty. I shoved aside the thoughts I had about my own situation and turned my full attention to him.

"We will have to cut corners," he said, "until I can straighten out the mess and see the extent of my loss. I suppose it serves me right for delegating too much responsibility to the wrong person. Though to be fair to myself, the man certainly made a good impression. I am not the only one he fooled."

"I know the sort of person you mean." I thought of how Edward Whitney had deceived not only me but my father who had been both delighted and relieved to find a man of such keen business sense, purportedly, who was a fine match for his only child. If my brother had not been killed, the jewelry trade would have been his responsibility and I would have been free to marry for love. But it was too late for might-have-beens, and I suddenly realized that my godfather had been speaking at length without a response from me.

My godfather looked apologetic. "Listen to me, going on and on. I must be boring you with all this talk of embezzlers. Tell me how you have been getting on. It is so good to see you."

I told him that I was doing admirably well, all things considered, and left it at that.

Accepting my statement at face value, he gestured across the table and introduced Miss Louise Rogers and her sweet-faced niece Susanna, who was about eighteen years of age. The conversation turned to the ball. It was clear from the sour expression on Miss Louise's tight face that she considered it a frivolous waste of time, money and effort.

"Since it is in honor of your birthday," she said to my godfather with a sniff, "I suppose it is alright."

The niece bit her lip and kept her eyes downcast. She gave the impression of dullness and I wasn't sure why Gloria had told me earlier in describing the guests to come that I would particularly like Susanna. The Rogers were relatives of old friends of my godparents who were unable to attend the ball, and so they had been invited instead. But as I was covertly watching Susanna, she suddenly smiled shyly at something my godfather said about the musicians who would play at the ball, and her whole face lit up. She looked my way and caught me studying her. I smiled, and she returned it. I began wondering if I had again misjudged someone by putting overmuch importance on a quick impression.

Others at the table included an older well-fed couple, Mr. and Mrs. Adams, who sat at the end of the table with my godmother. Laughter came from that end, and Susanna looked at them shyly. Before she could retreat back into her shell, I asked her, "Are you looking forward to the ball tomorrow night?"

"Oh, yes!" The sparkle in her eyes betrayed simmering anticipation.

I suddenly felt that Gloria was right: I had found a new friend.

There was a commotion in the hallway and the butler entered to announce the arrival of additional house guests. These were presented to us as Mr. and Mrs. McArthur and their sons Gordon and Samuel, both bachelors. They turned out to be relatives of my godmother's from Cornwall, Mrs. McArthur being her cousin from that distant region, which is why we had never met over the years.

Gordon and Samuel entreated Susanna and me to join them at a smaller table by the window. While they heaped plates at the buffet, Susanna and I gathered our skirts and settled across from each other at the new table. Claire watched us sulkily, clearly both envious and angry that she had been over-looked by the two bachelors at the dinner party. But then I saw her lean over and talk to Serena in confidence. Serena glanced my way, then coolly turned, dismissing me as being of no importance.

The young men returned and began eating.

It didn't take long to discover that the McArthur brothers were as dissimilar in personality as they were in appearance. Sensitive Gordon, with his face half-hidden by a bushy beard and sideboards, was soft-spoken and almost painfully shy. He and Susanna paired off quickly.

In contrast, older brother Samuel was almost deplorably barbaric, being tall and broad-shouldered with the ruddy complexion of one who is frequently out of doors. Wiry blond hair framed a clean-shaven face enhanced by piercing eyes and a ready smile.

Samuel proved so easy to talk with that I suddenly found myself relaxing. A thought insinuated itself in my mind: *Maybe he is the one!*

I asked if any of them knew who the remaining houseguest was, as I had counted and there were only twelve of us so far. In fact, my godmother had mentioned to me in private that there would be three bachelors but I did not mention this fact. The McArthur brothers numbered two, so the missing guest was the third bachelor.

"So who is guest number thirteen?" I asked lightly. But they had no idea.

Gordon McArthur said, "Are you sure it is not your husband?" He looked at my face in dismay and stammered, "Didn't I hear you introduced as Mrs. Whitney?"

I quickly explained. "You couldn't possibly have known. I am a widow. My husband died a year ago."

"But you're so young," Susanna said.

"Miss Rogers," Gordon chided, a possessive note already in his voice as he looked at her, "one can be widowed at any age."

Concerned, Samuel turned to me and asked, "Are we upsetting you by staring? But it was a surprise. My brother's hearing must be better than mine. I did not even hear the word 'Mrs.' when we were introduced." He took my hand in his and gave a small warm squeeze that I felt augured friendship between us. "It never occurred to me to ask if—"

Reluctantly withdrawing my hand, but aware of propriety, I said, "Please don't worry, any of you." I took in their somber glances. "This is a party, so let us go back to being of cheer. My husband was… much older than I and—" I broke off, not wanting to denigrate myself in their eyes by disclosing my utter lack of affection for Edward Whitney.

But it seemed that Samuel intuited my feelings, because he nodded simply and said, "You do not have to explain anything."

Perhaps, I thought to myself, he was even relieved to presume my love wasn't sustained posthumously. Then, taking the conversational reins firmly in hand, he related one anecdote after another concerning the McArthur shipyards.

My ears perked up like one of Gloria's terriers. I couldn't help thinking that someone in boat building might have a sound bank balance, and I should pay heed. There was little time between now and the arrival of over one hundred guests at tomorrow's ball. Some other woman might sweep this man away from me. I needed to stake my claim tonight.

Now that I'd found so easily a wealthy man, all I had to do was maneuver him into making a proposal of marriage, and then agreeing to a wedding without delay.

I had no time to tarry. Those debts Edward Whitney had burdened me with would soon become public knowledge. And who would want to marry me then?

CHAPTER 6

After supper, we adjourned to the front parlor for an informal evening of cards and music. My godmother's dogs curled up near her feet, content as always to be near her. Serena Harmon sang and played the piano.

I was seated on a long divan with Samuel McArthur on my left, and purely by chance, Thomas Harmon on my right. This latter situation had already earned me several fiery stares from our redheaded *chanteuse*. I recalled her earlier warning to avoid her husband, but felt she was being overly dramatic. Then Claire Lewis silently took up Serena's cause and shot a few cold glances my way as well.

Tiring of their puerile drama, I got up and went down a hall and through another room and from there outside onto the Manor's rear terrace leading to magnificent gardens bursting with young bloom and tender new growth.

As I turned to pull the door shut behind me, I noticed that Samuel McArthur had followed me, but while he was still at some distance he was waylaid by my godmother to move a large vase she had suddenly decided looked wrong where she had moved it earlier. He glanced my way, we shared a smile and he shrugged as if in apology for not joining me.

At first, I thought I was alone when I went out onto the covered terrace. I didn't notice that Samuel's father was there also, but soon I smelled pipe smoke and discovered him leaning against the balustrade.

"So you're the little goddaughter we have heard so much about for so many years, always missing the opportunity to meet." He eyed me closely through the smoky haze between us.

I flushed under his scrutiny, as if he could see right through to my newly hatched scheme to marry his older son.

Nervously, I steered our conversation through several general topics and finally, in a voice I hoped concealed my true interest, said, "I hear you are in the shipping business, Mr. McArthur."

He slowly nodded, intent on refilling his pipe, and spoke with the broad accent of a Cornishman. "I own two of the largest shipyards in all of Cornwall. And I am in the process of building a third." His straightforward manner took these statements out of the realm of boasting. He was merely stating the plain facts.

As he continued talking about the family business, in which his two sons were both an integral part, I felt I should pinch myself to awaken. I could scarcely believe my good luck, after so many months of the bad variety. Big blond Samuel McArthur was young, pleasant to look at, educated and polite, but most importantly for my urgent and practical needs, he had money.

Later, I was standing alone by the silent piano, idly watching the McArthur parents and my godparents play a game of whist. Others sat around the room, chatting together.

Claire Lewis sidled up to me. Her face was flushed although the room was not overly warm. "I have a secret," she whispered. She scratched at her neck. "Want to know what it is?"

I did, but I refused to admit it. "Not if it does not concern me," I said loftily, feeling self-righteous. *What kind of secret could Claire Lewis have, anyway, that would interest me?*

"It is about Serena Harmon," she said enticingly.

"Oh? What is it, then, if you simply must tell someone?"

"That is for me to know and for you to discover!"

As she scurried away, I noticed Serena Harmon watching us from the doorway. When Claire reached her, Serena yanked her aside and it was obvious from her posture that she wanted to know what Claire had told me. But Claire just tossed her head and wouldn't reply. Serena kept talking, growing angry, and I saw that Claire finally gave in and defended herself with a few words. Over Claire's shoulder, Serena cast me a dark look.

I felt uneasy suddenly, wondering what they could be discussing. Again, I was relieved that I had not confided in Claire at lunch about my financial problems. It appeared that she was all too willing to gossip about me with Serena, and I would have to be more cautious in the future.

Susanna Rogers and her aunt had been assigned to the corner suite directly across the hall from my own. On the way upstairs after the evening's entertainment was over, Susanna confided in me that she was happy to make my acquaintance since she had feared she would spend the visit with only her aunt for company.

When we reached the end of the hall, I invited her to come in my room for a little while to talk alone. But once I had her in the room, with the door shut, I propelled her to the dressing table, bade her to sit down and blurted, "Would you mind if I show you a better hair style? You have such a pretty face but your hair is…" I trailed off, fearful I had injured her feelings.

We both looked at her reflection in the mirror. She sadly patted the simple knot low on the nape of her neck. "My aunt says—"

"That it is frivolous and unseemly for a young lady of impeccable moral background to be overly concerned with such things as fashion and hair styles."

I laughed and she quickly joined in, biting her lip and glancing back at the door as if her aunt might suddenly burst into the room. "After observing your aunt this evening, I concluded that she is bent on turning every young girl into her own sanctimonious image." I released Susanna's brown hair from its pins, and it cascaded in waves to her waist.

"You won't tell my aunt, will you?"

"She will see for herself, because I will teach you how to style your hair, and her eyes will be agog as you sail out of the room and go down for breakfast, filled with self-motive and the knowledge that you are as good as she is and deserving of all you can enjoy in life!"

We fell into giggles again, and a happy thought struck me: with Susanna's obvious infatuation for Gordon McArthur, and his for her, plus my fervent desire to marry his older brother, Susanna and I might soon be sisters-in-law. I created several hair styles for her, until we both agreed on a becoming one that she could easily replicate.

I reflected that it had been a long day, and I needed rest. Stifling a yawn, I told Susanna that I would help her dress for the ball. I had to repeat myself twice because Susanna was intent on looking at a bouquet of waxed flowers under a large glass dome, and paid me no heed.

"You have pretty things," she commented.

I explained the room furnishings were not mine, but she insisted my taste was better than hers, and wondered wistfully if I would give an opinion of her ball gown now instead of waiting for tomorrow. I agreed to this and she hurried out, to return moments later with a burgundy taffeta monstrosity over her arm. As tactfully as I could, I pointed out a few simple changes we could make to the gown, and offered the loan of Ellen's excellent seamstress skills.

After Susanna left, and Ellen came in to help me get ready for bed, I told Ellen about Susanna Rogers and my intention of helping her look more attractive for the ball. She unbuttoned my gown then hung it in the wardrobe, leaving the wire crinoline hoop standing in a corner of the room like an awesome birdcage. After unfastening my corset, I slipped a green *crêpe* dressing gown over my lacy camisole and drawers. Ellen was the only one allowed to know these were patched and mended in a dozen places.

"I wish I had jewelry to loan Susanna," I said wistfully. "I'm sure she has nothing." I had brought an emerald necklace to wear, that had belonged to my mother. I had hoped I would not have to sell it as I had all her other jewelry and my own as well, but unless something changed, I would be forced to be practical and pawn the necklace or sell it outright.

This might be my last chance to enjoy wearing it, and so the gown I would be wearing was selected to complement the emeralds, being a gold and green concoction Ellen had helped me create from two gowns I had worn in the past. No one would know or suspect it was not the latest Parisienne mode.

Crossing to the wardrobe, I took a look at the ball gown, smiling as I anticipated Samuel McArthur's reaction upon seeing me in it. I looked for my jewelry case, intending to hold up the emerald necklace, but could not find it.

"Ellen, what did you do with the jewel case? You didn't leave it in London, did you?"

Perturbed, she looked through all my belongings and searched the room. Stark-faced, she announced, "It's gone!"

Frantic, I tore open bureau drawers, searched under chair cushions, repeated all the motions she had already made. "I can't believe this. Someone stole it."

"A joke…?" she began hesitantly.

"I can't think of anyone who would—" I broke off, remembering Claire's 'secret' about Serena Harmon.

Maybe the secret was that she had seen Serena steal my necklace. Or perhaps they had done it together, chortling together over a prank at my expense, and Claire had decided on her own to tease me longer, enjoying the secret she held over my head.

I was upset at the loss of my emeralds, whether a joke or not, because the jewels were an important part of my *ensemble* for the ball. I simply had to find my necklace in time to wear it, and appear to be wealthy.

Earlier, I had thought my recent spate of bad luck was turning for the better. Now it seemed more misfortune was in the cards for me.

CHAPTER 7

The next morning, I overslept. I had tossed and turned all night, fretting over the missing emerald necklace, and alternatively worrying that I wouldn't be charming and flirtatious enough to capture a proposal from young shipbuilder Samuel McArthur.

Half-asleep, I peered at the banjo shaped clock-barometer by the corner cupboard, which informed me the hour was half past ten and the weather was fair. The latter I confirmed when, yawning and stretching lazily, I flung open a window and inhaled the pungent country air.

It was a bright, clear, cloudless day. The house was peacefully quiet, as only a rural home can be, perhaps accounting for my being able to stay abed so long. In London, my bedchamber overlooked a bustling avenue. There, the early morning traffic awoke me by seven o'clock, eight at the latest, even on weekends.

The room behind me was still in disarray from my fevered search for the stolen necklace. The ball was this evening. What would I do if the jewels did not turn up by then?

I hadn't decided yet whether I should assume it was a prank, perhaps even confront Claire and Serena about it, or else alert my godfather to notify the local constable about the theft. It worried me that I felt so vulnerable about my financial status that I feared any probing questions about what jewelry I owned, what I had brought with me and etcetera.

Now, in the distance, I spotted a group of riders canting over the rolling green hills. Ruefully, I recalled having agreed to join Samuel and other guests for a nine o'clock horseback tour of the estate's vast acreage. In my upset over the necklace the previous evening, I had neglected to ask Ellen to wake me in time for the sport.

With a pang, I wondered if Samuel missed me, or if Claire Lewis had noticed my interest in him and had wormed her way into his affections already. I leaned out the window, trying to identify individual riders and determine if Claire was near Samuel, but I could tell nothing of significance from this distance.

Annoyed with myself, I turned away and began my *toilette*. My first thought was to hastily dress, get a horse from the stables and catch up with the riding party, but as a long-time visitor to the Manor, I could hardly claim to be overly curious about seeing the grounds. My motive might be forlornly obvious, and I had no intention of letting anyone guess that Samuel McArthur was the target of my intentions.

That famed naturalist from Kent, Charles Darwin, who first studied theology before quitting that course to study animals and plants during a long voyage to strange countries, had mulled over all his observations and produced his theory regarding 'survival of the fittest.' Well, I was in Kent now. And I was determined to survive. If that necessitated luring an unsuspecting male of the species into a marriage trap, then so be it. My interests would best be served by making sure my feathers were most attractive.

I put on a blue flowered challis dress. After braiding my hair, I coiled two loops and fastened them at each ear with sky-blue velvet ribbons. I must be as well-dressed as any fashion plate every time I left my room, even just to go down the hall for a visit with my godmother, in case someone else was in the hall or coming up the stairs. It wouldn't do to get caught with my darns showing.

With a glance at the clock, I accelerated the pace of my *toilette*, in hopes the housekeeper hadn't changed the practice of keeping the weekend breakfast buffet available until eleven o'clock. I was hungry, and anxious for a meal.

En route to the dining room, I paused outside the spacious oak-paneled salon opposite the double-doored entrance foyer on the ground floor, to be used as the ballroom tonight.

Intricately carved sidetables, magenta and canary-yellow upholstered chairs and settees had all been shoved against the walls, ready to be utilized by chaperones and those who were not dancing. By society's rules, I would be expected to join that group, as a widow and also as Claire Lewis's chaperone.

However, I had other plans.

I had already decided to wheedle my godmother into assuming my chaperone duties so I would be free to scandalize the gathering by dancing and partying as if I were a young marriageable maiden. In my mind, I still was one, my disastrous but brief marriage to Edward Whitney notwithstanding.

Looking around the salon, I saw the swaths of fabric on the walls and other decorations that had been the cause of the hammering the day before. Now four man-servants bandied jokes while rolling up the Oriental rugs which would be stored out of sight for the duration of the ball. Two young maids stood by with brooms and cleaning rags. It would be their thankless task to remove every speck of dust and every blade of straw, for my godmother kept straw layered under her carpets to absorb dirt and moisture, else suffer the sharp tongue of the Goodwins' autocratic housekeeper.

Watching them, comparing my situation against theirs, I reflected that if I did not find a husband this week, I might end up a parlor maid in a mansion such as this.

Shaking off the humiliating thought, I visualized how the salon would be later on. Candles would blaze in the *ormolu* chandeliers hanging at golden intervals along the walls and ceiling. Gaily dressed couples would swirl to the music of the small orchestra ensconced behind the Chinese screens in one corner. I would be in the midst of the dancers, laughing in the arms of Samuel McArthur, who had just informed me that he had no need of a dowry from me and would marry me as soon as the banns were read....

My girlish daydream burst as I was jolted back to reality by my godmother's voice.

"Loretta, you simply must help me." She piloted me down the branching hallway and around a corner to a small, seldom used parlor. "Yet another crisis! One after another the entire day, and now the gypsy—"

"What gypsy?"

"Didn't I tell you I hired a fortune teller for tonight?"

"No, but that sounds exciting."

"She requires a room decorated for 'mysterious' atmosphere, so I had a storeroom cleared out, but now she said that is too small and she wants this room."

I suddenly realized we were not alone. In a shadowy corner stood a stocky woman with dark hair and colourful garb. Around her neck she wore an odd-looking amulet of gold. She watched me closely, and stroked the necklace with a thoughtful air. I felt an uncontrollable shiver, as if she were casting a spell on me, but then brought myself up short in annoyance at my fancies, and turned back to my godmother.

I stayed a few moments longer, acting as mediator between the two women, helping to convince my godmother that the crisis was one with a solution, and then left to find my breakfast.

The food had grown cold and looked unappetizing, but I was too hungry to care and so I picked up a plate. A maid came in to begin removing the buffet dishes, but I convinced her to wait a few minutes, and also to bring me a pot of hot tea. While she was gone on that errand, I heaped the plate high with fish baked in tomato sauce, shirred eggs, corn muffins and orange marmalade, all the while slipping into another reverie, picturing myself the happy recipient of not just one marriage offer, but multiple proposals from a clamoring roomful of handsome and wealthy young esquires.

The maid returned, and poured me a cup of steaming tea, then began clearing the buffet so they could ready it for lunchtime when the riders returned.

Humming to myself, absently balancing plate and cutlery in one hand, teacup in the other, I headed for the window table where I had sat with Samuel McArthur the evening before, so the housemaids could polish the long dining table while I ate. I walked with slow measured steps, head bent to watch my precarious load, preoccupied by my thoughts about Samuel and wondering if he would propose to me tonight at the ball.

"Let me help you with that."

The male voice startled me. I sloshed scalding tea on my hand. Wincing, I jerked my head back and accosted the stranger.

"You've helped me enough, sir, already!" I hurried onward, but the man took plate and teacup from me and we reached the table at the same time. I sat down and wiped my hand, wincing from the burned skin.

He dabbed a fingertip into the butter on my plate and gently smeared the small burn with it. I felt a trail of fire, but my heart told me it wasn't from the burn which the tea had inflicted. Gulping, I looked at him more carefully, and couldn't help liking what I saw.

"Charles Weatherby, at your service." He smiled disarmingly, revealing dazzling white teeth. His auburn hair, droopy moustache and alert dark eyes combined to remind me of a fox. Everything about his expression was intelligent and amiable. His nose was long and thin, his mouth generous, his gaze solicitous. I could tell at once that he was a true Victorian gentleman.

With a slight bow, Charles took my teacup and went to the buffet.

Of its own volition, my head turned to watch him go. The man was about twenty-five years of age, dressed fashionably but conservatively in a tailored frock coat and gray checked trousers. Unlike those affected by the mashers and heavy swells to shock their elders, Mr. Weatherby's trousers were of a discreet pattern and conventional cut. No peg top mode for him! He wore no chains, stickpins nor rings. He sported no monocle nor nosegay. Yet I could tell from the starched frills on his shirtfront that he was no Puritan.

He filled a plate of food, refilled my teacup and poured himself one.

I couldn't help smiling almost foolishly, staring at him as he walked toward me and set the teacup in front of me.

So here was the missing thirteenth house guest… and third bachelor!

CHAPTER 8

While we ate, Mr. Weatherby explained that he had been delayed by business in London and had only just arrived. He was my godfather's new associate, this being only vaguely stated so that I wondered in what capacity he had been employed.

I let him know that I was aware of the embezzlement situation, and he admitted that he had been hired to look into it. But he was not forthcoming with any other information, and I admired his discretion as he changed the topic of conversation.

"Was the evening enjoyable last night?" he asked.

"The meal was delicious."

"And the company?"

I had the sudden intuition that he was accustomed to women fawning over him and protesting in florid phrases that it had been boring without him, and that everyone had remarked upon his absence. Perversely, I said, "The company was stimulating. The evening was a complete success."

He studied me for such a long time that I feared he could read my thoughts and know that I lied, that in fact the evening was a *fiasco* on several counts because of Serena and Claire. It seemed he could surmise my financial woes just from raking me over with a look, but of course that was absurd. Still, I knew I should be on my guard. A slip of the tongue would be my ruin.

My intuition told me here was a man whom feminine wiles would not sway. No tricks would lead him by the nose to the altar. But would I want to, anyway? I wasn't sure he was worth pursuing. I detested his somewhat smug attitude, and besides, he had caused me to burn my hand.

"You are much like my younger sister," he commented. "Always daydreaming. I'll ask again. Where are the others?"

My cheeks flamed. I hadn't realized he'd spoken before. "My godmother, Mrs. Goodwin, is in the kitchen. The other guests are riding."

"Why aren't you with them?" He laughed suddenly, realizing the reason. "You overslept. There are still creases on your cheek from where your head rested on the pillow. It's a shame you missed the activity."

"The real shame is that if only I had gone riding with the others, I could have avoided having my hand burnt and my feelings trod upon by your insults!"

He laughed, not at all dismayed. "You cannot blame me for the burn. When I first saw you at the sideboard," he said, "I called out a very cheery, and loud, good morning to you. That was before you picked up the teacup. I gave fair warning that you were not alone, but you snubbed me. So it is I who deserve an apology. From you."

I flushed, remembering that earlier I had been daydreaming about Samuel McArthur and would not have heard an army march through the room. However, I was not about to give Charles Weatherby the satisfaction of admitting he was right. He'd think my mind was always filled with frippery.

We talked for a while longer, about general subjects, but it seemed whatever comment I made, he would take the opposite view as if for the sport of jousting with me. Annoyed, I hastily finished my meal and rose. This was one female who was not going to succumb to his charm and blandishments.

"Good day," I said icily and swept from the room as quickly as my cumbersome hoops would allow.

But the fox caught his prey all too easily. He was quickly at my side, his hand cupping my elbow as if to escort me. His touch was warm and thrilling. I yanked my arm away, furious with myself for responding to him.

"You cannot be angry with me," he said in a most charming way. "Save every waltz for me tonight. And we shall dine together. You must let me atone for the burn on your hand."

I made a small dismissive wave and continued on my way, alone. But I was not to rid myself of his company so easily.

Taking advantage of the pleasant day while awaiting the return of the riders, I strolled the gardens, admiring the regimental rows of rosebushes and ornamental shrubs. The latter were pruned into amusing shapes such as swans and elephants. Such pruning was no longer the fashion, but my godparents felt no need to bow to the changing whims of society when the gardens were so pleasing this way.

I sat on a cold stone bench in front of a bronze sundial, admitting to myself that I was procrastinating. I had gone outside to think about Samuel McArthur and yet all I'd done was think about Charles Weatherby. I had to be practical, had to dismiss distractions and focus my attention on the shipbuilder. Mr. Weatherby had his charms, to be sure, but he was only an assistant to my godfather, whereas Mr. McArthur clearly had the family wealth that I needed.

Cold-blooded? Yes, I admit it freely, because my survival was at stake. I was not in a position to think of a love match. I had to think logically, like a man some might say, but I felt it was a woman's prerogative as well. Ellen had inculcated me with the beliefs of her religion, that both sexes are equal each to the other. A man would not hesitate to marry a woman for her title or her riches, so why should I spurn such practicalities in my own hour of need?

In order to carry out my plan, I had to get Samuel alone somewhere tonight. Here in the garden would be a logical place. I could feign being overly warm inside from the dancing, and in need of fresh air. Others would be strolling as well, no doubt, and so we two would simply wander off down a path and sit on a bench, such as this one with room for two. All distractions would have to be eliminated so his attention would be directed toward me.

But just the thought of being alone with him, and forcing myself into a flirtation I did not feel, made me nervous. What would I say? Ideally, I would simply state the truth: 'Excuse me, we barely know one another but I have debts to pay so will you marry me and take care of it all? You will? Oh, much obliged, sir.'

I sighed out loud, feeling overwhelmed.

"Is something wrong?"

It was Charles Weatherby again.

My head snapped around. "Stop following me!"

He sat beside me. "Beautiful day, ain't it? Look at the butterflies."

He pointed out the purple blooming buddleia and the butterflies darting about the shrubs. I couldn't help following his glance and smiling at the sight. I knew my godmother planted nettles in discreet patches of the garden to attract favorable caterpillars to the area.

Seeming to read my thoughts, he mentioned my godmother in the next breath. "Mrs. Goodwin told me you were out here," he said. "She saw you pass by but you didn't acknowledge her. It's a nasty habit, you know, ignoring people all the time."

I started to retort, then noticed he was silently laughing.

"I have been preoccupied of late," I said haughtily.

"I learned of your husband's death," he said softly. "May I offer my sympathy?"

I was taken aback, not expecting this gentleness from him. "Thank you. What else did my godmother tell you about me?"

"I actually met Edward Whitney on more than one occasion."

"Did you?" I tried to hide my sense of alarm and pretend only mild interest. "So you were... close friends?"

"No," he said, so hastily and firmly that it seemed he wanted to be sure I understood. "We were not." But instead of elaborating on the subject, he fell silent.

Again, that simple way he had of shutting the conversational door in my face. I knew I would not get any further remarks from him on this topic. But I didn't care. If he had known Edward, then perhaps he also knew that our marriage had been one of convenience, which had never been consummated. My husband had been a rake and a gambler, and I had been a *naïve* young girl sent into the lion's den.

We fell into a companionable silence, enjoying the butterflies. My thoughts drifted to the past, a time shortly before my brother had gone off to war. We had come here for a two-week visit and were playing out of doors. He spotted something too tall for me to see, and had lifted me up onto his shoulders to show me a bird nest in a myrtle tree branch. Remembering him and all else that had been lost to me, my eyes swam with unshed tears and my thoughts dwelt in the past for some moments.

There was a sudden small rustle next to me, and I was brought back to the present with a start. I realized that Charles was studying me. My cheeks flushed. It was anathema to know that I had been observed at such a vulnerable moment. But he said nothing untoward about my melancholy, and instead seemed determined to proceed on the premise that we were having a simple, delightful visit in my godparents' country estate. Seeming to realize I did not wish to talk, he spoke knowledgeably and with interest about various plants in the garden and a Shakespearean herb garden his mother had planted years ago. I stirred myself to show some interest in him, and inquired what area he was from.

"Here and there," he said.

Tactfully, I did not press him on the issue since he probably was ashamed to admit where he lived. No doubt a clerk in his position could only afford humble lodgings. Still, I could not help thinking that he had been at least raised decently, since he acted the part so well.

Then abruptly seeming to feel I was cheered up sufficiently, Charles stood up, and held out a hand as any gentleman should. I graciously accepted his assistance and we walked for a while together in the gardens, taking a path that eventually led down to a little stone bridge arching over a winding stream. The water was narrow but rather deep and spotted with large rocks and tangled marsh grasses. Nearest the bridge, the grasses were wildly overgrown, in marked contrast to the orderly gardens nearby.

I told Charles the local story about a young woman a hundred years ago who had leaned over the bridge to admire her reflection but leaned too far and fell to her death. Local superstition barred clearing away the vegetation because it concealed the water, thus preventing a similar tragedy from happening today.

"It sounds like an inventive excuse by an old gardener to avoid work," he commented.

I laughed and agreed that he was probably right.

Our meandering walk led us to the spring-house where butter, cheese and other perishable foods were stored. A servant's child, a boy of about nine or ten, squatted on the ground, playing with kittens.

"What have you got there, son?" Charles asked, bending down to the child's level.

"Cats, sir." The child was scornful that his elder didn't know what the common creatures were called.

"Yes, I see that," Charles replied, holding back a laugh. He picked up one of the kittens to admire.

I scooped up a ball of orange fur that was clawing at my hem. "Oh, Charles! Look at this one!" I held the kitten to my cheek and nearly melted with love for it. I glanced up and saw Charles watching me tenderly. My face was on fire as I smiled at him. For just a moment, it felt that I had been waiting all my life for this man, this day. But I forced myself to look away.

I could feel Charles's gaze still on me, and from the corner of my eye, it seemed he looked dejected but he rallied, and asked the boy, "Is it alright if the lady keeps the marmalade cat?" To me, Charles said courteously, "You do want the kitten, don't you?"

I nodded, but felt dismayed that the mood between us had subtly changed to one of civility rather than warmth, even though I knew it was for the better and indeed, that I was the one who had instigated the change by my coolness toward him.

The boy shrugged. "My dad says we've got too many."

His inadvertent glance toward the stream led me to surmise the kittens were to be drowned, and I held my little one all the tighter to me.

Returning to the Manor with my new kitten, Charles and I discussed a name for her, and finally decided on 'Ginger' to go with her colouring.

While we walked, I had time to reflect on the fact that Charles had been speaking privately with my godmother earlier. What if Gloria had not only told him I was outside, but had broken her vow of secrecy and told Charles about my debts? Nonchalantly, I asked him now if she had told him anything else about me when she said I was in the garden.

Instead of a direct reply, he said, "Is there something I should know? I know you live in London, you love to dance, you are afraid of spiders, you are generous to friends and—"

"How did you—? Oh. My godmother. You two must have had quite an interesting chat about me."

"Do you have anything to add? She didn't tell me anything I couldn't have found out from other sources. Please tell?" he said languorously. "I do love secrets."

"How fortunate for you." I began to move, but he held my arm and turned me to face him.

He tilted my chin up. Our gaze locked. I felt all at once that he would kiss me, and I wanted him to. I felt myself leaning closer towards him, as a flower might lean toward the sun without awareness. His eyes penetrated mine. When he spoke, it was barely above a whisper, words meant not even for the butterflies and birds to hear, but only me.

"I demand complete honesty in my friends," he said softly. "No matter who they are. Any secrets, Loretta?"

My lips parted. I had the sudden impulse to confess everything on my mind and in my heart. But then I took hold of my fancies and jerked away as if scalded once more. "You already know far too much about me, sir!"

I quickly walked away, hugging my kitten, desperate to avoid that searching gaze of his. I had nearly told him about Edward's debts! How could I possibly confide in a man whose personality changed from moment to moment, first sensitive, then caustic. I'd surely get nothing but censure. A more astute wife than I had been would have made herself aware of the gambling and carousing, and put her foot down in time to forfend disaster. I had been a complete ninny during my marriage, but I didn't need that pointed out to me by Charles Weatherby.

He called my name, and I glanced back to see how much distance I'd managed to put between us. Unheeding, I tripped over a gnarled root protruding in the path. The kitten leapt to safety as I tumbled to the ground, my wire hoops blowing inside out over my head, revealing to all the world, but most particularly to Charles Weatherby, that Loretta Whitney wears lace drawers with pink bows. Thankfully, this pair was not patched, but was fairly new.

I couldn't see Charles, but his laughter was loud and long. As I struggled to get up, I heard his footsteps coming closer at a trot. To my chagrin, I needed his assistance because the hoop skirt was hopelessly unmanageable by myself alone.

When I was finally upright, smoothing my curls as best I could, he gave a gentlemanly bow, handed the kitten to me, gestured toward the Manor and proffered his arm. "Shall we?"

I could feel him trying to suppress his laughter. He was so cocky and patronizing! I suddenly hated Charles Weatherby with all my heart, and decided to avoid him the remainder of my stay at Kenwick.

But inside the Manor, as I hurried away from him, that sly fox Mr. Weatherby called out to me, "Don't forget, Loretta! Dinner together tonight. And every waltz!"

"How impudent," I muttered under my breath, refusing to give him the satisfaction of a reply as I sped up the stairs with my kitten. My head ached, and I wanted nothing more than to lie down with a cool cloth on my brow.

I heard Charles laugh in the foyer below. "Running away from me again? You're making a habit of it, my dear."

CHAPTER 9

After lunch that day, during which I managed to avoid Charles Weatherby despite all his manufactured contrivances to be next to each other, I located Thomas Harmon alone in my godfather's study.

My purpose was to ask Mr. Harmon to intercede on my behalf with the gambling casino which, due to Edward Whitney's folly, was about to become the legal owner of my family's jewelry business unless I could convince them otherwise. It might seem strange to ask him, rather than my godfather, but Mr. Harmon was a club owner himself. He had connections, and I trusted his discretion. He would not tell my godparents anything I did not want them to know.

Although my godmother had advised me to avoid being alone with Serena's husband, in case the redhead should learn of it and erupt in a fit of jealousy, I felt this conversation could only take place in private and so I took the risk, pushing aside worry over any possible consequences.

I would deal with Serena later, if it should become necessary.

Mr. Harmon was surprised to see me, but as soon as I said I needed to speak with him in private on a business matter, he ushered me in and closed the door behind us. He put away papers he had been working on at my godfather's desk, explaining that he had done enough work for the day and was at my service.

Haltingly, I explained my problem in the broadest of terms, eliminating the facts about my true state of finances but making it clear that I did not have the resources to pay the debt unless I sold my home, which was mortgaged. He allowed me to speak without interruption, merely interjecting an occasional murmur of encouragement as if sensing how difficult this was for me.

I had found it far less embarrassing to talk without facing him directly, so I stood by a window overlooking a path a gardener was raking in preparation for the ball tonight. I tried to affect a casual pose and tone of voice, as if the result of our conversation was only of minor importance to me, but I fear my shaky voice betrayed my despair.

Gradually, I gathered courage from Mr. Harmon's sympathetic ear. Hoping I had not misinterpreted polite boredom for interest, I broached the possibility of a less extreme solution to my husband's casino debt.

"Perhaps they would agree to less stringent terms," I said and began faltering over my words since I was unfamiliar with the business world. "If they would only allow me to retain ownership of the business while fulfilling the debt. The firm has been in my family for three generations. You know my older brother would have taken charge, but… In any case, I should hate to see it pass into a stranger's hands owing to…." I didn't want to cast aspersions on the dead, but I could not think of a polite phrase to say about Edward Whitney.

"Yes, I see," Mr. Harmon said slowly, nodding to himself.

He waited a moment to see if I was finished. I felt drained, and couldn't speak another word. He crossed to where I was standing, and laid an affectionate arm about my shoulders. "A very pretty little speech, my dear," he said. "And one no man could resist. I would be honored to help you in this time of need."

"Thank you, sir. I would appreciate it if this matter could remain between the two of us. Even my godparents don't know how severe Edward's gambling compulsion was," I admitted. "Surely you will agree there is no purpose in making his sins common knowledge."

"One must be respectful of the departed." He tilted my chin with a fingertip. "You can be certain that I shall be the very soul of discretion. No one will learn of this conversation from me."

"Thank you." Tears of relief stung my eyes.

"Now, my dear, put all this from your pretty head and let me work out a solution. You shouldn't have to be concerned with such mundane matters. You should be worrying about what you'll wear to the ball or something suitable for a young woman's mind."

This was no time to argue about what was suitable for a woman, so I bit my tongue and thanked him again, more profusely than before. During this, I felt a sudden draft that blew a few tendrils onto my cheeks. I smoothed the hair off my face.

"I'll get the obstacles out of the way," he said, "and call on you when we are both back in London. Say in a fortnight? Some night when my wife is busy with one of her many social engagements, you and I will have a quiet dinner together. I know just the place—"

"I heard every word, Thomas," came Serena's formidable voice. "What is going on here?"

We both turned toward the door, guilt-stricken. Mr. Harmon quickly let his arm fall from my shoulder and clasped his hands behind his back as if to prove they had been there all along.

I recalled the draft I'd felt a little earlier, and tried to remember how far back into our conversation it had been when Serena must have opened the door. She had probably seen us from the garden path, or else heard voices from the hall-way, listened at the door and eased it open to confront us. Perhaps she hovered around her husband at all times, making sure to whom he was speaking in case she needed to intervene. I searched my mind anxiously. Could she have heard reference to Edward's gambling? If so, I had no hope that my secret would remain safe.

Serena stepped closer to me. "Didn't I warn you to stay away from my husband?"

"Now, dear," he began, in a diffident tone.

"Shut up, Thomas! Not another peep from you."

Suddenly afraid that he was going to tell her about my debts, I quickly cast him a worried glance. Serena intercepted it and her eyes narrowed in judgment. I felt I would perish with shame.

"You had best look worried," she said to me. "I suppose you thought I wouldn't catch up with you, but I have. I've warned you repeatedly—"

"Mrs. Whitney came to me for business advice—"

She cut him off with a contemptuous look. Through clenched teeth she shrilled, "A business matter that requires dining with her when I am otherwise occupied. I'll warrant that's a bold-faced lie. Since when are you involved in handling a widow's estate? You're not an accountant or solicitor."

"I know that, dear," he said in a placating tone, "but Loretta wanted to know if—"

I made a quick shushing motion that somehow caught his attention and not hers, before he could continue. He fell silent, looking abashed. I felt sorry for him.

Determining that he was not going to tell her anything of significance, Serena told him with a chilly look, "We'll discuss this later." She whipped around to face me. Her eyebrow lifted sardonically. "There had better not be a 'next time,' not if you know what's good for you, young lady. Your affair with my husband is over!"

Behind her, Mr. Harmon murmured protestations that there was no affair to end, but she ignored him.

My godmother had counseled me to ignore Serena's outbursts. But how could I? I was a fool to let her talk to me in such an odious fashion, yet somehow with the very subject of our old spats in the room between us, I became tongue-tied and ill at ease.

Serena sneered at me. "I saw you walking with Charles Weatherby in the gardens. Don't set your cap for him, dear Loretta. I happen to know he won't marry anyone unless the dowry is at least twenty thousand pounds."

I didn't think to ask how she knew this. In confusion from the doubts she'd inflicted, I backed out of the room, then turned and fled toward the stairs and the safety of my room.

CHAPTER 10

Running up the stairs, I wondered nervously what Serena Harmon meant by saying she'd make sure my 'affair' with her husband went no further. To what lengths would she go to eliminate someone she perceived as a rival? I could only guess that the next few days would prove to be exceedingly unpleasant if I were unable to avoid her company. It would be best if I were to leave sooner than planned, but of course I had no intention of leaving before tonight's ball.

I reached the top of the stairs and started to pass Claire's room. The door was open and she must have noticed my movement in the corridor because she suddenly called me in. As soon as I entered, she waved a piece of paper in my face. Recognizing it, I flinched. It was the note I had left on her bed with the magazine article on etiquette, saying I thought she'd like to refresh her memory of the latest social *mores*.

"'Fondly, Loretta,'" she read out loud in a snide tone that I had never intended the note to bear. She crumpled the paper and threw it across the room toward me. "I don't need your advice. Now or any time. I've been to a ball, more than once. I'm not a street urchin you've rescued."

"I didn't mean it to sound that way—"

"What did you think I would do tonight, Mrs. Whitney? Humiliate you in front of your society friends? You're a fine one to talk about proper behavior. Look at you, prancing around in girlish frocks the moment your year of mourning ended, acting like a debutante ready for your first season."

I sighed inwardly. First Serena, now Claire. What was wrong with these women today? Was there something in the water? Silly me, I had thought a trip to the country would be a refreshing change of pace from city life. Instead, chaos had ensued.

The headache I'd had earlier returned with full vengeance. I absently rubbed my brow, remembering there was something I needed to talk to Claire about and yet dreading it. If she exploded in rage over a polite note about etiquette, what would she do when I asked about my missing jewelry? I decided I would have to find out, because I needed to know the answer and I could not let fear of her outbursts deter me.

"Claire," I entreated kindly. "Please. Calm down. Never mind the magazine. It was thoughtless of me."

She gave a small shrug, somewhat mollified.

"I don't want you to take this the wrong way," I began hesitantly, "but I'd like to ask if you have seen my jewel case." Seeing her expression flare up, I hastily put in, "I'm not accusing you of anything, but maybe you saw it."

"You think I stole it!"

"It might have gotten mixed in with your things when our baggage was brought in the house, that is all I meant." It wasn't quite all I meant, but she was quickly growing hysterical. "Or maybe you noticed it standing in plain sight and put it away for safekeeping."

"Search my room!" she cried, her eyes gleaming wildly. "Go ahead, search it right now. I have nothing to hide."

"Oh, Claire," I said helplessly. "Don't be such a goose."

Coming closer, she looked at me a long moment, then noticed the small burn on my hand.

"I was clumsy with the teapot," I explained simply. "And I have a headache. So if you'll excuse me, Claire, I'm going to lie down and rest before the ball."

"Wait here." She dashed to the dressing table and quickly unlocked a drawer and took something from it. "I get headaches all the time," she said, handing me a small twist of paper. "A doctor gave me this. Be sure to take it all at once, as it is weak and ineffectual otherwise. You don't want to be sick at the ball, do you?"

"No, of course I do not." I faltered. I couldn't keep up with her mercurial changes. "That was very thoughtful of you, Claire." Thoughtful, yes. But she hadn't acted this strange way when Edward was alive, not to my recollection anyway. For a moment, I wondered if his death had unhinged her, but they had hardly been close enough to warrant such an extreme reaction, unless they had been lovers. The thought had crossed my mind before, when she questioned me so much about Edward, but it still seemed unlikely.

I thanked her for the headache powder, and left.

My hand was finally on the doorknob to my own room when the door opposite flung wide open and Louise Rogers stepped out into the hall to accost me. She saw me and her face fell.

"Oh. It's you, Mrs. Whitney. I heard a noise, and hoped it would be my niece but I can see I was mistaken." She wore a drab grey gown, buttoned to her chin, with long sleeves.

It was my supposition that Susanna and Gordon were off somewhere together, possibly taking a romantic walk on the grounds or reading poetry to each other in a secluded area of the garden, but I did not share my thoughts with this woman, knowing she would not approve. "Susanna is probably downstairs," I said, "with some of the other guests who were playing charades."

"I haven't seen her since lunch," Miss Rogers said, annoyed. "When she returns, I'll teach her a lesson she won't forget in a hurry."

I looked at her a moment in dismay, understanding more about young Susanna and what she endured at home. Life with her strict aunt must be wholly unbearable.

"She had better not be off with that McArthur lad," Miss Rogers said abruptly, "because he is nothing but trouble."

"He seems a very nice young man to me."

"All men are trouble!"

"I haven't seen your niece since last night, when she showed me her gown for tonight."

Her lips twisted in a foul grimace. "I heard about that! Shameful what women are wearing these days. Whatever happened to modesty? I don't know what this world is coming to, women dressing like daughters of the devil. Yes, Lucifer himself must have designed the clothes you call fashionable."

I hastily bid her a good afternoon and slipped into my room. It was a quiet haven and I was happy to escape her ceaseless complaints. Pitying Susanna the life she must lead with such a guardian, I drew the draperies closed, then eased out of my dress, crinoline skirt and shoes. Crossing to the marble-topped washing stand, I wrung out a small linen towel in cool water, pressed it to my face then draped it over a wooden dowel to dry.

Taking the twisted paper of headache powder Claire had given me, I opened it into a glass of water and stirred it by swirling the tumbler. Suddenly I lost my grip and the glass fell to the floor, breaking into pieces and splashing the contents out.

My head was throbbing so badly that after picking up a few shards of glass I left the rest of the mess for Ellen to clean up, and stretched out on the half-tester bed I'd slept in since I'd been old enough to merit a room of my own at the Manor. I lay there thinking uneasily.

On reflection, it seemed the entire day had been a long string of abrasive encounters, starting with the incident of meeting Mr. Weatherby in the dining room and topped by this irritating brush with Susanna's aunt. Sandwiched between were Serena Harmon, with whom I expected to argue at each encounter, and Claire Lewis, with whom I did not. Never before had the colorless and unassuming Claire Lewis caused me the anxiety and confusion she had in the past two days. I lapsed into a brown study, wondering what could be the cause of such rancor.

At a plaintive mewing sound, I looked down. Poor kitten, I'd left her on the floor and she was trying to get on the bed but was much too small. She was probably hungry again. I scooped her up and rubbed the soft fur between her ears. She snuggled against me, purring in contentment. Strange how comforting it was to have a warm living creature so readily offer trust and love without question.

I pulled the bellcord to ring for a maid. I would have her bring a bowl of cream and more food scraps. I had already made the kitten a bed out of folded towels.

It was pleasant to have something to do unrelated to my finances or the task ahead of me tonight. But even as my mind swirled with thoughts of how to make the kitten comfortable, I was thinking about Charles Weatherby as well. I realized my reaction to him was totally illogical. From one moment to the next, my feelings for him did a complete about-face. When I was with him, he was both charming and exasperating at the same time. I couldn't figure him out. And yet, my godfather trusted him enough to hire him for some sort of clerical task.

Still, there was no use becoming infatuated with a man who was a mere assistant or detective. And to think he demanded a huge dowry! He apparently had grown up in a cottage where his mother grew herbs to sell on market day, and now he had decided to marry well. Twenty thousand pounds! While I could empathize with his desire for a successful match, his dowry limit was like a boulder in my path to happiness.

I firmly pushed my thoughts away from Charles and thought about my missing jewel case. No doubt it was safe at home in London, and I was worrying unnecessarily, but it was troubling nonetheless. I didn't think a thief took it, because I had other jewelry out on the dressing table which had remained undisturbed.

But then my thoughts were interrupted by a knock on the door, and I was soon busy telling the maid what my kitten princess desired from the kitchen.

Later, after Ginger was settled in her bed with a full stomach, and a bowl of milk nearby, Ellen came in. She couldn't hide her delight at the kitten, but pretended to be annoyed that I had taken on another mouth to feed. After scolding me for trying to clean up the broken glass and risking a cut, she neatened my room and then left, but came back shortly with an herbal remedy for my headache made from marjoram, sage, catnip and peppermint, as well as an unguent for the burn on my hand.

"Thank you," I told her as she ministered to me. "I did not want to ask Claire for another headache powder. She would accuse me of something deplorable, no doubt."

Ellen told me to rest so I would be refreshed for the ball, then explained that she had been working on Susanna's dress earlier but did not have the right thread to finish it. She had checked with the housekeeper, and finally found what she needed, so the project would be done in time. "There is a lot of talk among the servants about your new cat," she added suddenly.

I was startled. "There is?"

"You shouldn't have taken it."

"I had the impression they were to be drowned. I would've taken all of them if I could. Why? Does the cat have a disease?"

"Not a disease…."

"Then what?"

"That girl who drowned in the stream so long ago had an orange cat just like this."

"I am tired of such nonsense. Many people have marmalade cats without anything bad happening to them."

"Don't be so sure."

"And don't you start up with your premonitions. You know I don't believe in soothsayers and superstitions. Next you'll be saying I'll drown too."

"Not such nonsense as all that. Look at yourself. A burned hand this morning. Then you tripped and fell and bruised your knees. Your jewel case has been stolen. You almost cut yourself on a broken glass—"

"But I didn't," I put in firmly. "And everything else can be explained. I was careless with hot tea, I wasn't looking at the path, and my jewelry was overlooked in packing and is safe at home. Why don't you light a lamp and finish Susanna's gown? It will need to be ironed as well, so save time for that." I yawned and turned on my side to rest. I heard her moving around the room, but moments later I heard her gasp in shock.

"Oh, just look at this," she cried.

I sat up. She held up Susanna's ball gown for me to see. At first I didn't notice anything and was about to complain at being disturbed, but then Ellen fanned out the skirt. At once I could see that the fabric had been viciously slashed into ribbons. It could never be repaired.

I was at a total loss for words. Who could have done such a wicked thing? Why would anyone want to cause distress to Susanna Rogers? She was such a quiet little mouse, so completely unoffensive.

"It must have happened when you were out of the room looking for more thread," I said, searching for the facts of the incident, and knowing it had to be when the room was empty. "But why would anyone… Wait! Whoever did it thought the dress was mine!" I was suddenly certain of myself. It made perfect sense.

My mind swiftly recounted what must have happened. Someone had come to my room, discovered it was vacant, slipped in, seen a ball gown laid out on the bed and assumed it was mine. So someone wanted to spoil what I had planned to wear, and perhaps keep me from attending the ball. After all, how many people would come to a country manor with more than one ball gown in their trunk? It would be unlikely the damage would be discovered until time to dress for the party, and that would be too late to borrow a gown from my much shorter godmother and try to alter it to fit me.

Ellen grew impatient with my continued silence. "Do you know who did it?" she asked.

Thinking out loud, I said slowly, "I must say I doubt that Miss Lewis is the guilty one."

"She does seem to have a sudden grudge against you."

"But she knows full well that I can send her home in a snap since she is here at my behest. I know how much she is looking forward to the ball tonight, and therefore I doubt she'd risk being forbidden to attend it. However… I have no such control over…." I lapsed into silence.

"Who, Miss Loretta? Who do you think did this?"

I looked at her and decided there was no harm in telling her my suspicions. "Mrs. Harmon threatened me this afternoon."

Ellen's eyes grew wide in alarm.

"I tried to stay out of her way," I said, in defense of myself, "but she is jeal… well, she has a wrong idea about me, and ruining my dress would be the type of spiteful thing she would think of doing. Don't you see? She had easy access to this room since hers is only two doors away. She probably was waiting for the first opportunity to come in here by herself. Then she saw you leave and came in to see what mischief she could do."

Ellen took up the dress and clucked sadly over it. "What will Miss Susanna wear?" asked the ever-practical northerner. "I cannot mend this. No one could." Her kind face was filled with concern. She, too, had taken a quick liking to the young Miss Rogers.

"There's only one thing to do," I said firmly. "The right thing. Find Miss Susanna and bring her in here. We are similar in girth and height, and our colouring is the same. If she's not back in her room, she may be outside in the gardens with Gordon McArthur, but be sure not to ask her aunt where she might be! Then, as soon as you locate her, we'll fit my ball gown to her and she will wear it tonight."

While Ellen was gone, I looked through the dresses I had brought with me, and also a few that I had left behind the last time I'd visited, before my marriage. Thankfully, I had not gained weight after the wedding as some women do, and I was confident that something suitable would still fit me.

Soon Ellen returned, and I was relieved to see that she brought Susanna Rogers with her, having found her in the library looking for a book to read. I noticed that Susanna's face was tear-streaked. I imagined her aunt was to blame, and asked if that was so.

Reluctantly, Susanna nodded. "When I came back to my room about forty minutes ago, my Aunt Louise began chastizing me for being gone so long, alone, and told me what happens to girls who flaunt themselves in front of men."

"Were you with Gordon earlier?" I asked gently.

Susanna nodded, blushing. "One of the gardeners showed us his topiary work. We were only gone an hour or two at the most. The time slipped away from me because I was enjoying myself so much. The gardener was with us the entire time. I was fully chaperoned, but she would not believe me. I know I should be accustomed to my aunt's leash by now, but she's been even worse since we arrived here. She seems determined to prevent my having a good time. But how does she expect me to find a husband? I wanted to tell her that, but I held my tongue, knowing how angry she gets if I remind her my parents' will left money for my care and she has not wanted for anything."

I impulsively hugged Susanna and knew at once that I had made the right decision about the ball gown. Telling her quickly about the damage done to her dress, I made it seem that the kitten had probably done it, playing while no one was in the room to scold it. In the telling, that theory began to sound like a reasonable supposition. I repeated it more firmly. "The cat did it."

There was no sense bandying accusations against Serena or Claire when I had no proof. I would discover the culprit's identity later, but now we had too much to take care of to waste the final hours before the ball on searching for the perpetrator.

While Susanna stepped into my green ball gown with Ellen's assistance, I showed them the yellow silk gown I had found in the back of the wardrobe from a party here two years ago. All it needed was to have the girlish scalloped neckline modified to remove the lace daisies and make it more suitable for a woman of my marital status. I knew the housekeeper would find someone to help with the sewing, someone quick with a needle.

"Why don't you let me wear that dress instead of this one?" Susanna suggested.

I almost agreed, but then I looked over at her, and saw how becoming the green was on her, and how her eyes sparkled with the pleasure of wearing such an elegant gown.

Ellen met my gaze and smiled encouragingly.

So I shook my head and told Susanna, "What use is that gown to me without the emerald necklace we left behind by mistake? I would think of it all evening and the ball would be ruined for me."

CHAPTER 11

I was resting for the ball, playing with my kitten on the bed, when I heard a soft knock at my door. Calling out to see who was there, I put on a dressing gown and when I heard Claire's voice in reply, I then opened the door. To my dismay, Serena Harmon was with her. The two swept in and perched on the edge of the bed. Both were dressed for the ball.

"We're on a mission of mercy," Serena purred, then she spotted the kitten and raced over to snatch it up and fondle the little thing.

Claire nodded. "How is my patient?"

"I'm feeling better," I replied warily, wondering what these two mischief-makers were up to this time.

It must have been my imagination that Claire seemed unsettled by my comment.

"I accidentally broke the glass with the powder you gave me," I explained, and saw the puzzled look leave her face, "but I do appreciate your offer to help."

Susanna had already gone back to her room to rest. After she left, Ellen and I had conferred, and decided she would complete the alterations on the green gown since she had already started on it, and one of the other maids would alter the yellow one since all it needed was the neckline modification which Ellen had pinned. Ellen had just left on her errand with the yellow dress in a protective sheet.

Now I sat at the dressing table, feeling uneasy as I watched my unwelcome visitors glance around the room with seeking eyes. It felt like an invasion, and yet I didn't know how to get rid of them. They were guests in my godparents' home, and hence my position was awkward.

Serena got up and fingered the fabric of the green ball gown. She and Claire exchanged a look I could not interpret, probably envy that the gown was so pretty.

"Lovely colour, isn't it?" I commented. "I selected the material to match my emerald necklace."

Serena wandered around the room looking at things. "Claire told me your jewel case was mislaid."

"I am sure it will turn up," I said meaningfully. I was still not certain we had overlooked packing it, and from the sly look on Serena's face, I wondered if she had taken it. "There were several pieces in it that I would miss, for sentimental value."

"Family heirlooms," Claire put in knowingly.

The emeralds had belonged to my mother, so I nodded. It didn't appear the subject of the jewelry would prove illuminating, so I told them about the gypsy woman hired to tell fortunes as entertainment during the evening.

When Serena put down my kitten, I told them the legend of the girl who drowned by the bridge. "And some of the servants seem to think this cat will bring me bad luck because that girl also had an orange marmalade cat." I carefully watched their faces, hoping to startle some reaction from them by telling the story, but they did not seem overly interested in it.

Claire stood up and took a few steps closer to me. "I just wanted to tell you that I plan to marry Charles Weatherby. So stay away from him." She tossed her head in perfect imitation of Serena and glided toward the door, Serena at her heels. Claire turned at the door. "By the way, Loretta. Or Mrs. Whitney, I should say. I'll be needing a dowry, and I expect you to provide it."

Serena snapped her fingers. "Come along, Claire!"

"Wait." I caught them at the door and confronted them with the tattered burgundy ball gown. "This was on my bed today, and when I returned to the room it had been damaged. Do either of you know anything about it? Maybe you saw someone come in here?"

"No," Serena said. "Not a soul."

Claire shook her head, seeming sincere. I was taken aback, so certain she would have given a guilty start. But perhaps she was a practiced liar and false reactions were natural to her.

Serena's parting words were, "Don't be late to the ball!" I shut the door but could still hear her musical laugh fade as she went down the hall with her new shadow, Claire Lewis.

For the past hour, I'd heard the deep rumble of carriages arriving as one after another they approached the Manor's entry, disgorged their passengers and rattled off to park near the stables.

The atmosphere crackled with excitement. Every few minutes I found myself drawn to the window which overlooked the front driveway. If I stood carefully to one side of the window, I could watch guests arrive without being observed, something I had learned at a young age when my godparents entertained but I was too young to attend the festivities.

Now I wished my suite were further down the hall, so my window would be directly over the entrance doors. But by craning my neck, I could see the parade of landaus, phaetons, barouches and an occasional curricle or cart, some with liveried footmen, others with a single driver in command of the horse or team.

I was anxious to join the party, but my dress was not ready yet.

As soon as Ellen had finished altering and ironing the green ball gown, she delivered it across the hall to an ecstatic Susanna Rogers and then went to have supper in the kitchen and fetch my yellow ball gown. I called across to Susanna to not wait for me, but go to the ball when she and her aunt were ready.

Waiting for my own gown, I had spent the time reading in my room, and then decided to start getting ready so all I would have to do would be put on the dress when Ellen returned.

I was sitting at the dressing table, brushing my hair, clad only in my finest embroidered camisole. My lace drawers were hidden by the wire hoop skirt which in turn was covered by a thin petticoat. On my feet were stockings and dancing slippers.

There was suddenly a rap at the door. I sighed in annoyance, certain that it was Claire Lewis and wondering what she wanted this time.

But it wasn't Claire. "Open up," a male voice whispered urgently. I thought I recognized the voice as belonging to Charles Weatherby and in my confusion I quickly slipped on my dressing gown and hurried to the door.

I didn't open it but whispered back, "Leave me alone! You can't come in. What do you want? I'm not dressed."

"Then clothe yourself, woman, because I am coming in!"

And suddenly the door opened. Charles strode in, elegant in his evening attire, but carrying a burden as he headed for the bed. I quickly glanced down the hall to be sure no one had seen him, and then eased my door shut. I hurried to the bed as he put Susanna down on it. She was pale and her eyes were closed.

"What have you done to her!" I cried.

He cast me a look of annoyance. "I have rescued her, after a fall on the stairs."

My heart leapt. "Is she—"

"No," he said more gently, "she is not dead."

"Where was she?"

"Just below the landing."

"How did you know to bring her here?" I asked, as I tried to examine her for injuries.

Susanna's eyes fluttered.

I bent over her and smoothed her hair. "What happened? Can you talk? Please explain."

"My ankle…." she murmured.

I removed her shoes and helplessly looked at her feet. Charles gently moved me aside, explaining that he had been around animals all his life and knew a bit of doctoring. He examined her ankles and decided she had a slight sprain in her left one. I gave him a spare stocking and he improvised a bandage around the ankle to give it support.

"You had better rest here a while, Susanna," I said.

"But Gordon is—"

Charles and I exchanged a quick glance.

"I'll let him know you will be down shortly," Charles offered. "I think your ankle will be strong enough to walk on, but don't overdo it by dancing all night." He turned to let himself out.

I quickly crossed to his side and laid a hand on his arm. "Thank you."

After he left, I hurried back to Susanna, who was trying to sit up.

"Oh, look at this dress!" she said in dismay. "It's all wrinkled now."

"I'm glad you are not in such pain that you can't have your priorities straight," I replied, laughing lightly to help break the tense mood. I helped her to a chair. "You'll have to be more careful on the stairs."

She frowned. "But I was being careful. I was dressed early but I didn't want to disturb you so I decided to look downstairs and watch the guests arrive. The oddest thing happened. I know I didn't slip. I was starting down, and suddenly I felt a hand on me. Someone pushed me at the top of the stairs! At once, I was falling, and trying to grab the handrail."

"You imagined—" I began, and then stopped myself. In a flash, I saw what must have happened. Susanna: my height, my hair colour, my green ball gown, in the dimly lit hallway at the top of the stairs…. Yes, it was entirely possible.

From behind, she could easily be mistaken for me. Particularly by someone who knew that dress was mine. Serena Harmon. Claire Lewis. Susanna's aunt and Ellen knew it as well, but why would they wish to harm me? Or did Miss Louise Rogers know it was Susanna and wanted to....? My thoughts quickly became muddled.

"What is the matter, Loretta? You do think it was my imagination, don't you? Why would someone push me?"

I did not want to cause her worry. She had enough troubles, trying to avoid her aunt's wrath and worrying now about whether she would be able to dance with Gordon McArthur. "Of course it was just your mind," I said, "playing a trick on you."

A little later, when Ellen came in with the yellow ball gown and I put it on, it seemed the seamstress is the one who had played a trick on me. Instead of a fashionable yet still modest *decolletage*, the bodice was now daringly low-cut.

Too stunned to speak, I sat at the dressing table, and looked in the mirror while Ellen quickly finished my hairstyle. I could almost hear the outraged comments from the matrons at the ball. Not only was I not dressed as a widow in half-mourning colours of grey or mauve, but now I did not dare bend over, or even breathe too deeply.

My only alternatives were to wear a plain dress, unsuitable for a ball, or else stay in my room and miss the golden opportunity this evening afforded for finding a husband. I tried to disguise the neckline with flowers or a scarf but nothing worked, and financial imperative gave me no real choice.

"Are you ready, Susanna?" I asked. "Lean on me, and we'll go down the stairs slowly. Just hold your head high, and no one will notice you are limping."

Sotto voce, I added, "And hopefully they will be too busy wondering about your injury to look at my dress!"

CHAPTER 12

I nearly lost Susanna in the noisy throng pressing in the front door. Taking hold of her arm, I led her through the crowd and into the ballroom. It was a scene of merriment even more delightful than my daydreams. Hundreds of candles lit the room and bathed the occupants in a soft glow.

All the men were attired in formal evening wear: plain unpatterned trousers, stiff shirts with standing starched collars and the *de riguer* cutaway coats. Many had adorned themselves resplendently with finger rings, cuff links, tie pins, collar studs and watch chains of gold, some set with gems such as onyx and garnets. More than a few affected the use of monocles and several even wore spectacles, perhaps desiring to start a new trend.

My heart beat faster as I noted so many men who were richly dressed. Perhaps I would find the task of procuring a husband easier than I'd dreamed. After all, I only needed one, and here were many candidates, with more entering at every moment.

Scents of bay rum, tallow hair pomade and perfume macassar oil mingled with feminine colognes and sachets to sweeten the air as couples danced to the orchestral music. The women lent gaiety and colour to the scene, in gowns of pink or white, blue, green, lilac or yellow like my own, fashioned in fine muslin, silk, satin or lace with snug bodices cut low at the neck and shoulders and voluminous skirts flounced from hem to waist with ruchings, scallops, tiny wreaths, rosebuds, pleats or knots of ribbon.

Garlands of blossoms crowned many of the girls' ringlets, braids and chignons. Their folding fans were carved or inlaid with painted flowers, and many wore posies pinned at the waist. I had tried pinning flowers at my bodice, but it was too scratchy, and my lace handkerchief kept falling out, calling attention to the area I was trying to conceal. So now I raised my open fan and held it casually, hiding my gown's low neckline.

Of a sudden, it seemed to me that time had been suspended for this one magical night, and I was poised on the brink of an experience I would never forget. I wanted the evening to be everlasting, so I could be sure to meet all of the bachelors and make my choice from among them. I laughed inside, suddenly bubbling with youthful optimism.

Flushed faces, sparkling eyes, the essence of a thousand flowers and spices, the sibilant shuffle of low-heeled dancing slippers, the snatches of gay *repartee* that reached my ears, all these impressed my senses with delight as dancers twirled past Susanna and me. I saw that she was searching the crowd with her eyes, and when she saw Gordon McArthur across the room, a smile lit her face. She was young, she was happy and she was in love.

Gordon smiled and waved to her. From the way he was looking at her as he tried to thread his way through the crowd, it appeared that her love for him was returned in full measure.

Flocks of young girls tittered in corners, comparing dance cards and no doubt whispering of new *beaux* to conquer. Somberly-clad matrons sat in chairs along the walls like so many plump and complacent hens twittering together, smugly buzzing, heads close to one another and bobbing as they pointed a quizzing glass or furled fan at a new subject for their gossip. I knew it would not take long for the busybodies to impale me with their thorny remarks.

As Gordon advanced closer, Samuel McArthur joined his brother, and the two approached us. An old-fashioned quadrille was forming. Within moments we four took our places just before the dance began. Sam's eyes seemed riveted to my bodice and I couldn't help blushing.

"Will you dine with me this evening?" he asked me.

"I'd be delighted," I replied, relieved that he had not asked anyone else while I had been upstairs.

Later, a waltz began, and Charles Weatherby materialized at my side to claim me for the dance. I tried to protest fatigue but he merely laughed and took me in his arms to sweep me away from Samuel's glowering look.

Although I knew that Charles was a fortune hunter like myself, else how would Serena Harmon know the dowry he required, I could not prevent my heart from beating faster as he held me close and murmured suave compliments in my ear. I felt that I could dance with him all night, and tell him anything. Indeed, within a few minutes, I found myself confiding in him that Susanna was wearing my green ball gown, and therefore I assumed that her accident had actually been intended for me.

He shot me a questioning look, and I added that she'd had the sensation of being pushed at the top of the stairs, but I put it down to the excitement of her first ball. Frowning, he asked if anything else strange had been happening to me.

"My jewel case is missing," I admitted, "but I am certain I will find it at home. And the reason Susanna needed a different gown to wear is that the one she had brought with her was somehow ripped beyond repair while in my room."

"Your corner of the manse is quite the hub of activity," he drawled.

I thought of something else, and stumbled. He smoothly helped me recover my footing and we continued dancing. I felt an explanation was in order. "I just remembered that I had to help my kitten up onto the bed when she was trying to leap up on it, because it was too high for her and she is too young to climb yet. The dress that was damaged was lying on the bed. She couldn't have ruined it with her claws, as I tried to convince myself."

He caught my meaning at once. "It was deliberate mischief against you," he said. "Why would you be the target for—"

"I don't know," I cut in hastily. "I really don't. It is a complete mystery to me." And yet, in the back of my mind all I could think of were Serena Harmon and Claire Lewis, each with reasons for being spiteful toward me. Serena, out of jealousy that I had designs on her husband, and Claire out of outrage that I did not mourn Edward Whitney's passing. Yet my fears were so nebulous, and it all seemed too trite to mention to Charles.

The music stopped but I remained in his arms. He looked into my eyes and said softly, "If you needed money, would you come to me?"

I was startled but quickly regained my composure. "Is this some new quizzing game?"

"Would you?" He saw that I wasn't going to answer and went on, "Do you want my help in finding out who is trying to harm you?"

Suddenly noticing the glances we were getting, I stepped away from him. "No one is trying to harm me, Charles." But my voice was faint.

Across the room I saw Serena Harmon talking with Claire Lewis. Charles quickly followed my gaze and turned back to me with a question in his eyes.

"Sometimes… strange things happen," I said lightly. "And we might think we know who did it, but it is better to just forget about it, instead of making matters worse by tossing out accusations." I inclined my head politely. "Thank you for the dance, Mr. Weatherby."

I left him as quickly as I could, knowing I had been right to refuse his help. He would only make matters worse, by telling my godfather about Susanna's damaged ball gown and her fall on the stairs. If I minimized the importance of these incidents and laughed them off as mere pranks, it would be the best for all concerned.

I had to use my energy for my own needs this evening, and not get embroiled in Claire's machination. I must remember at all times: *Survival of the fittest.* The more energy I expended trying to determine her motives, the less I'd have for my own plan to find a husband. So for now, I needed to turn my back on Charles Weatherby and promote my case with someone who had more potential.

About an hour later, I was glad to have a rest from dancing with several different partners.

Together with the McArthur brothers, Susanna and I were waiting in a queue to see the gypsy fortune teller in the decorated parlor.

Suddenly, a boisterous threesome of mashers pushed past us, trying to get to the head of the line out of turn. They were firmly but cheerfully turned away by some of the men, and left with comments of seeking out another punch bowl.

"It seems to me they had enough punch already," I said, to general laughter.

Samuel touched my arm. "Are you sure you want to keep waiting? We could go dance, and come back later."

"The line is moving up now," Susanna pointed out, and so we stayed to wait our turn.

Claire Lewis ran up to me just then, breathless and flushed, leaving a wake of annoyed glances. Everyone in my party had met her already, and we exchanged a few pleasantries with her. I assumed she would leave, but instead she insinuated herself in the line in front of me.

"I cannot wait to see this gypsy," Claire said. "I love fortune tellers, don't you? I don't care what anyone says about them. I think it is cruel they are persecuted so much. A girl I knew once went to a fair, and the gypsy said she would get married, live on a farm and have twin sons. And do you know what happened?"

"What?" asked Susanna, breathlessly.

"It all came true," Samuel put in sardonically.

Claire tossed him a cold look. "Just like the gypsy said. Every detail." Claire turned her glance on me. "Do you believe in fortune tellers?"

"Of course she doesn't," Samuel said in irritation. "It's a parlor game."

"That's right, it is only for entertainment," I added. "They say what you want to hear. To young girls, the fortune is marriage and children." I smiled at the McArthur brothers. "What will the gypsy tell you two, do you suppose?"

"I hope she doesn't say I'm going to have twins," Samuel joked. "It will ruin my figure!"

We all laughed, except Claire.

"Don't scoff," she warned.

Moments later, we were at the front of the line and with a helpless, apologetic shrug to the others behind me, I let Claire go in ahead of me. She seemed to take longer than others had with the gypsy, but perhaps I was just growing tired of the wait.

Eventually, she emerged. I gestured for Susanna to go in, since while waiting for Claire to finish, Gordon had decided he didn't want to take time for his own fortune and wanted Susanna to go with him and watch him play at cards, to bring him luck.

Claire quickly stopped Susanna from going in the door. Instead, she yanked at my hand. "Loretta is next."

Susanna stated that she didn't care who went first and so I hurried in, not wanting to delay the line further by squabbling over whose turn it was now.

An exotic, spicy fragrance assaulted me as I walked toward the vacant chair awaiting me in the center of the room. Looking around the parlor, I noticed the walls had been draped with yards of brightly coloured fabrics that billowed and sighed in the soft breeze from an open window. For illumination, there were flickering candles and shaded oil lamps. The room was dim, yet I could not overlook the coal-black cat curled up near a pot of burning incense on the floor. The cat hissed and arched its back as I passed.

The gypsy woman I had seen earlier sat behind a table draped in shimmering material. She had put on a turban and more jewelry since we'd last met. Lip rouge darkened her wide mouth. She was most impressive, in a mysterious way, and I could understand more readily now why my godmother had felt cowed by her earlier.

"Sit down," the gypsy said in a heavy accent. Her plump arms rested on the tabletop.

As I walked to the chair, shivers traversed my spine and I felt unaccountably weak in the knees, cowardly and yet splendidly thrilled all at the same time. I decided to enjoy myself, and when I sat, I gave her a coin which she tucked away.

She studied me for a moment. "You are too young for daughter so old as girl just here."

I frowned, then realized that for some reason, she thought Claire Lewis's mother was to be her next patron. I smiled, and corrected her mistake.

The gypsy gave me a blue deck of tarot cards and instructed me what to do with them, step by step. When I had finished laying out the rows of cards, she began the reading, explaining that each row represented a phase of my life: past, present and future, and her skill with the cards would reveal the course of events comprising my entire life.

I settled back, waiting to hear that I would marry a handsome man and be very happy. But instead, she said the influences in the cards revealed a quarrel or neglected friendship. She said my destiny was trouble, and that it would be dangerous for me to fall in love. Sweeping all the cards into a pile, she concluded, "No marriage for you."

"What?" I grabbed at the cards. "Show me where it says that." I turned over one blue card after another, suddenly frantic. I had never been given such a fortune! How could this be?

She quickly found the Sun card and then The Lovers. "The Sun was reversed, and combination with The Lovers is very bad. Means broken engagement. No love, not for you. You plan much, but," she said firmly, "no wedding."

Even though I logically knew it was a parlor game, the pronouncement struck terror in my heart. I had to get married! I felt utterly crushed, destitute of hope. My daydreams shattered into a thousand shards at my feet. I would be poor. I would have to support myself by being a governess or housekeeper, someone's servant.

Grasping at one last hope, I took out another coin I could ill afford to part with, and offered it to her. "May I have another reading?" I pleaded. "Perhaps the cards were… wrong."

She looked at the coin, and then my face. Something glittered in her eye as she considered me for a moment. "Is important you marry?"

Nodding quickly, I abandoned all fear of giving away my desires and influencing my fortune reading. "Yes, very important."

She picked up another deck of cards, black this time, and instructed me again in how to lay out the cards, shuffling, discarding, placing them in rows. Then she turned over the first card. "I see danger." She looked at me, and seemed to study me as if she were seeing me for the first time. She upturned another card, the Queen of Swords. "It is upside down. Means beware of hidden enemy, treacherous woman. Ruthless and cruel. The Moon in this place," she said, turning another card, "means false friend will betray you."

My heart skipped a beat. She meant Claire Lewis!

I leaned forward as she continued my reading. Everything she said added up to a warning of grave danger. Fear must have shown in my face, because she suddenly removed a necklace she was wearing. I realized it was the amulet I had seen earlier that day from a distance. Seen up close, it turned out to be a battered gold medallion, with strange figures and foreign lettering on it. She rubbed it softly between her fingers and muttered something under her breath in a language I did not understand, possibly Romanian from what my godmother had told me before. I wet my lips, wondering what she was doing.

Abruptly, she thrust the necklace at me. "Wear it for safety. No death." She made a washing motion with her hands. "No blame for me."

I took the talisman and looked at it. I knew its oddity would be remarked upon if I wore it around my neck, so I quickly thrust it into a pocket in the side seam of my ball gown with my handkerchief.

All at once, I felt a sense of comfort wash over me. I knew it was foolishness, an idea planted in my mind by the gypsy's words of danger and safety, but I didn't care.

As I departed the room, the fortune teller's final warning rang out, "Watch for *dusman*— enemy!"

CHAPTER 13

The rest of the evening sped by in a blur of disjointed episodes: dancing with one partner after another; walking on the terrace with Samuel McArthur; evading Claire Lewis and Serena Harmon when our orbits came in proximity; sipping fruit punch with my godparents. No matter how hard I tried, I could not forget the fortune teller's ominous words.

I felt like a sleepwalker, going through the motions as I greeted old friends, met new ones, danced and laughed gaily, pretending a joy I did not feel. Whereas at the start of the ball I had wished the night would be everlasting, now I prayed the party would quickly end. Instead, it dragged on and on, to the point of tedium.

Thomas Harmon came up to me and bowed. "You're looking lovely tonight. Would you care to dance?"

The words 'Are you insane!' were on the tip of my tongue but I did not utter them. Didn't he remember what his wife had said to me, about staying away from him? Instead, I merely said I was fatigued. As soon as possible, I made a polite excuse to leave him. As I walked away, I thought I caught a glimpse of Claire Lewis watching me, but then the crowd shifted and I felt perhaps it was only my overactive imagination.

The encounter with the gypsy had deflated my vitality. The rest of the evening I was like a wooden doll in the arms of my dance partners, distractedly nodding to their questions and falling out of step with the music, causing tangled feet and annoyed looks from nearby couples.

As he had vowed to do, that handsome fox, Charles Weatherby, claimed me for every waltz. He asked me more than once if something was wrong. Each time, I deflected his questions, but I knew he was not fooled. Indeed, he became annoyed with me, but I couldn't seem to care about his opinion. His interest in me seemed suddenly to be oppressive.

"I don't care for your company," I finally cried and pulled away from him to run outside. But before I reached the doors, Samuel McArthur approached and I found myself almost hysterical as he tried to lead me out to the dance floor yet again.

"Please, no," I said. "Let us take a turn in the garden."

We went outside and joined a few other couples strolling along the raked paths in the fragrant garden. Strains of music and laughter reached our ears and we wound along the paths lit with small oil lanterns.

He abruptly stopped at a bench and gestured for me to sit down. I did, but he remained standing. He towered over me, and I felt a sudden sense of intimidation. I shrank back slightly. "I demand to know what that man means to you," he said.

"What man?"

"That Charles Weatherby, as if you didn't know full well who I am talking about. He has hovered around you like a moth to the flame. I've watched you dancing together and I don't like the way he looks at you. I insist that you tell me if there is anything between you two. Am I wasting my time?"

I didn't like his manner. He was entirely too arrogant and presumptuous. "You insist?" I repeated in amazement. "Who gave you the right to insist about anything where I am concerned! Just because my godmother is your mother's cousin, that relationship gives you no proprietary rights in my life. Of all the smug, complacent attitudes! You had me fooled. I thought you were a gentleman but you're just a ruffian."

I quickly got up and moved toward the house. I could hear his feet crunching on the walkway behind me as he called out my name, pleading for me to wait. Reaching the door to the ballroom, I turned, not wanting to create a scene in front of the other guests.

"I guess I'm jealous. I can't stand the idea of him touching you. Forgive me for being rude?"

It would be churlish to refuse, so I bowed my head slightly, agreeing to his request.

Samuel was still my best prospect for a husband and I daren't cast him aside just because he vexed me. All men were vexing, after all. Even Charles Weatherby made me feel like screaming at times. I vowed to control my tongue and stop uttering every thought that popped into my head. So I smiled at him sweetly, bit back my annoyance and let him guide me back to the ballroom where we danced again.

Later, thinking anew about the gypsy's prophecy of danger and enemies, I became so overwrought that I could barely concentrate on flirting with the eligible men I met, and I know I made an unfortunate impression on many of them. No doubt they thought I was disinterested. As the evening waned, I had fewer dance partners, and indeed at one point I found myself standing alone, observing the crowd instead of being part of it.

Claire had enjoyed a successful evening, and I saw her dance by, her eyes bright, her face almost feverish. I was reminded of her behavior at the inn in Twelveoaks, and wondered what caused her to be so overheated at times, as if her heart beat with more fire than normal.

It was nearing midnight, and Samuel McArthur was walking toward me with a smile. During the course of the evening, I had received a proposal of marriage from an older man, which I politely turned down because I knew he was from the local village and did not have the means to take on both my support and my debts.

My relief at telling him no was somewhat confusing to me, then I realized that without intending to, I had begun comparing each dance partner against Charles Weatherby. No matter how much I protested to myself that he was both ineligible and impertinent, in my heart a warmth for him was blooming.

But now Samuel McArthur was coming closer. He was nearly at my side when his mother waylaid him. I saw her look in my direction then turn back to him, shaking her head and admonishing him about something. I felt faint with surmise that she was talking about me, unfavorably. My heart skipped in fear.

The significance of her possible comments did not escape me. He was my best prospect. If she did not approve of me, a proposal would not be forthcoming. I would have to be very careful around her the rest of the evening, make sure I did and said nothing she could take amiss. Now I saw her glance at my gown in disapproval. I quickly opened my fan and used it to conceal my *decolletage*, hoping she might be judging me harshly for this reason alone. If so, it was something easily rectified. I decided not to wait to learn if I was right about the dress. I sped from the salon.

Upstairs I went into my godmother's dressing room, knowing she would not mind. Familiar with her things, I searched the drawers until I found a lacy shawl to wrap around my shoulders and knot in front, making my costume more modest.

As I left the room, I noticed Serena Harmon coming away from my bedroom door down the hall on the opposite side. I quickly slipped back into my godmother's dressing room and shut the door. With my heart hammering, I listened with my ear pressed to the door until I heard steps descending the staircase.

Cracking the door to peer out, I ascertained the hallway was empty, and so I hastened to my room to see what Serena might have been doing. At first I didn't see anything out of place. I decided to bathe my face and freshen my powder before going back to the ball.

But when I approached the washstand, I found out what Serena had done. The lifeless body of my little kitten was in the washbowl. I cried out. Not knowing what else to do, I quickly picked the kitten up and lay it on a towel to see if it might by some chance still be breathing. I could tell at once that Ginger was dead.

What a cruel thing to do! So senseless, and cruel. Was it meant as a warning to me? Or perhaps sheer spite. No doubt Claire had indeed seen me talking earlier with Thomas Harmon, and had tattled to Serena.

At a loss, I didn't know what to do next. I stood for a moment, looking at my little pet, remembering sadly how Charles and I had found it together and played with it together, and named it… together.

"He will know what to do," I whispered out loud. I covered the sodden little corpse with the towel and hurried back to the salon in search of Charles Weatherby.

Samuel McArthur accosted me at the bottom of the staircase. "I saw you go up, and I've been waiting all this time. Come, the meal is being served." He held out an arm.

Frustrated, shoving thoughts of the dead kitten to the back of my mind, knowing I must remain on course with Samuel, I smilingly took his arm and let him escort me to the tables where guests were gathering to dine on a midnight supper.

Trying not to be obvious about it, I craned to look around the crowd and spy Charles in the room, wanting to ask him what to do about Ginger. Sighing softly to myself, I turned the other direction, and came face to face with him.

"Looking for me?" Charles said mischievously. Before I could reply, he went on, with a polite nod at Samuel McArthur, "You promised to dine with me tonight. Remember?"

I gaped at him, and remembered that silence is often construed as assent. When I hadn't replied in the negative this morning, to his thinking it might as well have been a 'yes' reply. I tried to think of something to say to the two men in front of me, but my usual command of the language failed me.

"Is this true?" Samuel demanded of me.

Gathering my pride along with my skirts, I stood up. "I had forgotten, but yes it is true. Forgive me?" And I left with Charles Weatherby.

As we walked away, I glanced back to see Claire Lewis quickly slide into the seat I had vacated. My heart plummeted. What if she managed to snare the marriage proposal that I had been casting my nets for since yesterday evening?

Charles took me toward another table, but on the way, I told him what had happened to our little kitten.

"Do you need me to—" he began, glancing upstairs.

I nodded gratefully, and we quietly slipped away, then went singly upstairs so that no one would be scandalized to see us go together into my *boudoir*.

Inside my room, I gestured toward the washstand and he quickly assessed the situation.

"You've had a shock," he told me, as he checked the kitten over. For a moment, my heart leapt with hope, but he sadly shook his head, confirming the cat's death.

"Will you…." I said, looking at the little kitten.

He understood my meaning at once, and wrapped the small body in the towel. "I will have one of the servants bury her in the garden."

"Near the bridge," I whispered, choking back a sob.

"Yes. Near the bridge." He looked at me sympathetically.

I looked at the sad bundle in his hands. "I appreciate your taking care of this for me. I'll be downstairs in a few minutes. We still need to eat, and I must be on hand for the birthday toasts."

He started to leave.

I stopped him as he passed me, and quietly said, "Thank you."

My godfather beamed happily at his wife as she presided over the presentation of a magnificent cake decorated with fresh flowers. Everyone applauded and called out hurrahs and cheers. Several of the gentlemen in the party took turns calling out ribald toasts and witty comments about Peter Goodwin's advancing age. He took it all with good humor.

Standing next to my godparents, I happened to catch Serena's glance. I shot her a questioning look, but she merely turned away.

The McArthur family pressed close, wishing my godfather well on the anniversary of his birth. I noticed that young Susanna Rogers hung back from the group, looking troubled. I found my way to her as quickly as I could and gently took her aside so we might speak in privacy.

"Is your ankle bothering you, Susanna?"

She shook her head. "Not that much. It's <u>her</u>." She looked pointedly at Gordon's mother. "I overheard her talking to another woman, I'm not sure who it was, but she said that it was clear to her that both you and I—"

"She mentioned me by name?" I cut in, horrified.

Susanna nodded. "She said that we obviously have set our caps for her sons, and she would do everything possible to stop any match, because she has in mind two sisters back in Cornwall whom she wants Gordon and Samuel to marry."

This was worse than I expected. How dare Mrs. McArthur flatly decree that Susanna Rogers and I were not good enough for her clan! I was not a blood relative of Gloria Goodwin, that is true, but I was not a charity case, and neither was Susanna Rogers.

I tossed my head, suddenly determined to marry Samuel McArthur no matter what it took. I'd show his mother that she didn't know what she was talking about.

"You and Gordon should elope," I said heatedly to Susanna. "That would teach Mrs. McArthur not to meddle!"

CHAPTER 14

The next morning, as I sat at my dressing table ready to enjoy a peaceful Sunday at the Manor, and hopefully close the trap around Samuel McArthur, Ellen rushed in, snatched the comb from my hand and finished dressing my hair.

"Have you heard?" she said breathlessly. "Miss Susanna eloped with Gordon McArthur during the night. There's three search parties out looking for them."

"Oh, no...." My glance met hers in the mirror. She stared back at me. Knowing she would get the truth from me eventually, as she always did, I ruefully admitted that it had been my idea. "But it was just something I blurted out! I didn't mean they should really elope. Oh, Ellen, what will happen to them when they are found?"

"It depends," she said sagely, "on whether they are married yet or not."

Impatiently, I jabbed a few pins in my hair, dressed hurriedly and sped from the room. I had to find out what was going on.

Loud angry voices drew me to the dining room. I hurried in, but paused in the doorway a moment, still unnoticed, taking in the scene. I was not surprised to see that neither Samuel nor Charles was there. They would've gone out with the search parties. Looking around, I saw that all the men must have gone.

"This is your fault, Mrs. Goodwin," Louise Rogers suddenly said. "My niece would be safely at home if you had not insisted in your letter that I allow her to come to this den of iniquity! You promised nothing would happen to her. Now look!" she added with black-hearted triumph.

It seemed to me that Miss Rogers was more interested in the drama than in her ward's safety.

My godmother shook her head sadly. I imagined she had already defended herself *ad nauseum* and had run out of things to say. How anyone could blame her was a mystery to me.

"I suppose it is my fault," Mrs. McArthur said from a chair at the table, "for not keeping my son under control better. It is not like Gordie to disobey us. I made it clear that he was to get permission before asking a girl to marry him. And now this!" She burst into tears.

"I shall have the marriage annulled," Miss Rogers said firmly.

Serena Harmon spoke up. "Does anyone know who saw them last? We don't even know how many hours they have been gone." She glanced over and saw me. "I bet you know something about this, don't you?"

The others turned to see whom she was addressing. I shook my head quickly. "I just heard about it from my maid, and I confess that I am completely mystified."

Miss Rogers turned her wrath on me. "Mrs. Harmon is right. You filled my niece's head with nonsense about the ball and finding a husband. You are the one to blame."

Shrugging as if I were at a loss to explain the elopement, I took a plate and hurriedly served myself, with the reassuring thought that Susanna and Gordon would have eventually considered elopement, and therefore I couldn't be faulted if they did turn out to be married. After all, it was just a suggestion I had made to Susanna. I had not coerced them to carry it out.

Taking my breakfast to the end of the table where taciturn Mrs. Adams was steadily plowing through a large meal, I joined her and allowed the conversation of the others in the room to swirl around me as the women speculated on whether the young couple had been found yet, and whether they were married.

Sunday passed slowly, and I fretted at the inactivity. Without Samuel McArthur on hand, I had no way to press my agenda further with him, and it made me nervous to have so much time on my hands to fret over whether I would be able to secure a marriage proposal from him or not.

Finally, the runaways were located and returned to Kenwick Manor in the afternoon, but it was time for dinner before all the searchers came back. The news of Susanna's and Gordon's marriage swept through the house like a fire, and I soon heard of it.

I hurried to find my godmother in her sitting room and burst in upon her with no warning, calling out, "We should have a special savoury in the newly-weds' honor!"

She wiped tears from her eyes before replying, and I could see she was not in agreement with me. "The subject is too painful to discuss. We will not speak of it at dinner."

But that subject was all anyone could talk about at the dinner table, in hurried whispers and furtive comments to one another, while pretending that we did nothing of the sort. I felt sorry for the new couple eating together with their heads bowed, thoroughly shamed by having caused such a ruckus. It seemed to me that they deserved at least some official recognition of their new status, if not an outright celebration.

Earlier, when I saw Samuel McArthur upon his return, I spoke with him and tried to ease his frustration at not being the first to find his brother. I told him soothingly, "Just think, one day soon every village and hamlet will have its own telegraph office, and in a case such as this you could be in communication with each other by coded message."

He glared at me. "Telegraph? A ridiculous idea! It will never amount to much. I should have gone east, as I first thought, but the others in my party talked me out of it and that is the only reason I did not find the runaways." He stalked away from me, and I watched, amused at his shortsightedness. It occurred to me how distressing a marriage with that man would be for a bluestocking and free-thinker such as myself, but I could not afford to abandon my pursuit of him.

Not long after the meal ended, my godmother reminded the gathering that it was Sunday evening, and time for chapel service.

The Manor's chapel was an outbuilding not far from the bridge where the legendary drowning had occurred a hundred years earlier.

Before entering, I took a moment to congratulate Susanna and Gordon upon their marriage. In better times, I would have pressed a monetary gift upon them. Or, even now, if I had my jewel case, I could give her my opal earrings as a wedding present. In reality, I had nothing to offer but my best wishes, yet they were so grateful for my good will, that they thanked me as if I'd showered gold coins upon them.

We walked in together with the others. The household servants were there as well.

My godfather began the service with a scripture reading that seemed interminably long.

Listening only vaguely, I glanced covertly around the room until I located Charles Weatherby not far from me. As if feeling my gaze on his back, he turned, and our eyes met.

I looked down, my cheeks flushing. In my mind, I could almost hear him laughing at my reaction, but the only noises in the room were restless shuffling of feet and my godfather's voice, which seemed to be getting weaker. From correspondence with my godmother, I knew that his health had been frail of late, although he himself denied it, and when he had confided in me about the embezzlement, I had realized at least one of the reasons for his debilitation.

I quickly stepped forward and told Peter Goodwin, "Let me finish reading for you."

He willingly gave over his position to me, and went to a chair Thomas Harmon hastily brought forward for him.

In honor of the newlyweds, hoping to inspire more charity towards them from the McArthurs and my godmother as well, I chose a passage from First Corinthians, and began reading, "'Love is patient, love is kind, and is not jealous. Love does not brag and is not arrogant, does not act unbecomingly; it does not seek its own, is not provoked, does not take into account a wrong suffered, does not rejoice in unrighteousness, but rejoices with the truth; bears all things; believes all things, hopes all things, endures all things.'" I looked up and shared a smile with the newly married couple.

The injunction that love is not arrogant struck me, and I thought of how Samuel McArthur seemed to strut and proclaim his right to me when Charles Weatherby had insisted I promised dinner and all the waltzes to him.

How simple it would be, if I could douse the flame of my feelings for Charles and simply alight the passion for Samuel, who had the means to make my life secure once more.

Then Serena Harmon briskly came up to me and took the Bible from my hands. There was nothing I could do but return to my place, although I felt she had acted out of turn in not letting me offer the Good Book back to my godfather to continue reading if he wished.

She quickly flipped through the pages and began reading Psalm Twenty-Three. "'The Lord is my shepherd, I shall not want....'"

In a few moments she looked at me with a chilling meaning in her voice as she read, "'Even though I walk through the valley of the shadow of death, I fear no evil; for Thou art with me; Thy rod and Thy staff, they comfort me.'"

She continued reading to the end of the psalm, but I barely listened. My mind was busy wondering what she meant by threatening me so openly. But glancing around, it seemed no one had taken her tone amiss, so I assumed I was the only one who noticed it.

After she finished, Serena moved back to her husband's side, presenting a calm demeanor to the casual observer. But to my eyes, her face was set in a cold mask, frightening in its severity and lack of good humour.

I was relieved when the service ended, and we all went back inside the Manor. I hurried ahead of the others, and went up to my room.

CHAPTER 15

The next morning, I hoped to find Samuel McArthur available for a *tête-à-tête*, but the men had gone out hunting after an early breakfast. The entertainment for the women of the party involved a rousing session of embroidery and crewel work in the drawing room.

Oddly enough, it was Claire Lewis who provided me with an escape. She glided up to me, scratching her nose. "I need to see you," she hissed. "In private. It's about Serena Harmon."

She suggested a horseback ride and we left the others. Upstairs, I quickly changed into my riding habit. On the way out, I suddenly recollected the gypsy's talisman, in the pocket of my other frock. I had kept it with me at all times since the gypsy had given it to me.

Feeling foolish, I hurried back and put the chain around my neck, tucking the medallion into the front of my high-necked riding dress. I patted it for good luck and raced down the stairs, thinking that maybe Claire would finally reveal to me what was behind all the madness of the past few days, and I would be able to put the matter to rest.

I was not worried about being with her. Perhaps that was arrogant of me as well as foolish, but I have always been a fine horsewoman and I was familiar with the terrain. If she tried to do anything to harm me, or vexed me with her lies again, I would simply ride off from her, and leave her to find her own way back.

At the stables, there was a paltry selection of horses since the men had ridden out on the fastest ones for their sport. But we were soon in the saddle, moving past the Manor's many outbuildings, across a wide field of grazing sheep and cattle and then up a small but steep tree-covered hill I had ridden on many times over the years during my visits to Kenwick.

On the top of the hill, we alit and rested our horses.

The activity had energized me. "Well, Claire," I said, "what is it about Serena Harmon you wished to tell me?"

Claire walked away from me and sat on a large rock overhanging a steep drop, her feet safely on the ground. "How's that cat of yours? The one Charles Weatherby gave you," she added needlessly.

"You need privacy to ask me that? I think you know the answer already. Don't you? You and Mrs. Harmon have gotten very close this weekend. Are you aware of what she's been doing to me? Have you been helping her? Is that what you wanted to tell me?"

Yesterday, I had tried to convince myself that a drunken partygoer had, perhaps on a dare, entered my bedroom during the ball, and without even knowing whose cat it was, played a cruel and violent prank.

Now, looking at Claire's set face, I knew I'd been fooling myself again. "Did you help Serena Harmon kill my kitten?" I asked her abruptly.

She leapt up. "It was Serena's idea. She did it! That's what I wanted to tell you. Be careful of her."

I reeled back, shaking my head, unable to understand. I knew Serena didn't like me, but to kill a harmless creature… I couldn't fathom her reasoning.

"Maybe she thought you needed to learn a lesson." Claire started toward her horse.

"Wait, don't go yet. What kind of lesson would killing my cat teach me?" I grabbed at her arm, and noticed how flushed her face was.

"I saw how you acted with Charles Weatherby at the ball, dancing so close together. It was disgusting! And you a widow. Poor Edward!" She glared at me, then mounted her horse. "I told you that I am going to marry Charles, so you need to stay away from him. And I will marry him, because I'll have a lot of money soon, more than enough for a dowry."

"What are you…" I paused and gathered my thoughts more cogently. "What do you mean, you'll be getting money? From what source?"

She looked at me with pinpointed eyes. "Stay away from Charles Weatherby. Or I'll see to it that you never get back those emeralds and opals!"

I stared at her as something struck me. "How did you know there were opals in the jewel box? I never mentioned anything but the emerald necklace I planned to wear to the ball. Only the thief could know the contents of that case. The thief, Claire!"

Her lips twisted nervously. Dismay flashed across her face and she started to kick the horse, but I grabbed the reins from her sweaty hands and stayed the beast.

"No, no," she babbled. "I told you already that I don't have your jewelry. You could've searched my room but you didn't want to. Remember?"

I did remember. I had trusted her then, because she had been nice enough to give me a headache medication.

"My mistake," I said. "I shouldn't have been so gullible. But we're going to rectify things now, aren't we, Claire? We'll ride back to the Manor and you'll give me the jewel case. Nothing can resurrect my poor kitten, but—"

"I told you I didn't drown your stupid cat!" She showed me scratches on her arms. "I tried to stop Serena, and look what she did to me!"

I did not allow her to sidetrack me. "You're going to pack your bags and leave Kenwick Manor at once. You can hire a carriage to take you home."

"No. I won't leave! I love it here. Charles—"

"You will leave. I don't care if you have to walk the whole way home. As for Charles Weatherby, he'll have to survive without you, though I sincerely doubt he'll even notice you are gone."

"I know he loves me. He does! And after what I told him about you, I know he can't wait to marry me instead of you."

I stared at her a moment. "What do you mean? What did you tell Charles?"

"I told him you don't have any money. I know it's not true, but how could he know that? So he thinks you have no dowry."

As she spoke, I feared Claire Lewis knew my secret, but it seemed she had thought she was lying to him. Ironically, she had told him the truth, but at least I now understood why he'd asked questions about my finances.

"I'm not a puppet, Claire, for you to manipulate at will. When the men return, you are going to explain to Charles Weatherby exactly what you told me, that you lied to him—"

"It's too late for you to do anything about it. He'd just think you managed to talk me into lying for you as part of a scheme to marry him. Oh, yes, Loretta, he believes that, too. I convinced him you've been plotting to become Mrs. Weatherby." She chuckled. "But that's the title I am going to have."

The expression on her face was suddenly one of peaceful satisfaction. She was not even trying to escape me. There was a sleepy, almost tranquil look in her constricted eyes.

My own emotions were in a turmoil. Her revelations were coming too quickly one upon the next to be absorbed all at once. How much of it was bragging, how much exaggeration? I had no way of knowing if she had told me a single word of truth.

Although I had entertained suspicions about Claire, sensing she was growing more hostile toward me, I never imagined she could be so treacherous.

Uneasily, I remembered the gypsy telling me to beware of a ruthless woman. I had thought at first she meant Claire, but then Serena. Now I didn't know what to think.

Outwardly, I was in control of my nerves. My hands weren't shaking, my knees weren't trembling, my voice did not quaver. But inside, my thoughts were turbulent, a confused eddy of horror, repugnance, disbelief, indignation and sorrow.

I wondered if Edward had ever realized how unbalanced Claire Lewis was. Perhaps he felt pity for her, and that is why he had invited her to the house now and then.

Numbly, I let go of the reins, and walked over to my own mare standing nearby.

Claire set off at full gallop.

Knowing she had nowhere to go but the Manor and I would catch up with her at the stables, I stood quietly for a few moments, thinking. Then I mounted and started slowly back down the hill, letting the horse walk while I tried to assemble my thoughts.

I had gone only a short distance when I heard Claire's voice yelling to me. Alarmed, I kicked the mare and we sped down the hill.

"Hurry," Claire called out, "I'm over here! Come this way! Help. I'm hurt." The sound of her voice led me to turn down a side path that was even steeper and filled with overhanging branches. I ducked, so the branches would not slap me in the face.

Moments later, it happened without warning: my horse stumbled hard.

The sudden jolt pitched me out of the saddle, and I found myself flying towards the edge of the cliff. I scrabbled and clutched at vines and shrubs as I tumbled, but I couldn't find a purchase.

I struggled desperately to save myself, but it seemed hopeless.

Then all at once, the necklace around my neck came free from my bodice and swung out heavily. The chain caught on a shrubbery branch and brought me up short. I was able to slow my fall enough to see that I was headed for a grouping of boulders.

In a panic, I groped at the plants on the hillside, and managed to stop my descent, but I was in a precarious position, clinging tenaciously.

At any moment, I might lose my hold and fall to the sharp rocks below.

CHAPTER 16

Searching desperately with the toes of my boots to find purchase, I encountered a small ledge to stand upon. From there I was able to haul myself up from one rock to another and climb to where my horse was waiting.

I was bruised and cut. I was thoroughly shaken and scared. And I was furious because I might have been killed.

My fingers closed around the gypsy talisman, in gratitude.

Then I remembered why I had ridden down that side path.

"Claire!" I called out. "Where are you? CLAIRE!"

The silence was broken only by the sound of birds, wind rustling the tree leaves, and the snort of my horse.

I checked over my horse, but to my relief the mare appeared sound of limb and nerve. As I walked around the area, searching for a reason for the accident, I came across a rope-like vine stretched across the path and tied to a tree trunk, about two feet up from the ground elevation.

Feeling stunned by the implication, I followed the vine to its other end. It was no longer tied to the second tree but there was a knot. My horse's strength had snapped the loop away from the tree trunk but the evidence was clear. Because of all the bushes, neither the horse nor I had seen the improvised tripwire in time to stop.

I held the vine in my hand, staring at the incomprehensible proof that Claire Lewis had deliberately lured me down this path with a false emergency, so that my horse would run into the outstretched vine and I would go over the edge of the cliff to the rocks below. No wonder she had not answered when I called out. She was long gone.

Shaken, I leaned against the tree, my mind barely able to grasp what had happened. And why would she want to do it? I could not think of any reason.

Slowly, I went to my horse and rode back to the Manor.

When I reached the stables, I asked the boy to check the mare over thoroughly as she had tripped on a vine and I wanted to be sure there was no injury.

I started to leave, but he hesitantly took me to my wagonette and pointed out what had happened to it while parked there since my arrival. Someone had slashed the seats, in the same way Susanna's burgundy ball gown had been cut.

"Did you see who did this?" I asked the lad.

He merely shook his head, seeming fearful that he would be accused.

Walking away, I murmured to myself, "It must have been Claire."

As I left the area, I wondered what damnable reticence had kept me from riding hell for leather up to the front entrance of Kenwick Manor and screaming until everyone came out of the house to see what was the matter. I would then declare: "Claire Lewis tried to kill me!"

But as I went into the house, I knew the answer: I feared that no one would believe me. The story was too fantastical. In fact, I could scarcely believe it myself!

On the first floor, I stormed into Claire's room without knocking. I was in no mood for observing social niceties. When someone has just tried to kill you, there is no need to stand on formality, or so I surmised.

"Hello, Claire," I said coolly.

She glanced up. Her face went white. I saw the flash of a needle before she swept what she was doing into a narrow box and thrust the box under some clothing on the bureau.

I stepped closer to her. "Have you finished your sewing, dear? What a busy day you've had. Plotting and carrying out attempted murder, then darning your stockings, or whatever you were doing. My goodness, one thing after another for a busy bee such as yourself."

She continued to stare at me blankly.

"I am not an apparition, Claire. Your little plot failed. I am still very much alive."

Her eyes flickered.

I fancied she was more amazed to see me than she was by the state I was in. I knew I made a strange bedraggled figure, with cuts bleeding and dusty, and my hair no doubt a veritable rat's nest. Holding out my hand, I said, "My jewel box." When she just sat there looking at me stupidly, I snapped my fingers in front of her face. "Get it now, Claire! I want it back."

With a sullen look, she got up and went to the wardrobe. I tapped my foot impatiently while she resurrected the jewel case from its hiding place behind a valise. As soon as she had it in her hand, I snatched it from her.

I knew at once that it was too light. I opened it. It was not empty, but the emerald necklace was not there among the several other items of jewelry.

"Alright, Claire," I said testily. "That was very clever. But how long did you think it would be before I noticed you still had the emeralds? Long enough for you to slip away, get a head start before I came after you?"

She glared at me with hatred in her eyes. "If the necklace is not there, then it wasn't there before."

"You're calling me a liar?" I laughed shortly. "That's rich. You're not going anywhere until my necklace is found."

"But I don't have it!"

"Then perhaps you had better find out who does, because you only have one hour, starting now," I added, glancing at a clock, "to find it before I notify the police."

A noise like a low growl came from her throat.

I went to the bell pull and rang it.

As soon as a maid came in response, I asked her to stay with Miss Lewis until my return, and, knowing how persuasive Claire could be, I let the young maid know in stringent terms that my godparents would be very displeased if Miss Lewis got out of the room.

On my way out, I turned at the door, and saw how curiously the maid was looking at Claire, and how malevolently Claire was looking at me.

In my own room, I quickly washed, and then began combing the tangles from my hair, all the while fuming over what Claire had done to me. I hurt all over, and bruises were starting to appear already. I knew that I needed one of Ellen's remedies for my aching muscles, but for now what I needed even more was to go to my godparents and finally tell them the truth.

I found my godmother in her sitting room, resting on a green brocade *chaise longue* with a cloth over her eyes. I tiptoed closer.

Just then, her two terriers leaped to their feet, and began barking wildly.

She removed the cloth, frowning at the interruption.

"I'm sorry," I said, shushing the dogs, "but it is very important. May I talk to you for a few minutes?"

Sitting up, she became aware of my appearance. "Loretta! What has happened to you?"

"I… had an accident."

She put her head in her hands and softly moaned. "What did I do to deserve this…."

I stifled an impatient sound. "I'm sorry," I repeated. "But I really need to tell you about this."

She looked up at me piteously, and I saw that she had been crying. Clearly it could not be because of me, as I had only just walked in.

"Why are you crying?"

"They… they're married!"

"Yes, I know. They came back yesterday. Are you still so upset over it?"

"No one in my family has ever done this," she said. "What a disgrace!"

I sat beside her and took her hands in mine. She did not seem to notice that mine were cut and bruised. "Try to look past that," I suggested gently, "and welcome Susanna into your cousin's family. Do you think you could do that? For their sakes? You are the one who can set the tone for everyone else to follow." I stopped cold. "Did your cousin Mrs. McArthur have something more to say about it, blaming you?"

Nodding, my godmother burst into renewed tears.

Seeing that my accident had been trumped by yesterday's news, I quietly left Gloria Goodwin to her tears and decided to find my godfather instead.

On the way to his study, I changed my mind, and asked a servant girl to locate Ellen and send her to me in the parlor where the gypsy had foretold her prophecies two nights ago.

I waited there, impatiently pacing, wondering what I should do about Claire, and about my emeralds. How dare she claim the necklace was not in the box and she knew nothing of it! She had to be lying. I knew to my regret that I should have insisted on searching her room, but I was so confused, it had seemed best to keep her prisoner and then get my godparents to help me. She would fear their authority, whereas I knew, all too well, that she scoffed at mine.

Perhaps it was the closeness of our ages, Claire being only three or four years my senior, but it seemed the problem went deeper. Her constant references to my deceased husband and her annoyance that I was not in deep mourning for him lent weight to the notion that Claire had formed a jealousy against me, and this had driven her to hatred.

Ellen rushed in. She took one look at me and cried out, "Which one did it?"

I almost laughed. Dear Ellen Armstrong, loyal to the core. What would I do without her support?

"Claire Lewis," I said. "She is in her room, guarded by one of the upstairs maids."

"You look dreadful."

I smiled. "There's no time for that now. I got my jewel case back. Claire had it. But the emerald necklace is gone. She claims she knows nothing of it, that it wasn't there before. Of course she's lying! Yet again. That is why I set a guard on her."

"You need to tell Mr. and Mrs. Goodwin."

"I tried to tell my godmother just now but she is still distraught about the newlyweds."

"I helped Susanna move her things from her aunt's room to the one she and her new husband are sharing now." Ellen shook her head, as if in awe at how things had transpired. "I've never seen two lovers so happy. They'll need that happiness to be strong as a shield, for the days ahead."

"Her aunt has been spitting nails," I commented dryly, thinking of how furious Louise Rogers was that the runaways had not been caught in time to prevent a marriage.

I told Ellen that Mr. Harmon had promised to go to London today and look into my financial problem. She confirmed that he had left already, and reached in her pocket to give me a note from him.

I took it. 'My dear Loretta,' the message read, 'I expect to return on Tuesday, confident that I will be bringing glad tidings. I have not forgotten your desire. I remain yours faithfully, T.H.'

I looked at it again, puzzled. "What does he mean by 'my desire'? Oh, of course, my desire for discretion. I suppose he was interrupted."

"He wrote the note hastily."

"And now, Ellen, I think you should sit down, so I may explain why I look the way I do, and why I need your help now, more than ever."

She sat.

CHAPTER 17

When I approached my godfather's study after leaving Ellen, I heard voices coming from behind the closed door. As far as I could discern, it seemed there were only two people in the room. Gordon McArthur's father was yelling about having the marriage annulled, and my godfather was trying to calm him.

I quickly shrank back into an alcove, and waited until I heard Mr. McArthur leave.

Hesitantly, I drew near to the open door and peeked in. My godfather was seated at his desk, staring into space, looking tired. All at once I felt very sorry for him. This party was supposed to be his birthday celebration, and it had all turned topsy-turvy. I determined that I would try not to worry him further.

He glanced up and waved me in with a weak smile.

I hurried to his side and kissed his cheek, then sat in the chair he indicated.

"Those two have caused quite a rumpus," he said, shaking his head, but looking more amused than not.

"I think they are truly in love," I told him. "I hope you will support their cause?"

He nodded, then took a surprised moment to look at me. I sat uncomfortably beneath his gaze, knowing my appearance required explanation.

"I went riding… and… and there was an accident." I thought carefully how to phrase this. "I would like to be charitable and say it was a childish prank on her part, but she is old enough to know that what she did—"

"She who, and did what?"

I gathered my thoughts and proceeded succinctly. "Claire Lewis, the woman I brought with me so she could attend the ball, and perhaps meet an eligible bachelor. She told me earlier that she had something to tell me, regarding Serena Harmon—"

"Not her again! Can you two not learn to be at peace?"

"I know. I'm sorry, but let me just tell you this part. I would not have gone out with Claire if she had not lured me by saying it was about Mrs. Harmon. So, we took two horses out, I knew you wouldn't mind, and when we had ridden for a while, up that craggy hill north of here, we stopped to rest the horses and talk. She told me that Serena had killed my cat and—" I stopped, seeing he was about to interrupt, and went on with my explanation. "I took one of the stable kittens Saturday, thinking to take it home with me to London as a pet, but then during the ball, someone went in my room and drowned the poor thing in my washbasin."

"Don't you lock your door when you leave the room?"

"The lock has been broken for years. I've never needed one here."

"Go on."

"A while ago, I accused Claire of killing the cat, but she said it was Mrs. Harmon's doing. The two have been very thick since meeting here on Friday. Anyway, I'll try to make this short. She admitted—Claire that is, not Serena—to having my jewel case which has been missing." I looked at his face as he tried to take all this in. "I know, I'm sorry it's long and involved, but I'm getting to the point. I told Claire that as soon as we got back here, she was to give me the jewelry and then go home, by whatever means she could find."

"And….?"

"Before I even mounted my horse, Claire took off at a gallop. I knew she had no other place to go in this area but back to the Manor, so I did not take chase. Although I realized later that I should have. Because she would not have had time to do what she did." Hastily, I went on, seeing the query in his eyes, "What she did was take a large vine and tie it between two trees on a side path and then call to me from that path as if she had hurt herself and needed me. Maybe she even prepared the vine ahead of time, so all would be in readiness. In any case, I raced to her aid, only to find myself flying headlong off the mare and tumbling down the cliff."

"Which explains your appearance. Are you quite sound of limb?"

"Yes, sir. I am battered, but sound. And of course, quite angry when I realized it was not a simple matter of my horse tripping on a stone. I have Claire in her room right now, under guard by one of the maids. I warned her that she must produce my emerald necklace within the hour, or you would notify the police. That was at least twenty minutes ago."

I sat back, exhausted by the telling.

He rested his elbows on his desk, steepled his hands beneath his chin, and mulled over my story.

I watched him anxiously, hoping I had explained myself cogently enough that he saw the gravity of my situation. The moments ticked by, and I shifted in my chair. Not only was I bruised and uncomfortable, but I was impatient to know what course of action he would recommend.

Suddenly there was a tap at the half-open door, and Charles Weatherby strolled in.

"Am I interrupting...?" he asked politely. Then he looked at me more closely and saw my condition. Concern washed over his features. "Loretta! I mean, Mrs. Whitney, what happened?"

I glanced at my godfather for help in what to reply, but he was still lost in thought, and so I merely said, "I fell from my horse." I waved away the comments he was about to make, knowing it would distract Mr. Goodwin from coming to a decision about my necklace and what to do with Claire Lewis.

Charles politely turned away and looked over a collection of Wedgwood figurines on a shelf. I wondered what business he had with my godfather, but there was no time to pursue the thought as I saw my godfather had come to a decision.

"Loretta," he said, "I am going to turn this matter over to Mr. Weatherby to handle. He has a young quick mind, and I think he will be a better advisor in this case."

"But, Godfather," I said hastily, "I wanted to keep the matter private, just between—"

"Mr. Weatherby has my full trust," he said firmly, getting up. "I will leave you two to discuss it."

I noticed the confusion on Charles's face, and felt a rush of pity for him. He had come in on an errand of his own, and had instead been drafted into helping me on a task that was still a mystery to him.

My godfather passed Charles on his way to the door. "I'll be in the library when you are finished here," he told Charles. "We can discuss our business then. It can wait. My goddaughter's situation is more urgent."

My heart beat so fast and hard I feared Mr. Weatherby would hear it from across the room as he quietly shut the door upon my godfather's exit, and turned to approach me, his expression grave. He pulled an armchair around to face me, and sat down. I looked at him, not knowing what to say.

He seemed to read my thoughts. "Start at the beginning."

Since he would never convince me to go back to the very beginning in my speech, to the debts Edward had burdened me with, instead I went back to the inn at Twelveoaks on Friday, and Claire Lewis's strange behavior.

I spoke quickly, and tried to be clear with my pronouns so he would know when 'she' meant Claire and when it meant Serena Harmon and when it meant the now-married Susanna McArthur, because the latter figured into my story as well, due to the mischief done to her burgundy ball gown, and the pushing on the stairs when she was mistaken for me. And perhaps even the vandalizing of my carriage, since it seemed to have been done by the same hand as the ball gown's ruination.

My mouth grew parched, but I kept talking, and he only interrupted to ask a pertinent question for clarification now and then. As I spoke, I began to see why my godfather respected this man for his business acumen. It occurred to me that Charles was hardly a mere clerk, but there was no time to ruminate further.

He seemed quick to grasp both the seriousness of my dilemma and the need for privacy. It would not do, and he agreed with me, to spread wild accusations about Claire Lewis when I had so little proof.

"What about the vine on the path?" I asked. "That is proof, is it not?"

He shook his head. "Did you see her put it there? Are you sure she was calling to you from that path, and not another nearby?"

I slumped in the chair, understanding the point he was making. "No. You are right, I have no real proof. It could have been there for some other reason. Children playing…."

"Do you want me to search her room while you keep her from leaving it?" he offered. "Perhaps the necklace is still there, and the matter can be quickly resolved."

I agreed to this, but first I needed to have a cup of tea and something to eat. I had eaten little all day, and I was feeling faint. "I told her one hour…."

"And she will have time to worry when you do not return on the dot."

He rang the bell for service, and shortly thereafter we had tea and sandwiches which I devoured with no thought for ladylike daintiness.

Charles watched me in amusement. At one point, he even reached out with his napkin to gently wipe my chin where a bit of cress had landed.

I smiled at him, totally forgetful of all my other problems, secure in the knowledge that he was going to help me, and that he… well, that he liked me. I had not been certain of that before, but now I was.

Suddenly, as if of one mind, we both held our teacups mid-air and looked over the cups into each other's eyes, smiling somewhat foolishly at each other.

When Charles had finished searching Claire's room, he turned to me in dismay, with nothing to show but his empty hands. I spun around to look at Claire, who had been sitting in a chair, wiping her brow with a crumpled handkerchief, watching the proceedings with a sullen air.

"Where is it?" I demanded.

"I told you I don't know!" Claire got up and began packing her bags. "You are so cruel to me. I don't wish to stay here any longer."

I exchanged a look with Charles, not knowing if I should try to stop her or let her go.

He gave me a look that meant: *What do you wish me to do?*

And I shot a look back that said: *I am not sure! You handle it!*

He did not need any more prompting than that, but quickly comprehended my meaning, and stepped up to Claire. He put her valise aside. "You need to stay until this matter is resolved, Miss Lewis, to our satisfaction. I do not think you fully understand the legal situation in which you have placed yourself."

"I am innocent," Claire spat out. "Now get out of my room."

There was nothing more to do but leave.

I had already sent the maid off when Charles and I arrived, and now the two of us went out silently. Claire slammed the door behind us.

In the hallway, I pressed my hand to my brow, suddenly overcome with a terrible headache.

Charles took my arm and led me toward my room. "I will proceed with a discreet search for your necklace. But you need to rest. Shall I call Ellen for you?"

Grateful for his sympathy, I nodded, and he left me outside my door.

CHAPTER 18

"Loretta dear...."

The voice calling my name repeatedly woke me from a troubled nap. It was still Monday, and my godmother was fetching me for dinner.

"Come, Loretta," my godmother said. "You cannot fool me like you used to when you were a child, shamming sleep to get out of doing something you did not wish to do."

I opened my eyes slowly, and struggled to sit up against the pillows, stifling a groan. I hurt all over from the fall off my horse earlier in the day. Everything rushed back to me and I excitedly asked her, "Did Charles find my necklace? Is that why you're here? Where is it?" I glanced to see if she was holding something behind her back.

She looked at me sorrowfully, and pressed a hand against my brow. "You don't seem feverish to me."

"Why would I be! I am not ill." I got up and drew on my dressing gown. Taking a seat in front of my mirror, I brushed my hair, trying not to look at the scratches and bruises reflected back at me.

"Claire told me all about your accident when you were riding together. That you were going too fast and your horse tripped. I have warned you more than once to be more careful."

I dropped the hairbrush with a clatter. "She told you...." I was stunned. Behind my back, Claire had apparently given her own version of what happened, a version that my godmother accepted as truth. And why wouldn't she? Who would believe my side of it? It was insane even to my thinking.

"Let me tell you what really happened," I said firmly. "Claire tried to kill me."

"Stop that right now!" She clamped her hands over her ears for a moment. "I won't listen to such things. Poor Claire told me all about the prank she played, hiding your jewel case. She told me how you didn't pay enough attention to the path so your horse tripped. It is a surprise you haven't broken an arm."

"But that isn't the way it—"

"The rude way you have treated Claire Lewis appalls me, Loretta. It is not the way your parents raised you, and it is not the way I expect you to behave in my house. Forcing her to stay in her room, with a servant barring the door, getting that Mr. Weatherby to rummage through all her clothes, looking for a necklace you already admitted you left at home in London. She is very upset, and I do not blame her a whit. She is lying down in my bedroom right now, with a nervous stomach."

"She's in <u>your</u>—"

"Her own room is too distressing to her. Poor fragile child, she could barely speak for the tears choking her. It shames us both, Loretta, that you treated her so shabbily!"

I suddenly felt the distress an innocent person on the docket must feel, wrongly accused but helpless to state the truth with any conviction because the other party had already laid out an airtight case in such a way as to make even the truth itself seem false.

She looked at me, and her face softened. Bustling over to me, she put her hands on my shoulders and met my gaze with a pitying one. "Poor dear. That fall from your horse has addled your brain. I have sent for Dr. Harris."

"What I need is a constable! To arrest Claire for killing my cat, stealing my emeralds and trying to murder me!" I hadn't meant to, but my voice rose in hysteria and I could see at once that my godmother thought I was babbling nonsense.

"Claire told me how she tried to rescue your kitten after it fell in the washbasin you carelessly left filled with water. Poor kitty, but poor Claire. I saw the scratches on her arms you gave her when she tried to help you after you fell off your horse. Of course the brain-fever had started already and you did not know what you were doing to her."

"I never scratched her! She told me they were caused by Serena Harmon. I see it now, she has scratches because the cat was alive and struggling to get away from her! I did not leave water in the basin, only a small bowl on the floor for the kitten to drink. If you think it is all so logical, Godmother, then tell me how did Claire happen to be in my room at the very moment a small kitten unaccountably 'fell' into a washbasin high up on the washstand?"

Mrs. Goodwin simply shook her head sadly. "You have already forgotten that you sent Claire to get a headache powder for you during the ball? And to bring you a warmer shawl?"

"I never—" I abruptly stopped, seeing that I was only adding to her conviction that I had lost my memory from the fall off the horse. It would serve no purpose to argue with her, or to explain that I had never sent Claire on an errand Saturday night.

I almost had to admire Claire for how cleverly she had mingled logic and half-truths with her lies, so that her actions shone with a halo of benevolence. I became determined that I would prove Claire Lewis's guilt, no matter what it took.

"Feeling better now?" Gloria asked, searching my face.

I managed a taut smile and a nod. "Thank you for your concern, God-mother. When you next see Susanna Rogers, that is, the younger Mrs. McArthur, please ask her to come see me. I wish to speak with her."

Patting my head, she promised to do so, then murmured a few kind words, and told me to go back to bed, and await the doctor. At the door, my god-mother paused and turned. "Rest assured," she said, "I made the child promise not to play any more jokes on you. Although I must confess I do not know what has happened to your sense of humor. You used to love pranks and cha-rades and games."

I began laughing at the ludicrous situation I had found myself in, and to my dismay, I could not stop. I was still laughing when Dr. Harris strode in. He took one look at me and quickly got busy in his bag, then moments later I felt a sharp jab in my arm. He had given me an injection.

"To calm her," he explained to my godmother who hovered nearby. "I have been using the new hypodermic system the past few years, and find the method of delivery most efficient. The morphine will make her relax."

She came closer, and patted my arm.

"You have had a nasty fall," he said to me, speaking slowly and clearly as if afraid I would not understand him otherwise. "Bed rest is the best medicine for a fever on the brain. I hope we will not find it necessary to shave your head. I have left another injection of morphine for you, and I will instruct your god-mother in its use. It is to be given later, in small amounts over a period of hours, to prevent an accidental overdose."

I wanted to go downstairs and find out whether Charles Weatherby had begun the search for my necklace, but I could see it would be useless to fight. I had never had morphine, but I understood it to be a strong opiate, and suspected that I would feel sleepy soon. "Don't shave my hair off," I pleaded, horrified at the prospect of a shaven skull.

My godmother tucked me in, and gave me a gentle kiss on my brow, as she used to when I was a child. Tears pricked my eyes. I felt awash with nostalgia for a gentler time in my life, when my parents and my brother were alive, and the whole world stretched before me with bright promises. Unable to help myself, I yawned, and my mind yearned toward a dream about my family. All I had to do was surrender to the morphia, and I would surely dream of them.

But suddenly, over my godmother's shoulder, I saw Claire Lewis in the doorway. I wondered how long she had been there. The sight of my enemy energized me. "Get out of here!" I screamed. I groped on top of the bedside table for something to throw at Claire to scare her off.

My fingers closed around a book and I quickly threw it, but my aim was off, as if my muscle movements were already uncoordinated from the drug, and so the book struck my dressing table, causing a few small glass jars to fly off and break.

Claire looked at me in great pity, as if we were the dearest of friends and she had nothing but the utmost concern for my well-being. "I wanted to see how you are feeling," Claire said. "But I can see your nerves are still overwrought, so I will come back later." She smiled sweetly at the doctor and my godmother. In return, they each gave her a sympathetic look.

Mrs. Goodwin sighed heavily as she picked the book off the floor and put it on a shelf. She glanced at the broken jars on the floor. "And you tried to tell me it was all a lie, Loretta, the way you treat her. Now I've seen with my own eyes. Shame on you." She left in a hurry, and I heard her in the hallway calling out Claire's name, and telling her to wait.

I sank against the pillows, frustrated and tired, but all at once I had a marvelous sense of euphoria. A floating sensation came over me as the morphine made its way into my system. I watched as the doctor packed his bag, shaking his head at what he had just witnessed.

"Claire Lewis tried to kill me," I said matter-of-factly. "It is true. But no one believes me."

"That's right, Mrs. Whitney. Get some rest."

"I feel feverish. But cold too. And a little itchy."

"That's the morphine," Dr. Harris said, not unkindly. "You must be more sensitive to it than most of my patients, since you have reacted so quickly, but it will help you feel better. I will check on you tomorrow. Send for me sooner if you need me."

I thanked him. After he left, I closed my eyes and tried to blot out my thoughts, but they had a life of their own and I fretted for a long time, fighting back a terrible nausea, until I finally slept.

During the night, I suddenly woke up, fully alert.

Some small noise must have disturbed me. Almost at once, I realized someone was moving around in the dark, coming toward me stealthily. I was afraid, yet even more terrified to call out and ask who was there.

Watching through slitted eyes, trying to keep my breathing even, I saw a shadowy figure approach me. I feared for my safety. But then, instead of striking me, the person cautiously felt around on the table beside my bed as if searching for something there.

My arm itched so badly it suddenly became all I could think about, and I must have made some rustling noise, trying to ease the itch, because the intruder suddenly left my room in a rush.

In the stillness, I began to wonder if the intruder found what he or she had been looking for, and a moment later, if anyone had even been there. Perhaps it had been my overactive imagination, from the medicine Dr. Harris gave me. It troubled me that I could not trust my own perception.

I lay against the pillows but sleep would not return.

I suddenly began to panic that in my helpless state I might be murdered in my bed, and no one would know until my body was found in the morning.

I tried to calm my hysterical thoughts, but they grew larger, and took over all reasoning. Suddenly all I could think of was being alone, and terrified that the intruder would return. I reached a hand for the bell rope but it was just out of reach. And so I simply sat up and began screaming for help.

CHAPTER 19

Ellen was at my side when I opened my eyes to daylight.

"I am so glad to see you!" I cried, grasping her hand.

"You're no sight for sore eyes, but you'll do," she said with a rare smile. "I have been worried about you. I heard, from more than one source, that you were hysterical."

I sat up in the strange bed and looked around. I was no longer in my familiar lodgings at the Manor, but a small plain room with a low ceiling. Two gabled windows were uncurtained and all I could see from the bed was sky.

There was a bentwood rocking chair near an old potbellied stove. Braided rag rugs were strewn over the bleached wood floor. A small table and functional bureau completed the simple furnishings. Other than a flowered pitcher and a washbowl, the bureau top was bare. The only book was the Holy Bible. On the walls were faint outlines against the faded wallpaper which indicated pictures or mirrors had once hung there. It seemed the previous resident had stripped the room of any warm or homey touches.

The austere surroundings alarmed me. I felt the room was unknown yet strangely familiar. It only took a moment to take all this in, and realize I had been moved during the night. I worried that I had been moved to an asylum, that my godfather had been convinced of my insanity and had agreed I needed special care and supervision.

"Where—" I began in alarm.

Ellen smiled reassuringly. "You are still at Kenwick. Third floor, in the servants' quarters, next to my room. You will be safe now, until you are strong enough to travel and go home."

I held tightly to her hand. "You believe me…."

She nodded. "I listened to all the rumours, and then I sifted out the truth. From now on, I will be next to you, and no one will harm you."

A little later, while Ellen was downstairs getting a lunch tray for me, my godmother came in hesitantly, carrying a workbasket which she put on the table by the rocking chair. When she saw I was awake, she quickly covered the distance between us and said carefully, "Do you remember who I am, dear? Can you recall my name?"

I smiled gently, knowing she must be worried about me, even though for some inexplicable reason she had chosen to believe Claire Lewis instead of me. "Of course I know who you are. Hello, Godmother. Thank you for coming to visit."

Her relief was visible. She hugged me tight, and brushed a few tears from her eyes.

"Will you stay a while and sit with me?" I asked, knowing it would please her, but also glad of the company. I had too much time alone, with my troubled thoughts.

Settling into the rocking chair, she began stitching the piece of embroidery I'd seen her working on at odd moments the past few days. "Dr. Harris will be along soon. Yesterday he told me I should give you another injection but we could not find the hypodermic. He must have taken it with him by mistake after saying he would leave it for me to give you."

"I don't need any more morphine. I will rest quietly. Ellen put a special liniment on my bruises. It doesn't smell good, but I believe it will be of more benefit than injections."

"The doctor will decide what you need, dear." She held up her embroidery work for me to admire, and I made a few comments about her progress on the piece, which was to be a small table covering in my godfather's study. "I had hoped to complete it for his birthday, but oh my! I never expected a house party to turn into such a hubbub."

"No one blames you for anything that's happened," I assured her.

She chatted amiably about the intricacies of eyelet stitches, french knots and bullion stitches, and I lay back against the pillows, content to listen to her. I knew that I must not mention Claire's name, or even hint that I knew there was a nefarious plot against me.

Despite my good intentions, I soon tired of her ceaseless prattle on the merits to be gained by a nimble needle and a few lengths of silken thread. I let my thoughts drift, and unbidden, they winged their way toward considerations of Charles Weatherby and his merits.

Of a sudden, my complaints against him had vanished, and I could not think highly enough of him. Yet there still lingered the troubling realization that he was a fortune hunter like me, and thus we could never make a match with each other.

Still, it was entertaining to imagine what would happen if we followed Susanna and Gordon's example, and gaily eloped. I imagined his tender kiss, and I sighed to myself. Even the way Charles spoke my name became like sweet music and in my mind I heard him say 'Loretta' in a verbal caress. My smile broadened.

With a start, I realized someone was indeed saying my name, but it was not Charles. It was my godmother's voice, and she wanted to know if I were having an attack, with all that twitching and sighing.

I blushed. "I must have fallen asleep," I replied hastily, "and started dreaming. I do admit to feeling a bit disoriented, here in the attic instead of my regular room, still feeling the effects of the morphine from Dr. Harris. I will be glad to never have another dose of it."

Feeling the warmth of the room as the sun grew higher, I pushed back one of the blankets covering me. I had been fortunate not to break any bones in the fall from my horse, and I had to remind myself the bruises would fade with time, and with Ellen's ministrations.

That same woman came in shortly with my lunch, and straightened the bedclothes. I ate the simple meal, fretting at my inactivity but knowing I should stay in bed at least a while longer.

My godmother methodically returned her embroidery to the workbasket. "Since Ellen has returned," she said, getting up, "I will leave you now so I may attend to my other guests. I came in, hoping to see that you had improved sufficiently to be trusted to come back downstairs, but I must confess I fear for Miss Lewis if that move should take place."

"For <u>Claire</u>! But I am the one—"

"You see, my dear? You are irrational. No one is sorrier than I am, to have to say so. Last night your screaming aroused the household, only to find you alone and hysterical, claiming someone had come in to harm you. Dr. Harris warned me you might have hallucinations. So that the rest of us could sleep, I had you moved up here."

"But someone <u>did</u>—"

She cut me off with a frown. "In the short time I have been here, your attention has wandered continuously. When I enquired about your symptoms you lied to me that you had been sleeping when it was clear you had been wide awake. You look at the ceiling when I speak, and you reply to commonplace questions either with an aggrieved air or a *non sequiter.*"

"Just because I wasn't interested in embroidery stitches does not make me a candidate for a straightjacket at Bedlam!" A moan of frustration burst out of me, unwanted. I wished I could explain myself better. "It is the morphine," I said, then quickly changed direction, desperate for her sympathy and understanding. "Last night, someone came in my room downstairs, trying not to let their presence be known. It was surely Claire, for who else would—"

"Enough, Loretta! I am not a physician but it is clear to me that you need a doctor's care, and are hardly in a position to approve or disapprove his treatment. If he says you require morphine, then so be it. All I want is my goddaughter returned to me in her entirety, not this strange young woman who rants about imagined attacks and insults. In your unbalanced state, how do you presume to think yourself capable of analyzing your own condition? No, don't answer me, child. I am only trying to do what is best for you. Now rest. Dr. Harris will be along soon."

It pained me to see my godmother so upset on my behalf, but she was wrong, and her sincerity did not make her right. If only I could get her to listen to me before Claire tried something else.

"You see?" Her voice came from far away then seemed to get louder as I heeded her words. "You are doing it again! Staring at the ceiling with that rabid look in your eyes, your lips moving as if you are trying to speak. I cannot leave you alone where you might hurt yourself or others. Who knows what you might do when you go into one of those trances of yours! After all, we wouldn't want a repeat of that episode in your room where you threw books at everyone."

"One book, at Miss Lewis," I said coolly.

"Next time it might be a lamp," she shot back, "and you would burn us all to death in our beds. I am not going to stand by and let you cause more harm than has already been done. Last night, we had to give you a strong dose of laudanum because you kept fighting us over the move and would not go peacably. We couldn't find the syringe of morphine the doctor was supposed to leave for me, and I must say you are stronger than you look. What a struggle you gave us all."

It hadn't occurred to me to wonder how I had gotten up here. Clearly someone must have carried me. Surely not my godfather. Perhaps one of the servants? I felt it important to find out, and asked my godmother.

Across the room, I noticed that Ellen was alert but holding her tongue. I realized she knew the answer but hesitated to speak out of turn.

"It was Mr. Weatherby," my godmother replied. "I suggested Samuel McArthur since he is so tall and strong, but your godfather said he trusts in the discretion of young Charles. In any case, no one was able to find Samuel. He was not in his room. I suppose he went for a stroll outside."

My heart sank. So Charles had seen me bruised and cut, drugged and limp in his arms. What an impression I must have made on him! Hardly the fair and lovely damsel in distress, but rather an hysterical invalid who smelled gamey from Ellen's liniments and potions.

I tried to remember any of the details, but I could not. It was incredible to me that people had come into my bedroom, dosed me with powerful drugs, carried me bodily up two flights of stairs and placed me in this small room.

Or rather, cell.

It was my prison. I saw that now. Ellen had made it sound like a sanctuary, a safe haven, but now I saw the truth of it. And I knew all at once, that if I tried to get up and run, there would be servants stationed here and there throughout the house to sound the alarm and stop my passage.

Sunbeams filled the windows, but they might as well have been iron bars.

CHAPTER 20

Susanna McArthur was very uncomfortable in my presence. She kept up a steady stream of chatter, hardly pausing for air, all the while looking at me out of the corner of her eye and quickly averting her gaze when I caught her at it.

Glancing around the small room where I had lain all that Tuesday, she commented, "To think that just a few days ago I despaired of ever marrying, and now I have the most excellent husband imaginable. We are truly compatible in all things."

"I am happy for you, Susanna." I started to get up, and winced to see she backed away at once, no doubt having been warned to expect the unexpected from me.

I padded barefooted across to one of the windows and looked out the dirty glass. In the distance, I could just make out the stone bridge from which that legendary girl with the orange cat like Ginger had met her unfortunate death.

I turned back to the young bride. I suddenly felt weak, and staggered to the rocking chair to sit. I had not eaten much, and when Dr. Harris came earlier he had insisted on giving me another dose of morphine despite my protests that I did not want or need it.

Easing myself into the chair, I said, "Would you bring that coverlet for my legs?"

Hesitantly, she draped it over my knees then hopped back out of arm's reach.

"What have they told you about me, dear Susanna? That I am gone mad? The truth is that I had a bad fall off my horse. And I am bruised. My mind is intact. My senses are as well, within the limits of the morphia the good doctor insists on dosing me with. The effects it induces are not altogether unpleasant, but I will be glad to discontinue its use."

She relaxed somewhat, and perched on the edge of the narrow bed. "I have heard so many different stories…."

"I wish I could allay your fears. I had asked to see you so that I might reassure you of my health."

In a rush, she came to my side and I held out my hands to her. She made a quick cry of dismay at the cuts and bruises, but took them in hers and kissed them. "I am sorry I doubted you," she said, "but you know how gossip can be."

Unfortunately, I did know, and the gossip about me was part of the confusion that I felt. I did not know whom I could trust other than Ellen. But now it seemed young Susanna was also on my side, and I was grateful for the support.

Out loud, I said, "Yes, I do have an idea of the kind of things that are being said about me. Please do me a favour, and pay no heed to what Claire Lewis might say. Or Mrs. Harmon. Would you do that for me? In the name of our friendship."

She hesitated, then cried out, "Of course I will. They are wrong to blame you, no matter what the facts are. We both, Gordon and I, are so thankful to you for suggesting elopement. I would never have given it consideration, as my mind was intent on doing everything aboveboard so his family would approve of me. Something that daring would never have crossed my mind!"

I was somewhat dismayed to learn she would never have thought of elopement, and thus I was indeed responsible for it, but I put that regret aside because, to my relief, it seemed the harmony between us was fully restored.

"We were in the parlor this morning," she said, "all of the women that is, with our handiwork. I am going to needlepoint a chair cushion for my husband, and your godmother helped me select a *gross-point* canvas and tapestry yarn from an assortment she had on hand."

"That was very nice of her, but typical of her generosity. Did anything of import happen in the parlor?" I asked offhandedly.

"Not of import, but only of minor annoyance. I told Mrs. Harmon that her new friend Miss Lewis—" she looked at me nervously to see my reaction to their names but I nodded calmly to continue—"had on Saturday borrowed several tortoiseshell hairpins from me and a pair of my best stockings and had not yet returned them. I wondered if she could use her influence to get their return, as I fear I am timid on that score, and we will be leaving the day after tomorrow."

"For your new home."

"Not yet. The McArthurs had planned to continue east on this journey and visit my father-in-law's family, then return to Cornwall later. As I am now the younger son's wife, I will be going with them. Gordon thinks we should have a celebration of our wedding when we arrive in East Anglia, since we did not have a wedding luncheon or anything here."

"That sounds like a wonderful plan," I put in quickly, not wanting to talk about the lack of festivities that had greeted her hasty marriage. "I hope they welcome you into the family in a way that brings you joy. You deserve happiness after all the years of living with that aunt of yours." I made a long face, and was pleased to see Susanna giggle. But I realized she had not finished telling me about the things Claire Lewis had borrowed, and I urged her to finish the tale.

"I had hoped Mrs. Harmon would agree to my request," Susanna went on, "but she laughed at me, and said that not only should I plan on never seeing those items again, but that Claire continued to borrow various things from her, including her new copy of *La Mode,* and had returned nothing at all. Can you sanction the audacity? I assume if Mrs. Harmon cannot get something of her own back, then I should forget the matter entirely and resolve myself to darning the pair of stockings I ruined during my elopement."

"Where was Claire during this? Weren't you afraid she would overhear?"

Susanna thought a moment. "Claire wasn't in the room, and now I cannot recall if an explanation was given as to her absence. She was the only one missing aside from you, and of course we all knew why you were not there." She clamped her hands over her mouth in horror. "I am sorry for my tone. I only meant that we all knew you were infirm."

I lapsed into thought, wondering what Claire Lewis had been doing with her freedom from supervision, by the other women at least. It seemed she had been free to go where she pleased far too often, and probably no one knew where she had been. I wondered to myself if Ellen would be able to find out the answer.

Getting up from the rocker, I accepted Susanna's assistance back in bed. Soon Ellen would arrive with my tea on a tray, and I would talk to her about all Susanna had told me. On this trip, Ellen had become more of a confidante than ever, and I relied on her good judgment in a way that I had spurned before. I would be sure to make amends to her for past wrongs.

"Your godmother has been so kind to me," Susanna commented, smoothing the blanket over my legs. "She said that now I am a married woman, I must start wearing a cap of lace and net. I asked if there was other advice she could offer, and she gave me several hints that will be useful."

"Hints?"

"Don't laugh at me, Loretta. I have no mother to tell me these things, and I do so want to be an excellent wife."

"I didn't mean to laugh. Go on."

"She said it's best to wash black lace in skimmed milk, and white satin in spirits of wine. She gave me her favourite recipe for almond cold cream, and told me never to wear curling papers in my hair around my husband, at least not until we have been married a full year."

"And did the men eventually join your party?"

"Yes, and they spoke of the civil war in America and the new tariff that will affect export business. My husband," she went on, beaming sweetly at being able to call Gordon that, "wondered how much longer it will take to finish the London Underground. I listened in, not making comments of my own of course, but because my husband was speaking!" Her face filled with wifely pride, and I did not dash her spirits with the type of lesson Ellen had taught me from an early age about equality of the genders. "Gordon said the earthworks have gone from Paddington to Euston Road in less than a year and a half, and it will probably be another year or more before the Underground can be used. But just imagine it! We will be able to visit each other so much more readily, won't we, when travel becomes faster and easier?"

I agreed that we would, but my thoughts instantly leapt to my uncertain future. If I had to become a governess, there would be no visits for me from the young McArthur couple. I would be out of their class, and off the social registry. No advice book for servants or young ladies would offer counsel to save me.

In a pensive mood, I drew the blanket closer to my shoulders, and wished Ellen would return and light a fire in the stove. The morphine made me feel chilled, and the evening had brought its own cold with it.

"And then," Susanna said, "that nice Charles Weatherby told us all about Mr. Dickens's new book called 'Great Expectations.'"

"Charles!"

"Yes. Charles Dickens. Have you not read any of his stories?"

"I meant Charles Weatherby. I had thought he was gone." I did not want to tell her that from one of these high windows I had seen his carriage depart in the distance, and had assumed he had forgotten all about me and left. I had not heard anything from him about his promised investigation into my horseback riding accident. After thinking it over, I had come to the logical conclusion that he was merely being polite to me because my godfather had asked him to be, and that nothing would come of it. Still, he had carried me up here, to safety, and I must thank him for that.

"Apparently he did go," she said, "but only on some errand or other, and has returned."

I couldn't stop myself from smiling in relief. Charles would believe me about the intruder last night, I was sure of it.

And so as Susanna continued sharing the household hints that Mrs. Goodwin had taught her, through my head ran visions of that charming fox, namely Mr. Charles Weatherby, listening intently to my every word, while stroking his dark red moustache and nodding sagely in agreement. He would outline a plan to avenge my honor and prove that it was not I but Claire Lewis who should be under guard and treated like a berserk prisoner.

Excitedly, I recalled Charles's way of getting straight to the point with every matter. I grew confident that soon the entire household at Kenwick Manor would be humbly apologizing to me for treating me with such scorn. Perhaps even Dr. Harris would be prevailed upon to admit his learned diagnosis of brain-fever was incorrect.

Then suddenly I realized that Susanna had shifted away from laundry and cookery, and was on the subject of Charles Weatherby again.

"I am so pleased you told me at the ball that you did not care for him," she said, "because that means it will not disturb you one whit to know that he was in the company of Claire Lewis this afternoon, talking with her most earnestly and at length." She looked at me, and frowned suddenly. "It does bother you, and now I have upset you."

"No, no! I am fine. Just a small… headache," I said, my thoughts swirling with questions over what this latest news could mean.

Charles Weatherby and Claire Lewis: a match? It was not only unthinkable, but unbearable!

CHAPTER 21

Loneliness engulfed me. I could not let Susanna see that her news left me miserable. It mattered little that I had earlier scorned Charles Weatherby's advances and made it clear his attentions were unwelcome.

There had been a spark between us in my godfather's study. I knew I had not imagined it, and I suspected that Charles had felt it too. *But what of it?* I asked myself. Sparks do not a marriage make, not in this practical day and age. I had to stick to my resolve to dig myself out from under debt. Letting my heart lead me astray was no solution.

Deep within I must have harbored a notion that Charles Weatherby would penetrate my charade and see for himself that I did care about him, but that his dowry requirement was an overwhelming obstacle.

My thoughts were in confusion but I managed to continue speaking lightly to Susanna of varied and sundry things.

I remembered Charles saying when we danced that we were two of a kind, and now I mulled that over, wondering what he had meant by it. At the time I had told him he was being foolish, but what if he had meant something more serious by it than idle conversation? Perhaps only that we were both fortune hunters. Then I flashed back to Claire's telling me that she had informed Charles I had set my cap for him and was eager to wed him. I had not suffered such humiliation since the first debt collector had appeared at my wreath-clad door and informed me of my penurious situation.

Charles Weatherby must have been laughing at me when my godfather asked him to help me. No doubt Charles had already decided I was a witless young woman who skipped from one difficulty to another, heedless of life's seriousness and only seeking pleasure or excitement.

How much easier it would be if I could simply tell Charles the truth!

Just as I was about to dissolve into tears, I managed to tap a reservoir of strength I'd never had to use before, and firmly reminded myself that I could not indulge in the luxury of wishing for a husband with whom I was in love. I had to be practical, at all costs. And I had to prevent Susanna McArthur from guessing my predicament and alerting her new brother-in-law.

I still had a chance with Samuel McArthur, and I was determined to capitalize on it as any businessman would a sound financial opportunity. Ellen had always spoken of gender equality, and now was my chance to prove a woman's mind could be as cool and calculating in business matters as a man's. I would not let my emotions steer my course.

Invigorated by my reinforced resolution, I firmly put aside thoughts of Charles Weatherby.

"By the way, Loretta," said Susanna, "I found out who was responsible for cutting up my burgundy ball gown."

"Claire Lewis!" I didn't give her a chance to affirm or deny it, but rattled on, wrapped in my own train of thought. "I <u>knew</u> it was her, all along. She thought the dress was mine. There's no one else in the house capable of such a malicious act. That girl! I little understand how I ever thought of her with affection or pity. She is a viper, a mean, spiteful and vicious—"

To my consternation, she broke in, "My aunt did it."

I stared at Susanna a long moment. "Your...."

"Aunt Louise did not want me to attend the ball," Susanna explained simply. "Oh, she said I could at first, but she made sure the dress I had to wear would be most unbecoming and matronly, so that I would be unattractive and the other girls would be the ones asked to dance. Then you stepped in, and offered to restyle it to a more modish look. This enraged her."

A frown creased my brow as I tried to adjust all the threads of deduction I had been weaving together. At once, I wondered if her aunt had also damaged my wagonette, but that made little sense. It only fit together if I thought the ball gown was slashed by someone who thought it was mine. Now, finding out that the perpetrator knew all along that it was Susanna's dress tore apart my scientifically constructed theory.

"And your aunt admitted this freely to you?" I asked, still disbelieving.

Susanna nodded.

"Then I think she ripped up my wagonette as well!" I quickly told her what the stable lad had shown me, and that it was logical the same person's hand had held the knife or scissors there as with her ball gown.

"But…this means you are accusing my aunt of being spiteful against you as well as me." She looked at me in concern. "Are you now going to accuse her of all the other things you've told me about?"

"Please, Susanna, do not be overwrought. I didn't mean—"

"Let us not talk of it," the girl suggested. "I can see it worries you, and your godmother specifically told me to cheer your spirits and lighten your mind of all concerns." She suddenly stopped, and I could see she was reflecting about something that troubled her. I was sorry I had mentioned my suspicions about the wagonette, if it was distressing her so, but before I could say anything more, she blurted out, "My aunt said something to me that I found most cryptic."

"What was it?"

"Well, it was later, and everyone in the room was talking about you. I am ashamed to say, it was the gossip that you have a brain-fever making you mad. I heard her say something softly, more to herself than to me, do you see what I mean?"

I nodded quickly, with a gesture for her to go on.

"She said something like 'That young busybody widow will never know I'm the one who did it.'"

I didn't like the term 'busybody' one whit, but did not allow myself to become distracted. "So she did slash up the wagonette, and thought she would not be found out. Thank you for telling me, Susanna. I know it must be distressing to you. Never fear. I won't reveal that you said anything. There is nothing either of us can do about it now, so it will remain our secret."

After she had left, rather than taking a nap, as I had shamelessly hinted to her that I was going to do, I started my plan. Yes, love endures all things, but so must someone in my position of financial unrest and insecurity. I must bear the price that my unfortunate marriage to Edward Whitney had forced upon me.

Ironically, there had been a young man of good family courting me before I was betrothed to Edward. I had felt myself in love with Robert, and he with me, but my father had decided his youth and inexperience were too great a liability. Practicality was needed in my situation, so that my husband would be able to take over the jewelry business from my father's feeble control, and not only continue the business but make it thrive for my own sons to inherit some day. I could not help but wonder what path my life would have taken, and where I should be today if only I had insisted upon marrying my young lover instead of the older man I did marry. I caught myself up short, almost hearing Ellen's voice telling me to cease with the plaintive use of the phrase 'if only'!

I heard voices in the hall. Ellen had returned and encountered the young newlywed in the passage. I craned to eavesdrop.

Susanna said something to Ellen but I could not make out the words.

"I know her well," Ellen replied, her voice rising in annoyance, "and I do not believe the things people are saying about her."

"How can you be so sure?" Susanna was clearly wavering in her loyalty to me, yet I could not censure her for it. She had known me but a short time and had little reason to disbelieve the others, especially when they all seemed to be in agreement against me.

"For one thing, listen to all the different stories Miss Lewis tells about the scratches on her arms. She first said it was from trying to save the kitten and Mrs. Harmon scratched her, now she says that Mrs. Whitney scratched her when she tried to help her up after falling off that horse. Young Miss Lewis has proven to be both unreliable and untrustworthy."

"I see," Susanna said hesitantly. "Thank you, Ellen."

When Ellen came in, I looked at her with new eyes. "I heard what you said to Susanna McArthur, and your trust in me is much appreciated, especially now when no one seems willing to hear my tale, let alone believe it fully." Even as I spoke, I remembered that Charles Weatherby had believed, or had pretended to at any event.

"I believe you," she said, placing the tea tray on my knees. "But you have no evidence that Miss Lewis is plotting against you. What you believe, and what everyone else believes seem to be two different things."

"What is your advice, then?" I said somewhat impatiently.

"Either forget the notion that Claire Lewis is trying to murder you and consider that she has played pranks that went awry, or—"

"Or?"

"Get real proof against Miss Lewis. Something that makes sense. Use your brain. That's what God gave it to you for, not to be thinking of folderol all day."

I let her words sink in. "Alright. I won't speak ill of Claire until I have some proof that will force everyone to realize I speak the truth."

Even I had begun to wonder if I had made Claire Lewis a scapegoat for all my fears. I had to learn to feel my way more cautiously and not be so quick to blame her for everything. After all, hadn't I just found out that Miss Louise Rogers, and not Claire, had mutilated Susanna's gown to prevent her from going to the ball? If the spinster was capable of such a cruelty, why did I persist in thinking that Claire was the only one capable of trying to kill me?

Perhaps Miss Rogers blamed me for the elopement and was seeking revenge against me.

And hadn't Serena Harmon warned me to be careful, and even read out loud Psalm Twenty-Three, warning me to beware of the valley of death?

Suddenly I thought of the note Serena's husband had sent me, and hoped it was in a safe place in my room downstairs. It had been in the pocket of the dress I wore before I had changed to bedclothes shortly before Dr. Harris's first visit.

Putting those thoughts aside, I knew I had to force myself to think of what was most urgent to take care of. The McArthur family would be leaving Thursday, limiting my time to secure Samuel's affection for me, if not a proposal of marriage. I had to focus. I had to renew my effort to find a husband.

"But sometimes, Ellen," I said, returning to her comment, "fashion and folderol is more important than it seems, when it helps as a means to an end."

There being no mirror in this small chamber to which I'd been banished, I had no true idea how I looked, but with a rueful smile, I looked at my scratches and remembered the view in my mirror downstairs.

Now that Ellen had returned, I would have her go down to my room and bring back powder, rouge, beauty recipes, hair ribbons and curling irons. I would put on a pretty frock, and then join the party this evening.

Since Samuel McArthur would not be coming up here, perforce I must go down to him, before opportunity knocked yet again… and then gave up trying to gain my attention and gave the opportunity to someone else instead.

CHAPTER 22

When Ellen came back, she brought with her all that I had asked for. A maid carried in a hip bath, and behind her were two more girls carrying large jugs of hot water.

After the three cheerful maids left, Ellen helped me undress and get into the bath. I winced at every touch, but steeled my nerves to the necessity of it. I had to be at my prettiest, well, the prettiest possible under these conditions, if I were to attract Samuel's attention and hold it. I knew he was more like a honeybee, seeking a pretty flower, than a philosopher seeking a partner. Confiding in Ellen, I explained my plan.

"He just might prove to be your meal ticket, too, don't forget," I told her as she began beating egg whites in a bowl, "so use all your art to gild this lily."

"It was difficult getting the pint of rum," she commented, glancing over the recipe in an old beauty book by Lola Montez. I had left the book here on my last trip to the Manor. "It says to beat four egg whites, let them dry on your hair then rinse in rum and rosewater."

"But I see you got the rum."

"Mrs. Goodwin came in the kitchen, thought you wanted to drink it, cried out in alarm that you had become dissolute, and when I said it was for a beauty treatment, she insisted on adding salt to it to prevent your weakness from overcoming you."

"My… weakness? For liquor it appears. I suppose she agrees with the doctor that I suffer from a brain-fever and am not myself at all now."

Nodding, she glanced at the book again. "I can't imagine the salt will hurt. The author says this treatment is 'one of the best cleansers and brighteners of the hair that was every used.'"

"Exactly what I need!"

Ellen carefully coated my hair with the egg whites. Then she brought out her pouches of various herbs and added juniper berries and rosemary leaves to my bath. When the water cooled, I stepped out and dried off quickly by the stove, then put on my dressing gown. I glanced around the room, and smiled to myself at the sight of all the beauty tools and potions. I was determined to look my best.

"Do you think all this will help?" I asked as I buffed my nails with carmine rouge.

"I hope so. If you get married, maybe you will smile again."

"What does that mean!"

"Worry over money has made you sullen and glum. Fear of Miss Lewis has made you jumpy and humourless. I would even welcome the return of your teasing and sassy ways of old. 'Twould be an improvement."

I laughed, feeling my mood lighten. My problems would be over soon, and I had to tell myself that any time my spirits flagged. I would charm Samuel McArthur, and maybe we would even elope as his younger brother had done. The new idea sent my pulse racing and I buffed my nails all the harder.

I knew it was true that I had grown too serious of late, with the burden of poverty crushing down on my young shoulders. It was considered a sign of gentility in a woman to be unconcerned with money and anything but her appearance, but with my husband's death all that had changed. My position was untenable.

It required riches to be a lady of leisure. Now I not only had a stack of debts to contend with but I was unprepared to embark on the lifestyle of a governess or lady's companion. I had been accustomed, with the exception of the past year of widowhood during which my troubles had compounded daily, to leading a life with little worry. I was used to being the lady of a large household, with many servants to do my bidding and a father or a husband to pay the bills.

Or so I had thought, until Edward's untimely demise.

Now I faced a life of poverty, a life in which I would have to fend for myself, no doubt becoming the servant to some other woman who had a position I once enjoyed. I faced a complete reversal of my way of living. And here I was at Kenwick Manor, where I had enjoyed countless good times in earlier years, but I was now straddling the two extremes, praying with all my might that I could somehow remain with both feet firmly planted in a life of comfort, and avoid the disgrace, shame and hardship of the alternative.

My only way out of misery was to marry a wealthy man, no questions asked. Particularly no questions about my financial status or my ability to offer a dowry. It was up to me to see that Samuel did not ask them.

We discussed these matters at length while I bathed. "And you wonder why I am not my cheerful self," I grumbled.

Ellen shook her head, not deigning to reply. She busied herself with preparing an elder flower eye wash which would be followed by a raw potato poultice to reduce the puffiness beneath my eyes.

I resolved that I would show everyone how bright and gay I could be, as if I had no worries at all. I knew they would be watching closely for signs of instability, and I would be careful to not give cause for worry on that score. I would be so sweet and endearing that it would be fairly disgusting!

I was stirring honey into the ceramic bowl on my lap which contained two apples Ellen had already mashed, when my godfather popped in after announcing his arrival with a light rap on the door.

"We are playing Baccarat in the salon," he explained, "but I came up to visit while I take a break from being banker."

I cast Ellen a meaningful, alarmed glance toward the disarray in the room. She quickly gathered various bottles of clove mouthwash, buttermilk lotion, cardamom bath powder and strawberry astringent into a basket and tucked it away behind the far side of the bed. When she passed me, I handed the ceramic bowl to Ellen, telling her, "We'll finish all this in a moment."

She nodded, and left us alone.

My godfather sat in the rocking chair. "Mr. Weatherby, whom you met in my study yesterday, asked that I give you his regards."

"Be sure to thank him," I said gravely, "when you return to the game." My heart leapt with the news that Charles was thinking of me, but I didn't want Peter to know my feelings. Then all at once I remembered what Susanna had told me about Charles and Claire, and I realized he indeed was a wily fox. It had not taken him long to find a new prey. I wondered if he knew something about Claire's wealth that I did not. I had never presumed her to be someone of means.

Breaking into my thoughts, my godfather said, "I withdrew from the game when young Mrs. McArthur came down from visiting you. She mentioned you were going to take a nap, so I did not come up right away. But since no one else volunteered to be your guard, that is no one properly qualified for the task, I came. I admit Charles offered but we couldn't take his proposal seriously.

Imagine such an indecent situation adding to the chaos your godmother has endured already." He gave a rueful chuckle.

But I was thinking of something else he'd just said. I was nonplused by his frankness in saying that I was being guarded. No one else had phrased it quite so bluntly, preferring instead to replace the sinister word with sugar-coated phrases such as 'keeping you company' or 'visiting the dear patient.'

My godmother, who had looked in on me once in a while, usually staying only a few moments after the first long visit she had paid, went so far as to say she was 'checking' on me.

Gordon McArthur had neatly avoided the issue by implying the sole reason for his brief visit was to thank me for all I had done for his bride. Susanna had lingered at his side, to lend an air of propriety to a man visiting me in my bed-chamber.

His father had sent up a message of good cheer, expressing surprise to learn I had reacted to his younger son's elopement in much the same way as his fretful wife had, that is, by taking to my bed with the vapors.

Exercising my self control, I had not laughed at the idea, but also did not enlighten the man as to the true facts of my *soi-disant* illness, namely that Claire Lewis had tried to murder me. Instead I sent a reply thanking him for his concern and well wishes.

A little later Dr. Harris had come in. I persuaded him that I did not need any more of the morphine. He questioned me at length, and seemed satisfied that I was no longer hysterical. I wisely prevented the name 'Claire Lewis' from falling from my lips, and soon he was on his way, greatly cheered at the progress of my brain-fever.

My godfather continued now, "You know how your godmother gets strange ideas at times, like this program of having you watched. I hope you will not hold it against her."

"I do not, sir."

After a few moments spent in discussing the weather, my godfather abruptly said that he understood from his wife that I had expressed an inclination to be on the marriage market again. I almost laughed at how awkwardly he phrased himself, but he was trying to be helpful, and so I smiled and then thanked him for visiting me.

As he got up to go, he added, "If you are looking for a husband, I'd put my money on Charles Weatherby. Good man. If I'd a son, I'd want him to be just like Charles. Yes, indeed."

Irritated, I snapped, "My understanding is he will marry Claire Lewis. That should make everyone happy. You all think she is such a paragon."

As soon as he left, Ellen returned from her room next door to this one, and picked up the bowl of honey and apple mash. "Don't let anyone else in," I pleaded. "If we keep getting interrupted, he will leave before I'm ready to go downstairs!"

She looked at me archly.

"You know who I mean," I said, "so don't give me those looks like I'm daft. I know what my godfather said about Charles Weatherby, and I also know you were listening at the door. You came in too quickly otherwise. But Samuel McArthur is my best chance, and even though I'm not a gambler, certainly not to the extent my late husband was, I'm betting all I've got on him."

"All on whom?" Serena Harmon drawled from the door, pushing it open. "I couldn't quite hear that last comment."

"Perhaps you were not meant to," I retorted. "Perhaps you were meant to knock."

Serena shoved Ellen out the door, slammed it and then wheeled on me. "I'll kill you if you don't stay away from my husband."

A sigh escaped me. "What now, Serena?" I was unsure of the reason for this renewed attack. I knew that Mr. Harmon had not yet returned from London, and even if he had, the continuous parade of wardens ensured my staying alone in this room without her husband being able to visit, should he even wish to.

Wordlessly, she held up a small paper, crumpled it and threw it at me. I picked it up, smoothed it open and recognized it as the note her husband had given Ellen for me.

"You took this from my room?" I asked, astounded.

"Claire gave it to me," she said.

"It's none of your business." I was suddenly filled with terror that she would uncover the truth about Edward Whitney, that he had gambled away my security, my home and my only source of livelihood.

Clenching her fists tightly at her side, she spat out, "It most certainly is my business. When my husband is lured by a woman such as you into arranging assignations, and writing love letters, then I will—"

"Love letters? What do you…" And then my mind cleared. I glanced at the note and the damning phrase he had written: 'I have not forgotten your desire….' Looking at her, I spread my hands in innocence. "Listen a moment, Serena. You have this all wrong."

She stepped so closely to me that I could smell her signature attar of roses perfume. "I'll kill you, Loretta Whitney, before I let you take him from me."

"Please, let me explain. My 'desire' was—"

"There is nothing to explain. The facts are clear. I refuse to listen to your lies." Snatching the note up, she cried, "This is all the explanation I need, all the proof one could want about an unfaithful husband. I will forgive him, because such is the duty of a loyal wife, but I will never forgive you!"

"I only—"

"Shut up!" With her hand on the door knob, she reiterated, "Leave my husband alone. Or you'd better take comfort in Psalm Twenty-Three, verse four! You remember it. I read it to you in the chapel."

"'The Lord is my Shepherd,'" I began.

Cutting in, she said, "Beware the valley of the shadow of death!"

And then she was gone, as swiftly as she'd arrived, like a tall red bird swooping in to devastate its prey and then abandon it, with the threat of returning to finish it off later.

I had lost my desire to pamper myself with the facial masque and other beauty potions. Now all I wanted was to quickly dress and go downstairs before Serena Harmon could spread any more poison about me.

Ellen returned almost immediately. "I heard everything by listening at the door. She came out of the room so swiftly that I did not have a chance to conceal myself. She realized at once that I heard it all."

"So she knows I have a witness. And she won't dare do anything to me. Brilliant, Ellen! I am proud of you for such quick thinking."

A slight breeze from the open window suddenly sent the lamp's flame flickering. I indicated the Holy Bible. Ellen opened it and found the Psalm in question. I gestured for her to hand it to me, and she did. I read the familiar passage to myself, just to be certain of it.

The book dropped from my hands to the bed. I shuddered involuntarily, suddenly not so certain that Serena Harmon would be daunted by the fact I had a witness to her death threat. I had to be careful of *The valley of the shadow of death…*.

CHAPTER 23

I was losing. Although baccarat is a popular game, it is a simple one, and requires no skill or decisions on the part of the player. And yet bad luck was still at my heels, and I withdrew from the game to sit and watch.

Perhaps it was my imagination, but as soon as I left the table, it seemed the general unease of the group lifted and the conversation became gayer.

Holding my head high, I feigned indifference. And I kept my head high when I saw my godmother chatting amiably with Claire Lewis. As if sensing that she was being watched, Claire turned her head slightly and shot a sly glance my way, a small smile on her lips. I knew the meaning of that smile, that she felt she had won, but I did not give her the satisfaction of looking away. I held her gaze until she was forced to turn her attention back to the card game.

When I had come in the room an hour earlier, there had been a sudden intake of breath at the sight of me. I knew it was not so much my appearance, as I had taken pains to hide the scratches on my face with powder, and I wore long sleeves and lace mitts to hide the cuts and bruises on my arms and hands, but the mere fact of my arrival in their midst. I was, after all, supposed to be safely drugged, far upstairs in the servants' quarters, where I could quietly play out the debilitation of brain-fever without inconveniencing anyone in the party with my mad ravings or mental disquietude.

To my dismay, Charles Weatherby was not in the room. From what I could gather by indirect questions about the players remaining, he had apparently left shortly before my arrival, as had Serena Harmon. I couldn't help wondering if they had left at the same time, but I felt helpless as to how to phrase the question without it being misconstrued as being prompted by jealousy.

My heart leapt at the news, however, because I felt he must be investigating my accident, and trying to find out Serena's part in it, if any. Perhaps he would have news for me later, after dinner.

Samuel McArthur abruptly left the game and came to my side. He sat on the couch beside me. "This comes of too much education."

I looked at him for a long moment, trying to extract the thought process behind his comment. Giving up, and completely at a loss, I asked what he meant.

"Brain-fever," he announced. "Dr. Harris told us all about it. Women are too delicate, too prone to illness at the slightest overtaxing of their mind or body."

"I see." An impish notion took hold of me, and I longed to unsettle his smugness by launching into an accounting of all the feminine wisdom lost to history. I could thank Ellen for teaching me the value of my mind, but at this moment, I had to bite my lip and play the role of a simpering and helpless female. Gritting my teeth, I smiled at him with a vacuous expression. I boldly laid a hand on his meaty arm and held his gaze for a moment. "We women need our strong men, that is true."

We were sitting far enough from the others to be able to speak privately if we kept our voices low, and I knew I should not dismiss this opportune moment. I flirted shamelessly with him, telling him how I admired men like him, how wonderful it must be to know so much about the world and its workings, when the women's sphere was merely in the home, as it should be.

Preening, he launched into one tale after another of his doings at the ship-yard he managed for his father, and which he would be given as a gift upon his marriage. He told me of boats, yachts and other vessels he had built, and the journeymen under his command. By clever prodding and questioning, I whipped the conversation in the direction I desired, and elicited the informa-tion that Samuel was madly envious of his younger brother's marriage because it meant Gordon would now be owner of the somewhat smaller shipyard he, Gordon, had only recently begun managing under their father's tutelage.

"That seems so unjust," I said to Samuel, giving him all my attention and sympathy. Inwardly, I exulted that my young friend Susanna would be secure in her marriage and would have no worries about money.

I kept up the conversation, stoking the flames of sibling jealousy, but still he did not seem to see that if only he quickly married, he could make the differ-ence between him and his brother vanish. Sighing to myself while maintaining a *facade* of its being idle feminine prattle, I said to him, "Just think, in a year or less, you will probably be an uncle, and you will have such delightful duties in that area, dandling your brother's son on your knee."

A frown creased his brow as he thought this over. "That means his child would be the heir to my father's fortune. We are not titled, but there is much at stake. I had always assumed I would be the first to wed, the first to..." he trailed off, blushing even, to my surprise.

"Yes. The first to have a child," I stated bluntly. What more could I do or say to plant the idea of proposing marriage to me? I felt at a standstill. I racked my mind for a new strategy to pursue. Perhaps a little coolness on my part would bring him around. He would be leaving on Thursday. That left me only tonight and tomorrow to secure him as my *fiancé*. I stood up.

He quickly rose. "Do you feel ill?"

"The air has become close, and I am going outside for a short walk." I took my shawl and moved away slowly, toward the french doors and the terrace with their steps leading to the topiary garden. I was tempted to turn to see if he followed, but I forced myself to act nonchalant.

He fell in step with me, and opened the door to the terrace, saying as he glanced over his shoulder at the others, "I imagine you've heard already that your Charles Weatherby of the waltzes has formed an attachment with Miss Lewis. You had merely to be out of sight, and he looked around for a new conquest. Such is his sort of loyalty. They make a fine pair, do they not?"

I slanted him a look and merely smiled. "Some might say absence makes the heart grow fonder, but I see you are a cynic." I was immediately sorry for my rash words since they obviously antagonized him. When would I learn to keep quiet, I thought, deeply annoyed that the rift between Samuel McArthur and myself which I was trying to mend had now widened again.

"I see I was wrong to believe you held some affection for me," he said.

We went down the terrace stairs at a slow pace, and I clung to his arm.

"You're not wrong," I said with all the sincerity I could infuse in my tone. "I spoke out of turn, and you misunderstood my meaning. I was agreeing with you, that one would think my absence would make a decent man show his loyalty and affection, but instead he showed his true colours, and ran from me."

Thankfully, Ellen was not at hand to overhear this, and I cringed inside, wondering how I managed to come up with such drivel.

After a turn on the garden path, we headed back into the house by a different door from which we had left it. When we entered, my eyes took a moment to adjust to the dimness. And then I saw that we were not alone. I quickly let go of Sam's arm and stepped slightly away from him. My heart skipped a beat.

"Hello, Mr. Weatherby," I said coolly. My mind spun madly. I wanted to know if he had interrogated Serena Harmon and discovered anything, but I could not let Samuel McArthur see me being cordial to his rival.

"Mrs. Whitney. Mr. McArthur." Charles bowed to each of us in turn, and his tone was politely impersonal.

Samuel quickly put a proprietary arm at the small of my back and led me away.

But as I passed, Charles Weatherby had the audacity to wink at me.

CHAPTER 24

"Ellen," I said when I was back in my regular room, hastily dressing for dinner, having decided on my own that my banishment to the nether regions was at an end, "have you ever felt like you were going to explode like a child's toy balloon? So many things, strange things, have been happening to me in such a short period of time that I almost believe Dr. Harris to be right: I must have brain-fever!"

"Nonsense," she said, powdering my face, trying to keep me still while I worked on my hairdo.

"Don't forget the rouge!" I was determined to press my advantage with Samuel McArthur during the evening.

The urgency of my situation had me too nervous to think about food, but I was anxious to get downstairs and socialize. I had decided that I would quietly enlist Susanna's help in wooing her new brother-in-law. Perhaps she would have some influence on him even though he was angry about his brother's marriage. After all, if she made it appear she had no interest in producing the family heir, he might be gulled into listening to her advancement of my cause.

Of course it would all have to be accomplished subtly, so that Samuel would not suspect he was being led by the nose like a bull.

My beauty regimen had been given short shrift earlier this afternoon, but now I would be ready for warfare. I had to battle for a husband, and time was fleeting. I needed to be armed with all my feminine wiles, and play by the rules society had set forth.

Too bad I couldn't be honest with Samuel, but he would not be the first man tricked into marriage, and doubtless would not be the last.

After Ellen left to have my dress ironed for dinner, I realized that I did not know what had happened to the gypsy talisman after I had been carried from this room to the one upstairs in the servants' quarters. I hoped that Ellen had put it safely in a drawer. I quickly searched for it, and found it in my jewel case. It was incomprehensible to me, but I immediately felt more at ease. Laughing at my foolishness, I nonetheless thrust the talisman into my pocket.

Waiting for Ellen to return with my gown, in the silence of the room, I drew comfort from the fact that my worries about money would soon be at an end. I would leave for London in the morning with the knowledge that Samuel McArthur and I were engaged to be married. Thinking thus, my troubles took on a new perspective. I felt he had been close to proposing when we had been interrupted by Charles in the hallway earlier, but tonight, after dinner, I would press my case, and I would succeed.

Resting a moment by the window, I recognized that I had given far too much importance to Claire's strange actions. Surely she had only meant to frighten and alarm me, for whatever immature and misguided reasons she might have, and I had imagined the rest. As for Serena Harmon, her husband would be taking her home and I would not have to see her again until my god-parents' next social event. By then I would be a married woman again, and she would finally come to realize that her jealousy was without merit.

From now on, I decided, I would be carefree. No one would be able to bother me.

But instantly I recalled Serena's threat to kill me, and Claire's malevolent behavior. I suddenly remembered that Claire had spoken to me the first day about Mrs. Harmon and said Serena had a secret. Then when we went riding, she again said it was related to Serena Harmon, but I had never found out what she meant.

Tonight I would find out. I would ask questions that needed to be answered, and I would not be turned aside. I would take charge of my life, and stop being a silly goose, jumping at shadows. Serena Harmon would not dare to do anything to me. She knew that Ellen had heard her threat, and so I mustn't give over to fear.

Feeling better for being stern with my overactive imagination, I relaxed my thoughts with the simple pleasure of using my rouge pot more generously than Ellen had.

But suddenly my peace was shattered by a rap at the door. An arrogant voice demanded entrance to my *boudoir*, and it could belong to only one man: the fox.

"Go away, Charles," I called out wearily, affecting boredom with him. Still, I tensed expectantly, certain he would knock at the door again. He was not one to go away so meekly.

There was no further sound from the hallway.

He was being strangely quiet, and I realized to my chagrin that I was disappointed. On the chance he might suddenly force the door, I leapt to my feet and went to it. Somehow, I felt cheated that he had given in so easily, and I brooded why he would have given in at once to my command to leave. If he had come to my door for a purpose, well then, what was it? And why had he not persisted? In a rush, I felt that I must find out what he wanted.

Piqued at my fickle reaction, I reminded myself that Samuel McArthur was the one I had decided upon, and I needed to be sure he did not catch me talking again with Charles Weatherby, especially not without a chaperone, and even more especially in my *boudoir*.

For a moment, I stayed firm in my resolve to ignore whether Charles was outside the door debating whether to knock again or leave, or whether he had in fact already walked away. But then my heart betrayed me, and I knew that merely saying I was not in love with Charles would not serve to change the fact of it. I couldn't entirely succeed in erasing the fox's face from my memory and replacing it with Sam's ruddy countenance, no matter how I tried.

I forced myself to remember that Charles Weatherby and Claire Lewis had been seen together, in a way that could only mean their attachment. Even Ellen had told me reluctantly that it appeared to be a match. It felt like a betrayal to me, as if somehow, something would intervene to allow Charles and me to be together. Alas, wishful thinking would not get me out of my financial dilemma.

But still, I simply could not stop thinking about whether Charles was at the door. I slowly opened the door just enough to peer out.

Charles Weatherby was there, smiling at me.

Before I could shut the door, he quickly put his foot in the gap and held the door open.

"Do you want me to stand out here all evening," he asked quietly, holding back a laugh, "and far into the nighttime, while everyone travels up and down the hall, watching us?"

"You cannot come in."

"I need to speak with you in private and I did not want a note to fall into the wrong hands."

Of a sudden, I realized he was serious. His eyes met mine. Then he smiled, and gave a hesitant touch to his own right cheek. "You're blushing more profusely on one side than on the other."

Recollecting I had not finished putting rouge on both cheeks, I hastily rubbed at my face.

"Is it about Claire?" I asked. When he nodded, I quickly said, "I will get dressed and meet you in the library."

As soon as he turned away, I shut the door and ran to the wardrobe, then recalled that the dress I planned to wear was being ironed. I had not brought a large trunkful of clothes to the Manor. Indeed, I had sold many of my better gowns over the past months and my personal wardrobe was not as lavish as it had once been.

Frantic, I went through old gowns in the back and found something serviceable that would still fit me. There was a mustard stain on the bodice so I quickly tied a few ribbons in a crisscross fashion to hide the old stain and hurried out, drawing a shawl around my shoulders to hide the fact that I had not been able to fasten all the buttons in back without assistance.

Racing down the staircase and then around a corner and toward the library, I had time to think about what Charles had said. He wanted to talk to me about Claire Lewis. For my godfather's sake, he had told me yesterday he believed me when I'd ranted about her trying to hurt me. But what if he had just been placating me? What if what he wanted to discuss with me was their marriage?

He knew that I had brought her to Kenwick, and that I was, in a sense, her chaperone. And perhaps he felt he should ask my permission for the match, or at least my nod of approval before asking Mr. Lewis for his consent. I had never been to Claire's home but she said she lived with her stepfather, not far from Twelveoaks, where we had our rendezvous at the inn.

I abruptly stopped outside the library door, which was closed. The nerve of that man! What gall, what effrontery! Talk to me about Claire? I suddenly knew why, and it had nothing to do with my emeralds or the attempts on my life.

My humiliation was intense. I had cherished the delusion that Charles Weatherby had formed some affection for me. At least it was a small comfort to warm the cold reality that I hadn't the dowry to marry him. All the while he was just waiting to speak with me about Claire Lewis, and his attachment to her.

With hot shame, I realized the intense look between us at my doorway had meant nothing to him. He was elated about Claire Lewis, not about me. I had puffed it up with my romantic interpretations that had no basis in fact but were firmly rooted in the novels I had read all my life. He didn't care about me, not one whit. More likely, I had misunderstood, and it was only his affection for my godparents that had him speak to me at all.

For the first time, I was able to see how ridiculous my reactions to him had been each time we met. Despite knowing my hope was futile, even today I had been entertaining the idea that somehow he would fall in love with me and waive his dowry requirement. *Twenty thousand pounds.* I could never sell enough gimcracks or Oriental rugs to come close to that amount.

Claire had already told him I had no money. So even though he never heard the words from my lips, he was certainly aware that his price was too steep for me.

Suddenly the library door opened. Charles stepped out and discreetly glanced up and down the hall to be sure we were alone. "I thought I heard footsteps, some moments ago."

"I don't care what you have to say to me," I told him frostily. "Now or ever. Leave me alone. You can figure out what you must do about Claire Lewis without my inept counsel."

I saw his look of confusion but I turned away and fled before he could convince me with his persuasive manner to help him marry her. But as I ran back upstairs to my room, visions of his face danced wickedly before my eyes.

Charles…tenderly buttering the burn on my hand the first time we met.

Charles…chuckling when I tripped in the garden and my wire hoop skirt flew inside out, yet helping me before anyone else might see me in such an embarrassing posture.

Charles…leering at me saucily when I stood in my dressing gown as he carried the injured Susanna to my bed the night of the ball.

Charles…leaning closer to hear about my accident and my suspicions about Claire Lewis.

And now, it would be Charles, laughing cozily with Claire as they gossiped about me, and agreed what a gullible little fool I was.

As I passed my godfather's study, Thomas Harmon suddenly popped out and gestured to me to come in the room. Sighing to myself, I followed him in. I was not in the mood for hearing any more bad news, and from the frown on his face, I did not expect otherwise.

"So," I said needlessly, "you have returned from London."

"Yes."

"May I assume you have news for me?" I asked. Seeing that his expression remained somber, my shoulders slumped.

He drew me to a chair and we both sat while he quietly told me about his efforts on my behalf. "They insist upon hard cash," he said. "Those are the bare facts. I am sorry. There is nothing I can do about it. Perhaps your godparents will advance a loan—"

I cut him off with a shake of my head, but did not give him the reason. I did not know if my godfather had confided in Mr. Harmon about the embezzlement and his own financial worries. It was not my place to enlighten Thomas Harmon on that matter if he was unaware of it.

"Thank you for making the trip," I told him, getting up, "and trying so valiantly on my behalf." I said a cautious word or two about my finances, and then parted from him.

Leaving the room, I reflected that, with the McArthurs already being well established in shipbuilding, perhaps they would not care about owning a jewel trade and thus the business would simply slip away from my own family like a pebble into a passing stream. Now I was more determined than ever to get Samuel McArthur to propose marriage to me. I had hoped to find an easier way out of my problems, but apparently it was not fated to be.

CHAPTER 25

I expected to find Ellen when I returned to my room but I had not been gone long, and she had not come back with my dress yet. Taking a glance at my reflection in the tall looking glass, I debated whether this old frock would suffice. At the wardrobe, I took out another choice and held it up in front of me at the mirror. It was in my mind to go down again immediately, hoping that Samuel McArthur would be on the prowl for late afternoon amusement, and be amenable to another stroll in the garden with me or a wooden jigsaw puzzle in the parlor while we waited for dinner to be announced.

I only had a short time remaining to secure his interest in me as his future wife, and with each passing minute without a proposal, I was that much closer to Wilfred Jennings' public announcement of my debts, and hence financial ruin.

While I was still debating which gown to wear, I heard Dr. Harris's voice at the door. Feeling like an errant child, I hastily threw the dress I held into the wardrobe and called out, "Come in."

"I expected to find you upstairs," he chided.

I did not explain that I had determined to rejoin the party, whether or not they all thought I had brain-fever. Indeed, if I were to fail in procuring a match, servants' quarters were all I could anticipate for the future, and I might as well enjoy this lovely guest bedroom while I was able.

After a brief examination, he said, "It seems the brain-fever has left as suddenly as it arrived. No more books, young lady. You're quite the bluestocking! And you see where it has led. Rest your brain. But you may stay in this room if it is more comfortable. I advise restricted activities. No sudden resumption of your social life. Visit the other members of the party for a few moments at a time, and join us at dinner if you wish. I have been invited to stay, and I will be on hand should you need me."

"Thank you, doctor."

His declaration that I could resume activities was what I needed to hear. Although he said I should restrict myself, there was no need for that. I hadn't time for it!

"Your friend Miss Lewis pleaded with me to let you be up," he went on. "She said you would convalesce faster if allowed to be mobile."

I was taken aback. "She said that?"

He nodded, and put the stethoscope in his bag.

All I could think of was to wonder what Claire Lewis had truly meant when she spoke to the doctor. I was positive that she didn't care if I got well, so there had to be another motive. The more I considered it, the more his statement perturbed me. Was there something in my room that Claire wanted access to, and could not obtain while I was in here? Perhaps when I had been in the room upstairs she had hidden something here for safekeeping, and now wanted it back. But what could it be, and for what reason would she hide something here?

At the door, he turned and said, "She was most concerned about you. Indeed, she quizzed me at length on the care I had given you, the medicinal doses and their amounts, the dangers if I had prescribed the wrong dose. Miss Lewis wanted to be sure I was taking the best care of you possible. Imagine, badgering me about milligrams and milliliters. I was surprised she knew the terms, but she lives near a health sanitarium and has done volunteer work there, reading to the inmates. Quite a good friend you have in Miss Lewis. I hope you appreciate her loyalty."

After he left, I turned over in my mind all he had said, and was finally forced to admit that perhaps I had misjudged Claire and unfairly leapt to conclusions about her. She had told me that Serena killed my cat and she herself had tried to prevent it. Why had I insisted that Claire was the guilty one? At the inn, she had been ill, and I was unkind to condemn her for it.

Had I grown so harsh in my fears about money that I had become a wicked person, relentlessly twisting facts to condemn someone innocent of all but the prank of hiding my jewel case? It troubled me that I could be guilty of such unpleasant behavior toward an old friend, and I vowed to be kinder to her at dinner.

Meanwhile, I thought, eyeing my reflection in the mirror, I had a *fiancé* to procure… *toute de suite*!

Breathlessly, I waited just out of sight while Samuel McArthur finished a game of cards with his younger brother. Then Susanna came to claim Gordon for a walk in the formal gardens before dinner.

Before Samuel could slip off to join others in the front parlor, I quickly dashed around the corner and bumped into him, as if by accident. Startled, he took my arm.

"Mrs. Whitney! I apologize. I did not see you." He looked at me earnestly.

I quickly opened my fan and rapidly fanned my face as if I felt faint. I glanced meaningfully at a satin settee nearby and he took me by the elbow to lead me there, as I had secretly wanted.

After making sure I was alright from our mishap, he said, "You appear to be feeling better from the riding accident." Yet he spoke hesitantly, and I recalled that he knew of the brain-fever diagnosis, and no doubt feared its lingering effects.

"Dr. Harris gave me permission to resume full activities," I lied blithely.

We spoke for a few moments of idle things. I brought up a subject I had become interested in, the abolition movement in America for which I had great sympathy. When I was still a foolish young bride, and thought I had wealth, I had sent funds in support of their cause. Something told me to hold back that last piece of information, however, and shortly I was glad that I had done so, for he was dismayed at my little speech.

"Against slavery? That is not a woman's concern. Next you will be telling me a woman should be prime minister! What foolishness that would be, a woman telling men what to do." He laughed loud and long.

My fingers tightened around my closed fan and it was only my long training in gentility that allowed me to stop the impulse to slap him over the head with my fan and lash him with my tongue. How dare he speak to me as if my head were filled with cotton! I knew his attitude was the prevailing one, but I railed against it.

Still, I knew that unless I were willing to be someone else's servant, a position that would definitely block me from ever supporting abolitionists or the new women's suffrage groups, Samuel McArthur represented the best chance at hand. I had to squash my true feelings, and ingratiate myself with him.

Swallowing my pride, I laid a hand gently on his arm, and cast my eyes down humbly. "You must forgive my foolishness. I was raised motherless, and perhaps my father was overly indulgent with his only child, planting seeds of the male sphere where they did not deserve to bear fruit in a silly woman's mind."

He patted my hand, readily appeased by my words. "I am glad you see reason," he said. "I had feared the brain-fever might be permanent."

"Not at all," I hastily assured him. "The doctor said there was no damage, and I am fully fit for all activities." I said this last with a lingering sweetness and docility that nearly gagged me, but it had its effect.

His ruddy cheeks grew ruddier. "I say, Mrs. Whitney! I meant to tell you that is a fetching gown you wear today. Lavender becomes your colouring."

"I noticed the other day that lavender is blooming in my godmother's kitchen garden…."

Taking the hint, he stood up and offered an arm for my assistance. "Let us pick some, for a nosegay."

We strolled in the garden, picking lavender and a few herbs I could later wrap inside a cone of lace paper to make a sachet, minus the silver tussy-mussy holder I had, alas, recently sold. At one point, we crossed the path of Gordon and Susanna and paused to chat with them briefly.

Once those two were out of earshot, I kept the subject on his brother's marriage, no matter how many times Samuel tried to change the topic to another one. I could see his growing frustration and confusion, but I had a purpose in mind and I relentlessly drove him toward it, as a lamb toward the shearing pen. I knew that by now Susanna would have told him she did not care about mothering the McArthur heir. I was about to turn her into a liar, and thus confuse his thinking and make him worry.

"Young Susanna confided in me," I went on, "that she is looking forward with joy to having a large family. We spoke at length about what a good mother she would be, and what an excellent father your brother will make. Don't you agree? Your parents will no doubt be pleased to have the new generation make its appearance in the family Bible in due course. A son is Susanna's fervent hope, to carry on the family name." I sighed and fanned myself. "My family was not so fortunate. I am the last, and the name died with my father."

Out of the corner of my eye, I watched with satisfaction as Samuel took in all this information and thought it over, consternation creasing his brow as the implication finally sank in that his brother's marriage was indeed a threat to him. I had already recognized that he was somewhat the dullard, owning nothing close to Charles Weatherby's quick wit and sharp mind.

But his slowness could not dissuade me from my appointed task. It was his inheritance that I needed to offset my problems. Indeed, his lack of perspicacity was in my favor, as it augured well for me in a future life together. I would gradually be able to mould and direct his thinking in the direction I pleased so that my new life would not be half bad. Joyless, no doubt, but not without its merits. Susanna and I would be like sisters, and I also would have children to occupy my time, children to love and cherish even if I cared little for their father.

"A new baby will bring such joy to your household," I commented innocently, stopping to smell a rose. I waited patiently, although my heart beat with less patience for his response. I could not think of anything else to say, short of asking him straight out to marry me, and so I remained silent, praying that he would speak the words I longed to hear.

At last, my patience was rewarded.

He looked at me, and slowly turned my shoulders to face him. I looked a question at him, feigning unawareness of his thoughts or intentions although he looked at me meaningfully as he took my hands in his.

"May I call you Loretta?"

I inclined my head in maidenly acquiescence.

He cleared his throat. "I am the elder son, as you may be aware. I feel I have a duty to marry soon. It has been a subject on my mind of late, but I felt I had time to choose my partner without rushing."

"My goodness! Are you saying that your brother's precipitous marriage has changed that?"

He looked at me carefully, as if weighing his thoughts before speaking. Taking my hand, he asked, "Will you marry me, Loretta?"

I acted startled and withdrew my hand. Unfurling my fan, I applied it rapidly to my face, which I hoped bloomed with girlish blushing. "I was not expecting—" I placed a hand on my bosom as if my heart were racing, which indeed it was, but with relief, not timidity. I made a show of composing myself. Putting my hand back in his, I demurely bowed my head and told him my answer.

With a shout of glee, he drew me to him for a chaste kiss.

Triumphant, I closed my eyes and humbly thanked God for my deliverance from poverty.

CHAPTER 26

During dinner, I kept a close eye on Samuel McArthur, and was pleased to see he was seated away from my enemies, Claire Lewis and Serena Harmon. Even though Dr. Harris had spoken so highly of Claire, I still had my suspicions of her, and had merely greeted her politely when our paths crossed going into the dining room earlier.

Before the meal, Samuel had stated somewhat vaguely to me that he would tell his parents about our engagement in the morning. We had both shied away from the idea of making an announcement to the whole party. I did not question his reasons, as I didn't want to give him cause for thought. As for myself, I did not want to give Serena or Claire any new reason for sniping at me the next time we were alone together.

The meal consisted of jellied eels, mussels in mustard soup, poached turbot, boiled vegetables from the garden, then for dessert there were broiled treacle roll, golden syrup pudding and assorted cheeses.

I tried to listen in on conversations going on simultaneously, but it proved impossible. Serena and Claire were seated one person apart, Mr. McArthur being between them across the table from me and down to the left. So I was able to watch the two women covertly, while seeming to glance idly about the table and carry on general conversation.

In thinking about their odd friendship, my mind turned to the realization that I had never discovered the secret Claire claimed to have about Serena Harmon. Passing them on another occasion, I had heard Serena say to her, "It's not part of our bargain." At the time, it confused me, and it still did.

I decided that I should trust Dr. Harris, who had intimated Claire Lewis was on my side now, so after dinner I would take the girl aside and find out at last what Serena Harmon's plot against me involved.

At one point, when I was talking to my godfather during dessert, I noticed to my dismay that Claire Lewis had cornered my *fiancé* away from the table and they were speaking in low tones. Samuel cast a quick glance in my direction and I hastily smiled and gave a small wave as if nothing could be amiss. Inwardly, I began worrying what she might be saying to him about me.

At the meal's conclusion, I arose to leave with the other ladies, but Dr. Harris waylaid me with a chuckled explanation to the others that he wanted to check on his patient.

He took me aside and carefully measured my pulse rate against his large pocket watch. Tutting to himself, he peered into my eyes. I squirmed beneath his frowning assessment. "Your heartbeat is more rapid than normal but I suppose you may stay up another hour or two. Do not overtire yourself."

I agreed to his conditions, privately dismissing any thought of obeying them, and hurried to reach the other women, who had already swept into the drawing room to work on embroidery and crochet until the gentlemen were ready to join us.

To my surprise, a large hand suddenly reached out and grabbed hold of my arm to stop me from going in the room.

It was Samuel McArthur, and the look on his face warned me that Claire had been up to her usual tricks.

"What's this I hear about you screaming half the night that only Charles Weatherby understands you," he demanded, pulling me to one side out of others' earshot, "and that you'd prefer to marry him instead of me."

My heart sank. I had to mend this rift quickly, but how? I racked my brain for inspiration. "Do not believe every morsel of gossip about me. You know how women can be, always searching for some new invention to talk about, whether it is groundless or not!" Inwardly, I felt ashamed of myself for making the female gender appear so full of guile, but in Claire's case, it was fact not fantasy. "Some people who claim to be my friend, and whom I have outdone myself to assist in every manner possible, might feel they are entitled to even more, and make malicious comments about me that are not founded in fact."

Well, it was the best I could produce on short notice, and from the hesitation in his eyes, I thought the excuse had made some sense at least.

Linking my arm through his, I began walking away from the dining room where the men still sat, enjoying postprandial liqueurs and talk of politics and finance.

"Of late, I have been a popular subject of conversation," I admitted with a self-deprecating laugh. "Country estates haven't enough grist for the gossip mill, so some look around and grab at the most minor incidents, expand them into the outrageous, and add their own words to the tale, with the uncontested claim that the other person spoke them."

Abruptly, he backed me against a wall in the quiet hall between the library and my godfather's study. He pressed his palms on the woodwork over my head, effectively penning me against the wall with his large body.

His ruddy face loomed over me, and his piercing eyes roved over my face. Huskily, he said, "You know why I want to marry you, Loretta. You are not a silly debutante, unaware of a wife's duties. You know what I'll expect, and you know your duty to me." A lusty grin punctuated his words. "I can't wait to hold you in my arms and make you mine."

He grabbed me and pressed urgent kisses on my throat and lips.

Crying out, I tried to escape him, but I was as trapped as a butterfly in a jar, my hands like helpless wings beating against his arms.

He laughed softly and held me even tighter.

"You'll be an asset to my business," he said. "I like to entertain, and a wife who is clever can help me rise to prominence. We will make a team, a strong team." He smirked at me. "My parents will think I've gone mad, wanting you as my wife. A widow! Used goods! A woman who has just suffered brain-fever, and may be disposed to other ailments. But I talked at length with the doctor before dinner. He told me that he saw no reason why you should not be a fit mother, and a healthy addition to the McArthur family."

It was hard to know what to say now to him. I resented that he had spoken about me to Dr. Harris as if he wanted to know the soundness of a mare he considered adding to his stable. But I had to agree with anything that kept our engagement viable, so I nodded as if the news was pleasing to me.

"I hope to have a large family," I put in modestly.

He beamed at me. "The doctor said you were just badly frightened by falling off your horse," Samuel continued, "and his word is good enough for me. After all, females were intended to be frightened easily. It gives us men something to look after when we are not busy making our fortune and defending our country's honor against enemies of the crown." He suddenly laughed in delight. "Like I told Dr. Harris, you're just a typical female and what other kind would I want to marry!"

"What other kind, indeed," I replied feebly.

If Ellen could hear what he was saying, and what I was agreeing about my gender's weakness, she would be outraged, and would remind me firmly that not only is God present in everyone, as an Inner Light, but that God created all humans equal, not just men equal to each other, but women equal to men.

I knew better to hold my tongue than try to educate Samuel McArthur at this time. Perhaps later, after I had borne him a son and helped his business thrive, I would be able to teach him a broader view. But for now, all I could think was how odious he was, and how I detested his touch.

He looked at me for what seemed a long time. Slowly, he said, harking back to his earlier subject, "If the gossips were right, and it is indeed Charles Weatherby you wish to marry, would you tell me so? Honor me with your honesty?"

I did not answer quickly enough. Some stubbornness in my heart prevented me from denying my affection for Charles. I opened my mouth, knowing I must say something, fast!

Before I had a chance to speak, he cut in, his voice taking on a cold edge. "Let me put it thus, since you did not comprehend: Do you want to marry Charles Weatherby? Do... you... love... him?"

Samuel McArthur was my lifeline, the means by which I could escape genteel poverty. I knew that I dare not tell him the truth. He would not understand. It would wound his vanity too much, and even if he did not break our engagement but actually married me, he would taunt me with my love for Charles the rest of my life, at the slightest provocation. I sensed this about him, and felt I was right, that he was this type of man, a vindictive one.

My heart rent with the agony of denying the love I felt in my heart for Charles Weatherby. I had tried already to deny it to myself, but it had grown anyway.

In that awful moment, the bare breath of time that elapsed before I responded to Samuel's question, I knew that I must proceed with the logical plan which entailed marrying this man, even though I held little affection or esteem for him. He would pay my debts, and had not requested a dowry.

With a pang, I knew I could not say the same about fortune-hunting Charles, and hence must kill every bit of my desire for him. I had to stop yearning for someone I could never possess! With a heavy feeling, I acknowledged that my situation had grown too involved to ever allow a match with Charles Weatherby.

Even if I were able to convince Charles that the times I rejected him I hadn't really meant it, that I had lied about my feelings for him, there was still the matter of the dowry, and I could not produce twenty thousand pounds for the privilege of being Mrs. Weatherby.

My voice caught in my throat but I hastened to tell Samuel McArthur, "No, I neither desire nor love him. Those were rumours because I was forced to dance with him as an obligation to my godfather."

"You do not sound convincing," he said, his eyes narrowing. "I will not tell my parents of our betrothal until you are able to assure me that your heart does not belong to another man."

Impatiently, I snapped, "I neither want nor love Charles Weatherby. I would not marry him if he begged me. Now," I went on firmly, "the subject is closed. Promise you will stop listening to gossip about me!"

His arms dropped to his side.

I quickly stepped around him, almost breathless in my relief at being freed from such proximity, not allowing myself to think ahead to our wedding night when he would be even closer to me.

In moving away from Samuel, my view of the library door was suddenly clear, and in its doorway stood the fox, Charles Weatherby, smiling slyly at me, apparently having witnessed the entire conversation.

Our gaze met and I knew my suspicion was correct. White-faced, I stood numbly, unable to move, pleading with my eyes for Charles to simply go away and leave me alone.

Instead, he sauntered closer towards us and I knew in a moment, Samuel would be face to face with the man I had just denounced.

CHAPTER 27

Samuel McArthur still faced in my general direction, away from the library, so he remained unaware of our witness. He grabbed my arm. "I am not finished with you yet, my dear bride-to-be, so do not be in such a tizzy to leave."

As if magnetized, my eyes remain locked with the gaze of the fox as Samuel jerked me to stand in front of himself, apparently not noticing my focus was elsewhere. With relief, I saw that even though Charles Weatherby did not walk away, he also did not come any nearer to us, but stayed to listen to what transpired next.

"I can see you have a lot to learn," Samuel said. "You had better understand that I expect you to obey me, and not walk away when I have not yet dismissed you."

I nodded mutely, suddenly filled with dread for myself and my future. I could not look the fox in the eye, but kept my head bowed as I stood meekly in front of Samuel McArthur.

"'Yes, sir,'" he prompted crisply.

Suddenly intimidated, I repeated softly, "Yes, sir." I felt my cheeks flame in humiliation that Charles Weatherby had seen this.

"Good," Samuel said, and his voice changed quickly from bland to biting, "You say you've closed the subject of Charles Weatherby. I have not. You now understand it is my word that is law, not yours? I am the one who decides what subject is closed and when."

"Yes, that's right, Sam… Samuel… Mr. McArthur?" I said this last with hesitation, watching his face until I got the name right and he finally nodded in acceptance. He did not even want me to call him by his first name?

Suddenly, I did not dare ask for clarification. Whereas normally I was not so easily cowed, I found myself afraid of this man, but equally afraid of the power Wilfred Jennings held over my head with those debts.

"You have told me more than once that Mr. Weatherby means nothing to you," he began, "and yet at the ball it was with him you dined and danced half the night. My dear," he said with a short laugh that held no merriment, "you must think me a simpleton. I assure you I am not so easily hoodwinked."

"Whatever do you mean?" I bluffed, my voice seeming false even to my own ears. I glanced up at my *fiancé*. "I told you it was a duty to my godfather. Mr. Weatherby works for him." I held my breath, wishing I had the nerve to move my head so I could see Charles again, but he was just out of my line of vision and I still held the hope that he would depart before Samuel McArthur realized he was there.

"I have told you that I am willing to marry you," Samuel said, "despite the many rumours that would put off a lesser man. It suits my needs to have a wife at this time, and you will suffice. Now in return, all I ask is that you denounce this fellow Charles Weatherby. You have not been convincing thus far and I still have doubts as to your feelings for him."

He waited with an expectant air, but for all that my mind urged me to comply, my heart refused to do his bidding. The words hovered on my tongue but I could not speak. I was as someone struck dumb by a gypsy spell.

Unbidden, my fingers went to the talisman in my pocket and I rubbed the old medallion as if it were imbued with some power that might transfer to me, and give me the right words to speak. It would not be the first time Charles had heard me disavow my feelings for him. If I had ever imagined that I might be able to make amends to him, I knew now that such dreams were in the past and had best be forgotten for the dreams that they were. It was time to put aside girlish fantasies, and take on the responsibilities of a woman who happened to be in debt through no fault of her own.

Magnanimously, my *fiancé* said, "I am sure I will be able to forgive you if you have been indiscreet. We will put it behind us and make a fresh start. After all, I am perfectly aware that you are a widow and familiar with the marriage bed. I must insist that you admit exactly how you feel about Weatherby because your words and your expression are not in agreement."

Suddenly I saw Charles move, and stroll toward us. My heart leapt in terror. I gazed at him in a silent plea to leave me alone. He did not stop. My pulse ran wild. My breath came in ragged gasps.

"I'll confess that I am puzzled on the same score, McArthur," Charles drawled, breaking into our conversation as easily and casually as if we had been discussing the weather.

Samuel snarled at him. "I assume you've heard all this?"

"As much as I cared to, and then some. But we were discussing Loretta's feelings for me."

I did not want to look at Charles, but his eyes seemed to compel me, and I met his gaze, my heart leaping with the anxiety I felt deep inside. I wanted to run away, but knew that Samuel McArthur would never allow me to leave, not with the honorific of *fiancée* attached to my name.

"<u>We</u> were?" Samuel replied to him archly.

"When you find out how she feels," Charles said, "do let me know, won't you? I assure you, I am interested in the outcome of your *tête-à-tête*, seeing as it affects me."

"It does not!" I quickly asserted. "Go away. You heard what I said to him. Just leave me in peace."

"Where were you," Charles addressed Samuel McArthur, "when Loretta was ill and the whole house was in an uproar, seeking someone to carry her upstairs to sleep the night next to her maid and not disturb anyone if she should cry out in a nightmare?"

Was it my imagination, or did Charles seem to be arguing on my behalf, with sympathy toward my situation? It was unfathomable.

"I did not hear the commotion," Samuel McArthur said, his customary swaggering returning after a moment of hesitation that I surely imagined.

"Methinks the gentleman protests overmuch," Charles said, smiling slowly, his expression like a fox which has outsmarted its prey and now moves in for the kill. "You did not hear because you were not in the house!"

"No. That is… yes, I was—"

"Out for a midnight stroll? I have it on the best authority you were in the company of the housekeeper's daughter in the wine cellar."

I stared at Charles, wondering how he had found out such a thing.

"At that time Mrs. Whitney and I were not engaged to be married," Samuel quickly put in.

"But you were pursuing her," Charles said, "from the first day of meeting. So shame onto you, sir. Your own conduct has not been above reproach and yet you interrogate Mrs. Whitney for dancing with me in a crowded ball-room?"

I pressed my hands to my ears, then cried out, "Please! Stop, both of you. Just stop the wrangling. I cannot stand it a moment longer. I am not a mound of taffy to be yanked and pulled by both of you at the same time."

They looked at me a moment, surprised by my outburst. It was amazing we had not drawn others to us, but our voices had not been as loud as all that, and I supposed that accounted for our continued privacy. But how I wished Charles Weatherby would give up and walk away. I couldn't understand what he was trying to accomplish. At first it seemed he would stir up trouble between Samuel and me, and then he defended me. I did not know what to think of all this.

Samuel McArthur took my hand in his and gave me a conciliatory look. "I am sorry if I upset you, dear. But you still have not answered my question."

Without volition, my hand pulled away from his touch.

"Do you love him?" Samuel demanded of me.

"No," I said quietly, barely breathing, unable to look at either man.

I saw Charles stiffen. He said to Samuel McArthur, with a slight bow, "There you have it, man. Straight from the lady's lips. So you two will be married. Have you taken care of all the arrangements? The banns? The honeymoon accommodations? And—" he paused and shot me a glance and I suddenly knew to my dismay what he was going to say next— "the dowry?"

"Dowry?" Samuel repeated with a puzzled frown. "We haven't had time for any of those things. My mother will help with the details you mentioned. But I know Loretta is of good family, and has a house near Hyde Park. I am sure there are no problems."

The fox gave a sudden bark of a laugh. "Then your mind must be at ease."

I started to cut in with some kind of protest, I knew not what, but suddenly Samuel McArthur stared at me. His voice was tight and clipped as he said, "What is going on? He speaks in codes that have meaning for you. What does he know, that I do not, and should?"

Without warning, Samuel snatched me into his arms and kissed me roughly.

I shrank back and without thinking wiped my mouth on the back of my hand in disgust. At once, I arrested my motion but I was not swift enough to hide it.

"Tut, tut," Charles chided. "Don't be stingy with kisses, Loretta. That's not how you comport yourself with me."

"What!" Samuel roared and all in one motion he lunged with a ham-like fist directed towards Charles's head.

But Charles ducked and caught Samuel by surprise with a thudding blow to the mid-section. The McArthur bully doubled over and slowly sank to the floor, to lean against the wall like a giant ragdoll with his eyes closed.

In the distance, I heard a male servant call out, "Look! A fight!"

"Did you kill him?" I whispered to Charles, stunned by how quickly events had unfolded.

Charles laughed shortly. "I knocked the breath out of him. He will get up in a few minutes and be none the worse for it." He turned his attention back to me.

I could not read the expression in his dark eyes but I felt sure there was no derision for me there. It confused me. I expected to see scorn or even hatred and disdain.

He gently took my arm and led me away from a few servants and house guests who were coming to investigate the commotion. Glancing back, I saw Mr. McArthur lean over his son, and look sharply at Charles.

"We have to talk," Charles said to me simply.

Tears came to my eyes. I turned my head and looked back down the hall, in time to see two men help Samuel McArthur to his feet. My heart sank. It was highly unlikely my engagement would be announced in the McArthur family tomorrow. Even more unlikely that I would find a rich husband in time to avoid financial ruin.

And it was Charles Weatherby's fault. I would have to be a governess or a lady's companion, because he had sabotaged my engagement to Samuel McArthur, the one man who could save me from my pending doom.

"Talk?" I repeated, my voice cracking. "What is there left to talk about? I might as well be dead now."

We were near a hallway which I knew led to the servants' stairs, and so I quickly gathered my skirts in my hands to speed up alone, knowing I could reach my room from this direction. A maid coming down with laundry hugged the wall to let me pass, her face registering surprise that I had not used the main staircase.

Charles stood at the bottom of the stairs and bellowed up to me, "When are you going to stop running away from me?"

Breathless, starting to weep and furious at myself for such weakness, I paused long enough to turn my head and call back down to him, "Never!"

And in my heart, I added the rest of it: that I would never stop running from him, because I knew that I could never have him.

CHAPTER 28

Hoping it was not a lost cause, hoping to renew Samuel McArthur's trust in me, I took the bold move of writing a sweet note to him, sealing it, and slipping it under his door then hurrying back to my room. I did not want to risk his having time to reflect about Charles Weatherby and decide that my fealty was too divided to take a chance on marrying me.

Samuel sent back a note in reply, asking to see me at once in the front parlor.

To my utter amazement, when I met him there, Samuel McArthur took my arm in his. My mind swirled with things I could or should say, but my mouth was silent.

Was he such a dimwit that he had forgotten the altercation with Charles Weatherby? Were we still engaged? I found it unbelievable if it were true, but I did not know how to simply ask the question out loud.

He took the matter out of my hands. "I spoke with your godfather," he said. "And he assured me that your relationship with Mr. Weatherby is strictly of a business nature. You do understand that man will not be welcome in our home after we are married."

Stammering, I told him I understood full well, and I clung tighter to his arm, feeling my heart lift up with a prayer to my guardian angel who surely had made this come about.

As we started to leave, I cast him a questioning look, with a small frown. Hesitating, but compelled to know the answer, I asked, "Will you announce our betrothal at breakfast?"

He frowned. "I should ask Mr. Goodwin for your hand, and then tell my parents."

I hid my exasperation. "Fine! Do it now and announce our engagement in the morning, first thing." Suddenly afraid he might suspect my motive, I hastily added, "I cannot wait for everyone to share in our joy!"

My godfather's weeklong sixtieth birthday celebration would be officially over tomorrow tonight, with all the house guests leaving on Thursday morning.

The Goodwins had invited me to stay longer, but I was anxious to go home and see to my affairs. I had much to take care of before I could become Mrs. Samuel McArthur, including restoring more rooms in my house to at least a semblance of normalcy, so he would not suspect anything about my financial status before we married.

When I moved back downstairs to my old room at the Manor, Ellen offered to sleep in the adjoining dressing room which had space for a cot. I appreciated her offer to guard me, but when I noticed her preparing the cot, I suddenly grew annoyed, feeling like a child with a nursemaid at her elbow around the clock.

Something in my heart told me I was angry at Samuel McArthur and the fact that he had been the best I could find to marry, but having no other outlet for that annoyance, instead I berated Ellen for being underfoot.

She eyed me closely.

I hated when she did that, because it had always seemed to me she could read my very thoughts and that is how she was always one step ahead of my childish plans and foibles in years past. But now I was an adult, and I wanted to be alone tonight, to cry myself to sleep and not have her listening from close at hand.

"I see you are not happy about this engagement to Mr. McArthur," she commented drily, folding the clothes I had discarded.

"After all that has gone wrong, I feared he would rescind the offer but it still holds." I looked at her a moment and tried to force happiness into my voice. "Just think, no more worries about money! I shall be able to pay back wages to you and Dora, and resume a more normal life."

"So you told him about the debts?"

I studied her impassive face.

"Did you tell him about the bills you have to pay?" she persisted. "That you've sold most of your furnishings and dismissed all but two of the servants months ago? That he not only will be getting a bride but another man's debts?"

"This is no time for honesty. I am serious, Ellen Armstrong. Do not get overly virtuous and feel you have the right to go behind my back. There will be plenty of time after the wedding to apologize and to economize my own spending in recompense."

"What if he asks for a dowry?"

I had been worried about the very same thing, but I snapped at her for bringing it to mind. "I will be vague, if pressed, and let him think the house is wholly mine."

"Risky business, if you ask me," she said, turning down the bed for me.

"But I didn't, so keep your opinion to yourself. He won't be able to do anything about it, once we are married. I will be safe."

"Unless he or his family demands an annulment."

I stared at her in horror. "You've been listening to Louise Rogers too much. That is all that woman talks about since her niece married without her permission. She should be happy Susanna made such a good match."

"You need to start your marriage on the right foot. Tell him about the debts."

"But what if he refuses to marry me?" I cried. "Oh get out, Ellen! I am sick of talking to you. Your advice is unwelcome. You don't know how carefully I have thought all this out. I know what I am doing, and I don't need you," I added ungraciously.

She looked at me with tears in her eyes, startled by my uncustomary rudeness. Her voice was soft and reproachful. "You have never ill-treated me before this."

And yet, knowing I had been rude and hurt her feelings, nonetheless I was like a wayward child, too stubborn to change direction. "Go upstairs to your room in the servants' quarters," I said peremptorily. "I don't want you sleeping here with me."

She hesitated a moment.

"Leave!" I cried with undisciplined fervour. "I don't want to see you. And don't come back til morning."

But by morning, I wished with all my heart that I could take back those harsh words I'd spoken to her, and beg her forgiveness.

CHAPTER 29

As I lay in bed, trying to fall asleep that night, I reflected on the gypsy fortune teller's prediction that I would not get married, and yet now I was engaged, not a week later. Suddenly uneasy, but laughing at myself inwardly for being superstitious, I hurriedly got up and found the talisman the gypsy had given me for good luck.

After looking at it for a moment in the moonlight coming from a window I had left open for air, enjoying the scent of the orchards and the spring gardens, I tucked the strange medallion beneath my pillow, and then went to sleep, free of the anxiety that had beleaguered me for months. My debts would be paid, and I would carve out a decent life for myself in Cornwall.

It comforted me greatly that I would soon be sisters-in-law with newlywed Susanna, as I had grown fond of the girl in this short time, and knew we would become true sisters, allies together in that family, no matter what my marriage turned out to be, or even what our shared mother-in-law would prove to be like at close association.

Although Susanna was my age, because of my marriage at barely age seventeen, and the past year of worrying over financial matters, I felt older than my nineteen years. But now I had the promise of a bright future, and on that hope, I fell asleep.

Charles and I strolled hand-in-hand through a lush private garden where magnificent roses bloomed in every imaginable hue from shell pink to deepest crimson.

Turning a corner, we passed beneath a rose-covered bower where honeybees buzzed and sunlight streamed through the latticework.

There was no need to speak. Our thoughts were as one, and the beauty of the garden declared our peace and happiness. We stopped, and turned to face each other. He bent his head to kiss me, and I eagerly met his lips. Parting reluctantly, but with some sense of urgency, we left the arbor and hurried down a different path.

All at once, we were in a thicket. There was no outlet. I began to panic, and clutched his hand. He gripped my fingers as if to reassure me. I turned my head, thinking to go back whence we had come, but the path had strangely disappeared. There was no choice but to go forward and hope the overgrown copse would soon clear.

He moved in front of me to shield me from the backlash of branches he parted to allow our passage. The path suddenly twisted and became so narrow that my wide skirts were torn by brambles and impeded my walking. Now and then I had to stop to free myself from thorns. Sometimes the only way I could do this was to rip at the cloth, not caring about the dress but only desperate to keep up with Charles and not lose sight of him.

Gradually, the thicket changed and I found myself deep in a forest where the towering trees blocked the sunlight. It was cold suddenly, and I shivered. Then all at once the feeling of oppression lifted. The air was filled with birds, swooping from one branch to the next, their chirping and chirring breaking the silence. As we continued walking, now side by side again, I noticed that wild creatures approached us without fear. I pointed this out to Charles and together we delighted in the fearless rabbits, deer and squirrels.

I spied a clearing in the distance and raced toward it, leaving Charles behind. I felt an urgency to get there. In the center, a unicorn appeared, having come from behind a clump of blooming shrubbery. I cried out in delight, but the unicorn startled and fled.

Charles came up behind me and took me in his arms to comfort me. All at once, I realized he had brought a large basket. Now he spread out a blanket and a picnic upon it in the middle of the glade. We ate blackberry melon, Banbury cakes, Blue Leicestershire cheese, Scotch eggs, and gooseberry tarts with custard sauce. I did not question how the food had appeared. It all tasted delicious to me, the finest feast a queen could desire.

Later, he fashioned a swing for me out of sturdy vines tied together and looped over a tall branch. I sat it in and he pushed me higher than I had ever dreamed of flying. Then I saw a solitary fox enter the glade where we had picnicked. I told Charles to stop swinging me.

The small fox stood in front of us and made a yipping bark. To my immense surprise, Charles barked in reply, and the two conversed for several moments in this strange language. There was a chorus of answering yaps from within the forest, and soon the clearing was filled with more foxes.

Charles stood in the center of the clearing and spread the remains of our picnic in a circle around him. The foxes approached and began feeding.

Suddenly I was swinging high above them, with the singing birds, and from my vantage point, I saw how my lover's auburn hair blended with the colour of the animals' fur, and I knew that he was a fox too, but in human form.

After the food was gone, the animals sat in front of Charles, their fluffy long tails waving excitedly and their alert little faces pointed toward Charles as he began barking at them. After a series of yelps, yips and yaps, Charles concluded, and the foxes vanished into the forest.

The swing was gone now, too, and I was walking with Charles toward a chapel near a stone bridge. I asked him what he had talked about with the foxes and he said he had told them about his secret love for me. After a sweet kiss, he promised that by the end of the day our love would be a secret no longer.

My heart soared as I understood the hidden meaning in his words. At that moment, I was happier and more contented than I had ever imagined possible.

The afternoon shadows lengthened as we reached the chapel steps. I reached down to lift my skirts, and noticed that my gown had changed to white satin with a French lace overskirt. A bouquet was in my hand, and I looked up to see my father waiting at the entrance to escort me to the altar. Within the chapel, I saw that Charles was waiting for his bride.

I wanted to run to my groom, but my father was suddenly clutching my arm too roughly. His light support beneath my elbow had changed to a vise-like grip that was painful. I heard him mutter darkly, "Hold still," and he pushed at the sleeve of my gown.

I turned my head to tell my father to let go of me, but just then my flesh was pricked by a long thorn plunging deeply into my arm. I cried out.

My eyes fluttered open.

For an instant, I was confused to see that I was in bed, instead of in a chapel marrying Charles Weatherby.

In a flash my mind registered the salient facts, to wit: I had been asleep and dreaming, but something had awoken me suddenly; there was someone in the room with me; I did not know who the intruder was; there was only moonlight through the window to cast strange shadow shapes as the intruder moved about; I had dreamed of roses yet now the scent of real flowers was in the room; in the dream, a thorn had pricked my arm.

A quick logical thought succeeded all this, and I knew at once that I had just received a hypodermic injection such as the type Dr. Harris had given me. That sensation of a thorn or needle had been too real to be imagined.

Roses....

I inhaled the scent again.

And I remembered Serena Harmon's favourite rose cologne, the one she always wore.

All these thoughts took a brief moment as I saw the cloaked figure bending over me. I knew it must be Mrs. Harmon. She had injected me with... what? A poison? A drug?

The valley of the shadow of death....

My heart skipped in panic. I forced myself to feign sleep so Serena would not realize I had awoken and was aware of her presence. But why had she not left after giving the hypodermic?

Then I had my answer: the moonlight glinted on something she held in her hand. A needle. She was going to give a second injection! All at once I realized it must be morphine. I was feeling the effects I had told Dr. Harris about, and recalled all too clearly his comment that I must be overly sensitive to the drug.

By the way in which I was already feeling a floating sensation, I had a horri-fied suspicion that the dosage I had just received was stronger than what the doctor had given me, and I struggled to fight its effect.

Part of my mind wanted to know why I was so positive Serena was trying to give me a lethal dose. I had no time to dwell on the thought. The hypodermic was coming closer to me, and at any moment, the drug would be in me, and I would be dead from too much of it, too soon.

I tried to move my arm but the muscles had already relaxed from the first injection and were uncooperative. I tried again, and pushed against the cloaked figure. Suddenly my arm was pinned down to the bed.

"Ellen!" I started to cry out again for my maid, then memories of the previ-ous evening flooded me, and I remembered that I had told her to sleep upstairs, that I did not need or want her. "Help! Someone come and help!" My voice was not strong. I despaired of anyone hearing me except the woman at my side, trying to get me to hold still. I wriggled and squirmed, forcing my body to move.

Suddenly I remembered the gypsy talisman beneath my pillow. I don't know how I found the strength, but I thrust my hand under the pillow, withdrew the heavy medallion and swung it by its chain toward my attacker. Just before it hit her, I felt the prick of a needle on my skin, and I managed to pull back, away from it, to keep it from going further into my skin.

I had watched how Dr. Harris made the hypodermic mechanism work, and I knew Serena had to press the plunger to force the liquid into my arm.

With relief, I heard the hypodermic clatter to the floor. The cloaked figure bent as if searching for it.

I was overwhelmed with a sense of weariness. I felt nauseous and the room had grown colder. I knew it was the morphine, affecting my senses in this fashion. But suddenly I felt euphoric and free from worry. This must be the sensation the users of morphine sought, and it was pleasant, but a seed of doubt pressed itself forward urgently and I knew that it was important to call out for assistance and make Serena Harmon leave me alone.

"Help!" I cried again. "Ellen!" Was it my imagination, or did my voice suddenly seem louder than before? I could not tell, but in my panic I kept calling out for help again and again. Surely someone would come.

Apparently Serena decided the same, because the cloaked figure abruptly abandoned her search and raced from the room, closing the door behind her.

I drifted into a troubled sleep, wondering petulantly why Ellen had not come to my aid.

CHAPTER 30

A hand shook me, and I heard my name called repeatedly. Sleepily, I mumbled, "Come back later, Ellen," turned over and buried my head under the pillows. I felt something in my hand, and realized it was the gypsy talisman.

In slow waves, everything came back to me. Groaning from the lingering effects of the morphine, I sat up and greeted my godmother, who had been trying to waken me.

"You must get up now, dear," she said.

I peered at her, and saw the frown creasing her brow, and the way her hands were clenched together, as she did when she was upset over something. There was a movement near the door, and I realized Susanna McArthur had come in as well.

She quietly approached Mrs. Goodwin and whispered in her ear, but I heard her say, "Have you told her yet?"

At once, I became fully awake. "Told me what? What news have you?"

The two women exchanged an uneasy look, neither wanting to speak. Finally, my godmother took my hands in hers. "Your Ellen has died."

I shook my head. "That's not possible." Confusion washed over me, and I knew that my godmother would not state it if she did not believe it to be true. "Perhaps it was someone else, who looks like her...."

"No," Susanna put in, "she has been identified."

Tears filled my eyes. "She died, defending me from Mrs. Harmon," I said softly, more to myself than the others, but they heard and quickly began telling me that I was wrong.

"Ellen was found outside by one of the gardeners," my godmother said. "It was an accident... I suppose."

"Tell me what you mean," I demanded.

"She must have been walking on the bridge," she went on, "and leaned over too far, perhaps looking at something in the water. Or else…."

"Are you saying she drowned? And you think it was suicide? That's mad!" I instantly regretted my outburst. "I am sorry, Godmother. I did not mean that you are insane, just that I find the idea of Ellen's killing herself to be completely unacceptable. She had no reason for it."

"Then it was an accident," Susanna said.

"We were… friends," I said, knowing it would be hard to explain my old relationship with the curt northerner who had been governess, mother, confidante and companion, not just maid or servant. I hastily thought of what money I had brought with me. "I'm not sure I have enough with me to pay for the funeral. If not, may I borrow—"

My godmother quickly replied that she had already begun preparations, and would help me with the expense if I did not have the funds with me. The funeral would be this afternoon, since there was no one who needed to be notified for it and the sooner done the better.

Glancing at the clock, I realized it was nearing the lunch hour. I had been asleep far longer than usual, no doubt due to the morphine. But since Susanna was still at the Manor, I did not have to worry that my *fiancé* had left without saying goodbye and arranging to meet again on his way back to Cornwall from East Anglia. They would pass through or near London, and I would suggest that we should get married at that time so I could simply join them for their journey home and not require more traveling by the family for a wedding at a later date. At least, I hoped he would be agreeable to my logic.

Now, however, I had the loss of Ellen Armstrong to absorb.

I got up and opened the wardrobe, thinking to wear the black bombazine she had insisted on bringing in case I recanted my notion of not wearing widow's weeds. I would put it on for the funeral. At the same time, I had to be practical, and look suitable for the announcement of my engagement. Even Ellen's death could not change the need for a new husband.

Selecting a plain gray frock that was not overly wrinkled, I started to draw it out, but was unsteady on my feet and clutched the door frame. The gown fell in a heap to the floor.

"You need a maid to help you dress," my godmother said. "And I will send in a tray of tea with her. You are weak, no doubt from lack of breakfast. I tried to awaken you earlier but you were in the grip of such a deep slumber that I left you in peace. The news of Ellen's death could wait, I decided. You have been under such a strain, Loretta, that I feared the return of your brain-fever. But I knew you might want to attend the funeral, you see, so I came in again."

I reassured her that she had done the right thing by waking me, and that the brain-fever had not returned. As I began hastily dressing, Susanna looked around the room curiously. My godmother opened a drapery to the sunshine, and Susanna stopped suddenly. Bending to look under the bed at something that caught her attention in the light, she retrieved the hypodermic that had fallen in my struggle with Serena Harmon. She held it up curiously.

My godmother recognized it for what it was. "No wonder you slept so soundly. The medicine Dr. Harris left for you Monday! He told me it was enough to sedate you two or three times if I was careful not to dispense all of the medicine at once."

I took the hypodermic from Susanna McArthur, and she seemed all too glad to be rid of the sinister object. I held it to the light and saw it still contained a liquid. I had no way of knowing if part of the second injection had gone into me or perhaps some had leaked out on the floor when the hypodermic had fallen from Serena's grip. I carefully discharged the drug into the washbowl and laid the hypodermic aside.

Turning back to them, I told them about my struggle with a cloaked figure in the night, the injection I received and how I had fought off the second injection. "I screamed for Ellen and she must have run in here from the dressing room cot. No, wait, she was sleeping upstairs. I mean—"

"Your thoughts are confused after all," my godmother said. "Ellen was found outside. Do you suppose she helped you fight off an imaginary attacker, then ran out and flung herself off the bridge? You had a nightmare. They can seem real upon waking, but it was your imagination. Why would Mrs. Harmon wish to hurt you? And how could someone give two injections when there is only one hypodermic, the one that you secretly hid and claimed someone took? Poor dear! Brain-fever causes strange rambling, or so I have heard, and therefore I am not blaming you. But I must insist that you refrain from any more accusations. Before this it was Claire Lewis who wished to kill you, and now you claim—"

"But Serena even threatened me! The news of Ellen's death drove this from my mind. Let me tell you what happened. Mrs. Harmon came in here last night, stealthily, while I slept, disguised in a dark cloak, but I knew her by her cologne. She gave me morphine and here is the proof—" I dashed to the washbowl and held up the hypodermic in triumph. Finally, I had proof to substantiate my story.

"That is quite enough," my godmother said, looking at me in distress. "When you have finished dressing, come downstairs for lunch. I will expect you to remember your position here, and hold your tongue when you are ready to accuse blindly and without provocation."

She turned to Susanna and said, "Dr. Harris warned me the brain-fever could reoccur in times of uncertainty or upset. Clearly her maid's death has unhinged her mind. I will insist that she stay here a few weeks and recuperate under the doctor's care."

"No!" I cried out. "I must dress. I need to see Samuel McArthur and I have to go to the funeral."

Ignoring me, Susanna told my godmother, "I had even believed some of the things she told me. She convinced me Claire Lewis was scheming against her, but now her story changes again."

They looked at each and nodded, in mutual understanding that I was ill and my rantings were those of someone with an unsound mind.

I grew alarmed about what my godmother had just said to Susanna, about my staying under the doctor's care. I knew that Dr. Harris had patients at a sanitarium not far from the village. What if that was the method of treatment he would suggest to my godparents, and in their love for me they agreed to it? I had to stop those wheels turning before they led to my being locked away with no say in where I went or when.

Samuel McArthur would never go through with a marriage to an asylum inmate!

"I feel like I've awoken from a bad dream," I said quickly, smiling ingratiatingly at both of them. "I had strange thoughts of someone trying to hurt me. I told you about my dream, though, didn't I?"

"You did not say it was a dream," my godmother said skeptically.

I laughed as if at myself. "Can you imagine how silly it would be, one of my friends sneaking in here to try to do me bodily harm. You didn't believe any of my nonsense, I hope. I am sorry if I made it seem so real. I was sleeping, and the dream lingered overlong."

I could see confusion flit across their faces.

Pressing my advantage, I hurriedly indicated my state of undress, and pleaded, "Now someone please help me with these buttons! And help me braid my hair into a neat chignon. I don't need to wait for a maid. If you'll both help me, I'll be ready to go down to lunch with you and we'll put my nonsense behind us like the dream that it was. Look, Susanna, take that ribbon I meant to give you earlier. It will be a remembrance of our first meeting here at Kenwick Manor."

As they buttoned and fussed over me, I added on impulse, "You will have to pretend surprise later, but I will tell you a secret now. No, don't frown, either of you. It's a lovely secret. Samuel McArthur and I are going to be married! Yes, Susanna, we shall be sisters soon. And, Godmother, I will be the bride of your cousin's son. Isn't that the most delightful news, to offset the sorrow of Ellen's death?"

CHAPTER 31

After going downstairs with my godmother and the new Mrs. McArthur, I had asked to see my maid's body, and a servant took me to the dim room where she was laid out.

Alone with Ellen, I quietly prayed for the repose of her soul, and begged her forgiveness for the harsh and childish words I had spoken to her the previous night, not knowing they would be the last words she would hear from me. Filled with regret, knowing her accident would have been prevented if she had been safely home with me in London instead of here, trying to help me find a husband, a campaign she had not condoned, I silently left her.

Searching out the Goodwins' housekeeper, I thanked her for the care that had been taken with Ellen's body, and pressed some coins in her hand to show my appreciation. I could little afford the money, but I could not live with myself if I ignored my duty on Ellen's behalf.

A short while later, going into lunch, Claire dropped back from accompanying the elder Mrs. McArthur, and gently stroked my arm. "Poor Loretta. I hear the brain-fever has returned."

Just as quickly as she had appeared, she slipped away, and was already seated at the table when I entered the dining room.

I took a chair as far from her as I could get, and hoped that Samuel would soon come in, and sit across from me where a seat remained empty. I avoided looking in the direction of my godmother, because Charles Weatherby was at her left hand, and the two were engaged in a lively dialogue, punctuated by laughter now and then. Sourly, I reflected that he had quickly recovered from any dismay he might have felt at my engagement to Samuel McArthur. Soon that latter gentleman made an appearance, but instead of taking the chair opposite me, he sat further down the table. I tried to hide my discomfort that he did not even come over to greet me, and I cast a smile his way. To my consternation, he actually appeared to be avoiding me.

As the meal progressed, I barely ate, merely going through the motions, chatting idly with people around me, trying not to worry as a lull in the conversation would appear now and then, and yet Samuel McArthur still failed to rise and announce that he was going to marry me.

It must be that he is waiting until after we finish eating, I consoled myself, grasping at a reason for this delay. All I could think of was the fight between Charles and him the previous evening, and my latent uncertainty about the whole thing. Had I managed to convince Samuel McArthur of my fidelity to him? Glancing toward that end of the table once more, Claire Lewis caught my eye and it seemed that she smirked as she gave a small nod to me and flicked her gaze toward Samuel.

My heart grew cold. I tried not to show my alarm, and merely met her smile with a polite one of my own, but it did not escape me that she felt smug and satisfied about something. In her meddling, she might have said something to Samuel McArthur that had turned him against me completely. I had to remember that while I slept hours longer than anyone else had, Claire herself had no doubt been up and busy with her own plans.

I forced myself to continue eating and join the conversation with a sanguine composure I did not feel. I noticed that Mr. Harmon tried to avoid my eye each time I looked in his direction, and sighed sadly to myself, wishing he did not feel guilty for not being able to help me, but even more, wishing he had better news for me. I had been anxious for his return yesterday, hoping for the best, and had been disappointed instead.

I thought about Ellen. Life would go on, as Ellen had often pointed out, and I would simply have to adjust myself to what came next. I wondered apprehensively what the future held for me now.

But then I saw Samuel McArthur push back his chair and come to his feet, and I put aside my oppressive musings.

He raised his glass as in a toast, and I felt relief wash over me. Here it was then, at last.

"Attention, everyone," he called out, smiling. "I would like to say something."

All eyes turned toward him, and the room grew quiet. I shifted in my chair so that he could see my face, and smiled eagerly at him, trying not to look too anxious since the others were supposed to be surprised at his announcement. I glanced quickly at my godmother and we exchanged a small nod of anticipation.

"I want to thank our charming hostess and generous host for having us here," Samuel began, "and for introducing me to the woman I am going to marry."

Excited whispers swept the room.

I shifted in my chair, preparing to stand.

He held out a hand. "To my betrothed. Claire Lewis."

With a thud, I sat hard, stunned.

Claire stood, and bowed her head modestly.

From nearby, I felt Susanna McArthur's eyes on me, but I could not force myself to turn and look at her.

Following the lead of my godfather, I raised my glass and joined in the toast to the happy couple, as Samuel went around the table and took Claire's hand in his.

Holding back the desire to scream in frustration, I managed to smile, turn to the people next to me and join in the prevailing delight that this houseparty had brought wives to both of the McArthur sons. What an unexpected joy for all concerned, or so it seemed. I struggled inside to make sure that no one saw that I was anything but happy for the girl I had brought to the ball.

I knew one person at the table who would not share the jovial mood. My gaze sought out Susanna's aunt and I knew that her grim look matched my feelings.

As quickly as it was reasonable to do so without attracting unwanted attention to myself, I left the room with the other women, and yet did not go into the drawing room with them. I had to be alone with my thoughts.

It took only a few moments to find a quiet corner in my godfather's study. I felt I would not be disturbed here, since the men would be talking in the dining room still. Sitting in a chair, I leaned my head back and finally let myself see that my all my bold plans had failed. Not only that, but I had lost Ellen. Guilt hammered at my thoughts as I remembered I had told her to go away, had declared I wished never to see her again… and now I never would.

Thinking of Ellen, I wondered at length why she would have been outside, either late at night after leaving me, or early in the morning shortly before her body was discovered. Had she been unable to sleep, disturbed by my heated words, and gone for a walk at dawn? Then had she been overcome with despair over my crossness at her, and leapt off the bridge to her death?

A scornful noise escaped my throat.

That wasn't the Ellen Armstrong I knew, the stern northerner who told me that strife and disappointment were challenges to prove your mettle. I was certain that she had not killed herself. Could it have been an appalling and unfortunate accident? Maybe she had dropped something and been on the side of the stream, straining to reach it, then had fallen in and been caught by the weeds and current, unable to surface, the weight of her wet gown dragging her under, and no one about to hear her cries for help.

It occurred to me that she might have been crying out at the same moment I had been, during the night.

Was it possible that someone had deliberately killed her? But why would anyone want to harm a middle-aged servant? That question led to the obvious answer: because she was <u>my</u> servant. And for some reason, anything connected to me was at risk for being stolen, damaged, pushed down stairs, slashed, drowned like the kitten… and, maybe, drowned like Ellen herself.

After the kitten died, the legend of the girl who drowned off the bridge had raced through the Manor like a wildfire, with predictions that something might happen to me. Several things had indeed happened, none pleasant.

I came to the conclusion that I needed to stop thinking of whether it was Claire or Serena who wished to hurt me, and be aware that both of them were trying to, perhaps for separate reasons. I pushed aside all the things others had told me in their defense, trying to convince me of my brain-fever. That was nonsense. I was thinking more clearly and logically than ever. Ellen would be proud of me, I suddenly realized.

The tears I'd been holding back, suddenly gushed forth and I sobbed into my hands. After a few moments, I sniffed, groped in my pocket for a handkerchief and became aware that a large freshly laundered one was dangling in my line of vision. I looked up.

Charles Weatherby stood before me, a sympathetic look on his face.

Embarrassed at how I must look, I hastily took the handkerchief and wiped my eyes and nose.

He drew a chair close to me and sat down. "I looked for you after lunch."

"How kind of you," I muttered.

"Last night, you thought you were engaged to Samuel McArthur, and I gave him cause for doubt."

"Yes, you did!"

"Is that why you were crying? Over him?"

"Ellen, my maid, died this morning. Or perhaps last night. The doctor has not seen her yet, to tell us how long… if she was in the water only a few hours, or longer."

I could see he had not heard of this.

"I think Serena pushed her off the bridge," I told him, not caring if he believed me or not. "She tried to kill me last night."

"Ellen did?"

I snapped, "Mrs. Harmon! She came in my room in a cloak with a hood over her head, but her rose cologne was like a calling card and I knew it was she, trying to give me an overdose of morphine."

At his request, I detailed what had taken place, and my godmother's belief that I had hidden the hypodermic after the doctor's first visit, and had injected myself, with the drug being responsible for my fantasy that someone mysterious had come in and attempted murder.

To my relief, he did not laugh when I was finished, and did not try to produce alternate explanations for what I said had happened.

The clock chimed, and I became aware of the hour. If I were to attend Ellen's funeral, I needed a carriage to the cemetery by the village church.

CHAPTER 32

A little later, after freshening up in my room, I hurried out to the stables and carriage house. In the yard, I passed Miss Louise Rogers. She gave a start at seeing me. Thinking of my slashed wagonette, I called out impetuously to her that she would not get away with it.

Leaving her dumfounded and frightened, I went on to the carriage I had arranged to borrow from my godfather, not wanting to ride in the slashed interior of my own wagonette. There I found Charles Weatherby waiting for me.

He tipped his hat. "May I accompany you to the funeral?"

I saw no reason to refuse him, so I nodded, and he helped me into the open carriage.

We followed behind the coffin. A few of the servants who had known Ellen from our many visits to Kenwick Manor were in attendance.

During the drive, Charles offered no explanation as to why he wanted to attend the burial of a servant, and I asked no questions. I kept my hands in my lap, holding the bouquet I had asked a gardener to prepare for the funeral, and let my thoughts wander over the years, thinking of things Ellen Armstrong had said to me since childhood.

Whether wisdom or foolishness, it didn't matter now. The sum of it was that she had tried to offer her experiences to me, and had been loyal to me even when she disagreed with the path I had chosen. I knew it had distressed her that I was going to marry Samuel McArthur without informing him of my debts. Well, now that would not happen, because the engagement was off. I found it scarcely imaginable that Claire Lewis had been able to insinuate herself into his affections to such a degree as to upset my own position with him, and yet that was the reality. I suddenly recollected her stated intention of marrying Charles Weatherby and wondered what had become of that plan. Then I shut her out of my thoughts, as the entire subject was too distressing.

For a moment, I had the notion that Ellen had taken it upon herself to inform Samuel McArthur of my financial predicament. Perhaps she too had slipped a note under his door, but one inviting him to meet her by the bridge to discuss something of importance. Then, at the bridge, she had told him about my debts, and the burden he would be taking on. I knew that she would have flaunted her outrage at the law which says a woman becomes a man's property upon their marriage. Had he been so angered over my deceit, or at her words of female equality, that he had struck her, caused her to stumble back and go over the low wall of the bridge to her death?

The scenario played out in front of my eyes as if a playwright had penned it for performance by actors on a stage. My logic was flawless. I must consider the possibility of this explanation for her death.

"You are deep in thought," Charles said, touching my arm. "But it is time for the service. We are keeping the vicar waiting."

I looked up and to my confusion saw that the small crowd was waiting for me. I hastily exited the carriage with his assistance.

Approaching the grave-site, I placed the bouquet of flowers upon Ellen's simple coffin. She had lived simply and frugally all her life, and now I was too poor to give her a proper funeral and lunch in her honor. I felt she would understand, and I hoped she would forgive me, not only for this simple service, but for the wrongs I had done against her.

The ceremony was brief, but we paid our office of respect and affection for Ellen Armstrong. I knew that she would have understood my inner relief when Mr. Weatherby insisted upon paying for the funeral, and pressed upon the vicar an additional sum for the church.

As we returned to the carriage, I told Charles, "I intended to pay." I added, patting my reticule, "I have the money right here."

"I am sure you do," he said, in a tone I thought was impertinent, but perhaps I was too overwrought to judge correctly what anyone else might intend by their manner of speech.

I had certainly been wrong before, more than a few times, in my assessment of another person's private meaning or intention.

While we were still alone, I stopped Charles. "Why did you attend the funeral?" I blurted out, unable to hold my tongue. The question had weighed on my mind all through the service.

"I admired Ellen," he said simply.

"But you did not even know her."

He arched a brow, intimating that I was wrong.

I quickly asked him, "How did you come to—"

"We spoke a few times, and I sought her out once or twice."

"For what purpose?" I asked, growing uneasy at his words. Ellen would not have betrayed me to him, I was certain of it, but he was skilled at asking questions and she might have inadvertently been indiscreet about me to him.

"She was fond of you," he said.

"I know."

"She was a wise woman. In her simple way, she discarded confusion and saw to the heart of the matter."

"What… 'matter' would that be?" I asked, feeling sick inside. So they <u>had</u> discussed my debts. How humiliating! "Will you tell me what you discussed with her? I have the right to know."

"No, my dear, you do not. It was between Ellen and myself."

No amount of wheedling on my part pried further elucidation from him. He stayed calm, seeming unaware of my growing upset over what they might have talked about. The strain of attending Ellen's funeral close on the heels of Serena's attack on me during the night, my broken engagement and now being in the company of the man I loved but could never have, began to have an affect on me. I grew more irritable. "So don't tell me, I didn't want to know anyway! I was just making conversation to be polite."

He smiled infuriatingly, and I wished I could deduce what he was thinking.

Calming myself, I wisely changed the subject away from me, and back to Ellen in a more general fashion. "Have you heard that the servants believe Ellen's death was inevitable?"

"Why is that?"

I reminded him of the legend of the girl who fell off the bridge and drowned. "Then when my kitten was drowned, the gossips said I would be next. Now that Ellen has died, they admit to confusion over whether it would actually be me or my maid, and now the prophecy has come true. Or maybe they still expect me to die as well," I added. I felt a sudden chill, and rubbed my arms.

"You are not superstitious, are you?" he asked.

"Of course not!" In my pocket I felt the weight of the gypsy talisman that I carried with me at all times, knowing it was foolish, but feeling it could not do me any harm… and might help. After all, had it not saved me when I tumbled down the cliff, and its chain caught on a branch, giving me just enough time to stop my fall and climb to safety? And had it not been a quick weapon during my fight against Serena Harmon last night? I felt it was a deep shame that the talisman's magical powers did not extend toward making my debts vanish, so I could let Charles Weatherby know my true feelings for him.

CHAPTER 33

During the return journey, Charles and I were silent but for a few unremarkable comments about the weather. The day was overcast, but there was only a mild drizzle, and we would be safely indoors before the rain came. Both of us were conscious of the driver's presence, and did not speak anything we did not want him to overhear.

The manicured lawns, big stone manor and whitewashed outbuildings of Kenwick swung into view as we turned onto the road leading to it.

At the carriage house, I noticed that the McArthur family's brougham was already being readied for their trip in the morning. Wryly, I thought of the dreams I'd had, that they would be my new family, and I would be joining them on their later return to Cornwall.

Leaving those thoughts behind as being moot, I started toward the Manor, with Charles Weatherby at my side.

Along the way, while we were still in the gardens, I decided to tell him about the other things that had been happening. Hesitantly, I began, "I hope you will not feel it is simply my female foolishness—"

"I do not think women are foolish," he said gravely. "The male sphere and the female sphere should overlap, not be separate."

Surprised, I couldn't help smiling at him. I also couldn't help wondering if that was what he and Ellen had discussed together, the equality of the genders, but I felt it would serve me little to try to bring back the topic of his talks with Ellen again, so I continued with what had happened last night, and my thoughts about it.

He frowned. "This is very serious. And you are certain you were not asleep and dreaming?"

My cheeks coloured at the memory of the dream I had about him, with the yipping foxes… and the wedding chapel.

Quickly, I said, "I am certain. She has entertained a jealousy for a long time, and has even threatened to kill me. Last night, she saw her opportunity, and she took it. Only my… good fortune," I said, having started to say 'my gypsy talisman,' "allowed me the strength to fight her off and call out for help, so that she feared discovery and fled."

The silence lasted so long that I finally spoke again, "Maybe she is the one who killed Ellen. Maybe Ellen told her to leave me alone, and so she pushed her off the bridge, and then—"

"And then ran upstairs," he said, gently mocking, "put on a cloak, hurried in to you, without being at all breathless, tried to inject you with morphine in a dose that she suddenly knew would be just the right amount to kill you, then fled the room and went down to breakfast the next day with a smile on her face. I breakfasted across the table from Mrs. Harmon and I assure you that she did not look like a thwarted murderer."

When he put it that way, it did sound inconceivable. My thoughts were awash with theories and still no proof. I had thought about the hypodermic, and my godmother's assertion that I was the one who had hidden it away, that it was the missing hypodermic Dr. Harris had left for her to give me, and that my talk of a second hypodermic was part of my brain-fever.

Feeling I might as well share these thoughts with him as well, I did.

During this, he led me toward a bench near a group of statues, and we sat together.

"I wish someone believed me," I said as a final note, dejected, heedless of the pretty flowers and the chirping birds.

"I believe you," he said quietly.

My spine straightened by itself and I looked at him with such relief that I wanted to pour out my thanks but feared being overly sentimental. "Thank you," I said simply.

"However," he began, "I do not think you are right about Mrs. Harmon."

"You don't?" I cried, feeling betrayed all at once. "Why ever not?"

"Because," he replied, watching for my reaction, "I know that she did not leave her bedroom last night."

"But her husband was back from London already…." Shocked, I realized the implication of his statement.

My eyes stung with tears. I fought off a feeling of despair and wounded pride. I had, with great difficulty, been living with the determination that I must avoid Charles Weatherby, a resolution made necessary by the fact that I had fallen in love with him, and could not marry him since he was in need of a fortune, just as I was.

It had been hard enough on my heart to see him time and again and have to turn away from him, to be forced by Samuel McArthur to denounce Charles in his hearing, but now… to have Charles admit without shame that he had been in Serena's *boudoir* the night before, it was too much to bear.

Vexed and out of spirits, I was determined that he would not see me cry.

Tossing my head back, I laughed lightly. "Others told me you had formed an attachment with Claire Lewis. What a bluebeard you have turned out to be, Mr. Weatherby! It must have hurt you to hear she will marry Samuel McArthur."

It took a moment for me to realize that he was chuckling to himself as he tugged at his droopy red-brown moustache, and watching me sidelong with that alert fox-like gaze that I had come to know so well the past few days and had even seen in my dreams.

"Do you always leap to conclusions on such slim evidence?" he asked drily.

"When the conclusion is that obvious," I retorted, "who could not take the leap?"

Now he laughed out loud. "You are jealous!"

"You are ridiculous."

"You think that Mrs. Harmon and I…. Well, before jumping, at least see your conclusions are based on more fact than what I gave you. All I said is that she did not leave her room."

Haughtily, I asked, "How would you know, unless you were in there with her?"

"Because, my dear," he said, delighting in drawing out his words, "after hearing your accusations against her the other day, your confusion over whether she and Miss Lewis were plotting together against you or separately, I took it upon myself to keep an eye on her comings and goings. In other words, I listened at her wall, and I heard two people snoring."

I felt foolish but did not want to admit to the feeling of relief and happiness that had suddenly filled my heart to realize he had not formed an affection for Serena Harmon.

"So maybe it was Claire after all?" I was utterly confused now, not knowing what to think. "I was so certain it must have been Serena Harmon."

"You have overlooked an important fact," he said. At my questioning glance, he went on, "Mrs. Harmon has threatened you repeatedly. You told me earlier that this is nothing new in your relationship with her."

"She's always accusing me of something."

"So she's threatened to murder you before this?"

"Oh, probably. I don't remember. Yes, I think the last time I saw her, she told me she'd slit my throat if I wore a certain blue gown to dinner when she had planned to wear one that was a similar colour."

Smiling, he said, "So time and again, she's made threats she never actually carried out. If she wanted to kill you, she would have done so long ago. Why wait til this particular gathering to make serious attempts against you?"

"Maybe she decided she could not take any more from me. Even though I never did anything...."

"What is different now, about this party, that would make her suddenly determined to carry out a threat that in the past proved to be baseless?"

"But if Serena is not the one, what about the rose cologne?" I said, musing out loud. "No, it had to be Mrs. Harmon in my room. I know I am right. And there is something I haven't told you before: the night my kitten was killed, the night of the ball, I saw Serena come out of my bedroom."

"How did that come about?"

"I went to my godmother's dressing room for a shawl, and as I was leaving, I saw Serena coming from my room."

"Coming from it, and then closing the door? Or just turning away from the closed door?"

I looked at him, and saw the reasoning behind his question. "I can't be certain now, whether the door was open or not. I remember being sure it was my room, and not hers, as mine is at the corner and hers is two doors away, but...."

He patted my hand. "It is not important. Maybe you will remember later."

We looked at each other a moment, and I suddenly felt the urge to tell him all about the debts my husband had burdened me with, and how hard it had been the past year, finding out how much money he owed, that he had even gambled away my inheritance and I was left with nothing. I had brought wealth to the marriage, and Edward Whitney had squandered it.

Bitterly, I knew I did not dare share my thoughts with Charles Weatherby. He was a man in need of a rich wife. I was a woman in need of a rich husband. What use was it to go against convention and try to make a friend of him? It would only lead to my heart aching more than it already was.

"Something on your mind?" he asked gently.

I shook my head.

"So you are certain it was Serena in the cloak?" he persisted. "Perhaps I was mistaken about her activities, or she went out a window and climbed a balcony." He shrugged. "I am not a detective. I thought I was helping, but I seem to have added to your confusion."

"It had to be Serena Harmon. I know I am right."

"And so you no longer suspect Miss Lewis of trying to harm you?"

"She did try. I am certain of that."

"Then she stopped," he suggested.

"It would seem so."

"Why?"

I looked at him, stumped by his question. I did not fathom why Claire had given up when she had seemed set on a course to destroy me. "I… I do not know. What do you think?"

"Firstly, I don't believe that someone stops a certain way of acting without good cause. You were sure she was trying to harm you. Now you are just as sure she magically changed her mind. It does not make sense."

"I know," I admitted miserably. "But I don't see why two women would be… and that reminds me!"

He was startled by my sudden change of course.

"I forgot to tell you that I found out Louise Rogers, Susanna's aunt, is the one who destroyed her ball gown. I had guessed someone thought it was mine, but I was wrong. Miss Rogers hoped to prevent her niece from attending the ball."

"Why?"

"Out of sheer spite, I suppose. Because Susanna is young and marriageable."

"And her aunt is not?"

We both laughed.

"Back to our detecting," he said, "the logical conclusion is that Miss Lewis has <u>not</u> stopped trying to hurt you."

"But she hasn't done anything…" I trailed off, thinking to myself *Other than stealing my* fiancé!

"I think it was Miss Lewis, not Mrs. Harmon, in your room last night," he said, cutting into my thoughts. "You said you did not see a face?"

"She wore a cloak with a hood, or maybe it was just a blanket thrown over her head."

"But you are sure it was a woman, not a man?"

"I saw her hand. Even in the dark I could see it was not a man's hand. Also, the perfume was definitely feminine. Rose perfume. It was Serena's cologne," I added stubbornly. "She wears it all the time."

We fell silent, each thinking our own thoughts. I knew we should get up and go into the house, but I hesitated to leave him, knowing this would probably be our final meeting. Tomorrow we would be leaving, no doubt in different directions. It was unlikely I'd see him again, my fox.

Finally, Charles broke the silence, speaking slowly as though the idea was taking shape along with the words, "Serena's cologne... but was Serena the one wearing it?"

His question sparked a memory and I cried out, "I'm a fool!"

"Don't berate yourself, woman, just tell me!"

"Susanna complained to me Sunday that Claire had been borrowing things from her, and not returning them—"

"And borrowing also from Mrs. Harmon?" he quickly suggested.

"Yes!"

We looked at each other, and this time it was with the excitement of realizing how well our two minds worked together.

"We should help the detectives at Scotland Yard!" I cried out happily.

He smiled at me, just as excited by our cleverness in solving at least part of the puzzle together.

"Claire wore the rose cologne," I said. "It is so simple. I should have seen it sooner, but there were too many details."

"Of course, too much confusion. That is how these things go unsolved, but now you know whom to be on guard against."

"Then it was Claire who killed Ellen," I said gravely. "I sent Ellen from me last night, with harsh words."

"Which you are heartily sorry for now," he put in kindly.

I nodded. "But I know Ellen. She probably hovered around my door, wanting to be sure I was safe, guarding me."

"As I should have done," he murmured under his breath.

I darted him a glance, but decided I should pretend I had not heard. However, my heart heard full well, and leapt with joy. He cared about me. This, too, was obvious now.

"But she could not have killed Ellen at my door," I pointed out. "Ellen's body was found by the bridge. She drowned."

"Is there something she could have said to Ellen," he mused, "to lure her outside?"

"I can't think of anything. It's all too much, all at once." So much had changed, now that I eliminated Serena Harmon from the picture. I had to shift all the facts and theories once more, and try to determine the order of events. "I spent so much time lately suspecting Mrs. Harmon, that I feel I've over-looked something important about Claire. Or more than one thing," I added helplessly.

"That is understandable," he said. "Still," he added, glancing toward the McArthur carriage in the distance, "Miss Lewis will be leaving your life soon, and you will not have to worry about her."

I nodded. And then we were looking at each other, and somehow, we both leaned closer as if drawn to each other by mesmerism, and then we were kiss-ing.

We drew apart slowly, our eyes locked. Time meant nothing.

He looked more like a fox than ever, and I felt I was in a dream again, but the wind against my cheek told me I was awake.

"Will you do me the honor," he began, taking my hand in his, "of becoming my wife?"

The assent rushed to my lips, but I instantly recalled his requirement of a twenty thousand pound dowry. Leaping to my feet, I cried out, "No! I cannot!" and hurried into the house, knowing from the silence behind me that, this time, he did not follow when I ran from him.

CHAPTER 34

There was no reason for me to stay until morning, so I was packing. And, I must confess, crying too, moaning to myself that if only I had money, I could have accepted Charles Weatherby's proposal of marriage. It was all Edward Whitney's fault, I decided bitterly. He had no right to leave me with such oppressing debt.

As if Ellen were beside me, I suddenly felt her saying to me that I should go to Charles and explain the truth to him. But I rejected that thought the moment it appeared. I had no intention of debasing myself, and admitting I was a fake.

I had maintained a *facade* of wealth since Charles and I had met in the dining room, when I had burned my hand... and started falling in love with him....

Drawing myself up short, I reminded myself it would be folly to tell a fortune hunter that I was penniless. What purpose would it serve? *He wants twenty thousand pounds*, I reminded myself again and again, as I tossed my clothes in fury into my valises.

But all of a sudden, as I closed one valise, I remembered Claire Lewis taking my jewel case from where she had hidden it in her wardrobe, behind a valise somewhat similar to mine.

"My emerald necklace," I murmured out loud. That was what I had been unable to recall earlier. In the confusion of the attack on me, then Ellen's death and the funeral, the necklace had slipped my mind. Claire had asserted that she did not know where it was, and something about the way she said it carried the ring of truth.

So who had it?

Charles had professed a belief in Claire's scheming to murder me, but as he reminded me before, I had no proof. It always came down to the fact that it was my word against hers, and everyone believed her!

A small voice inside whispered: *Charles believes you.*

Annoyed at myself, without regard to orderliness, I tossed dresses, stockings, glove boxes and riding boots pell-mell into the gaping mouth of my trunk. I picked up a hat and sailed it into a waiting striped hatbox. Hairbrushes, combs and toiletries followed, with only a bit more care on my part, to ensure nothing broke or spilled. The bureau near the door to the corridor was soon empty and I tackled its cluttered top.

That is when I discovered the second hypodermic.

It held a horrible fascination for me. With a shudder, I picked it up gingerly from the plunger end, and held it at arm's length as though it might, under its own power, turn and assault me with its needle. There was still some liquid in it, but not much, and I suspected it was the one that had been used on me first, then tossed aside in the haste of leaving the room.

I walked to my washstand and looked at the other hypodermic, the one Susanna had found under the bed. I carefully took both hypodermics and hid them inside a shoe, realizing I would rather be foolish now than risk wishing later I had indulged my fancy that someone still wanted to find those hypodermics.

Remembering the bizarre effects the morphine had on me, and the laudanum too, the strange way the drugs distorted reality and made me feel fuzzy and out of control, I shuddered to think what would have happened if Serena… no, wait, Claire… had been able to give me as much morphine as she had tried to do.

All at once, I realized I had proof against Claire with the two hypodermics, and I could get more proof: by finding Serena's cologne in Claire's room. I knew she might have packed already, while I was at Ellen's funeral, but there was a chance I could uncover her treachery, and at least satisfy myself rather than leaving Kenwick with so many questions still unanswered.

Overheated from rushing around my room packing, I poured cool water into the basin, splashed my face and reached for a linen towel. In the mirror over the washstand, I suddenly caught sight of my flushed face, and realized while looking at myself curiously, that it was exactly how I had looked after Dr. Harris had given me morphine.

Trying to piece it all together, I wondered why the reflection nagged at my mind, as if trying to open the door to another memory. And then, I recalled how Claire looked at The Hare and Hound when I first saw her, after not having seen her since my husband's funeral a year ago. Her face was flushed. Like me when I had the morphine drug in my body, she had no appetite at that lunch, and at other meals here at Kenwick Manor. She was thin, flushed, and sleepy. Then at other times, she was hysterical and overwrought.

Could Dr. Harris have given her a dose of morphine when he came to see me after my horseback riding 'accident,' so that she would calm down after relating how terrifying the event had been from her viewpoint? But that did not explain the other times when her behavior had been erratic. Where would a girl like her get morphia? It was incomprehensible to me that she could be a habitual user of opiates, and so I put the mental puzzle aside for the moment.

Sitting at the dressing table, I realized I had never uncovered a motive for Claire's hostility toward me. There seemed no reason for her to wish me ill. After all, she should thank me for bringing her to Kenwick Manor, not try to kill me! In the instance of Serena Harmon, her motive was totally driven by jealousy and her illogical assumption that I was in love with her husband. But what about Claire? What Machiavellian logic drove her behavior?

Claire had admitted indirectly to a jealousy against me over Charles Weatherby, but now she was engaged to Samuel McArthur, an occurrence I did not even want to think about further. Her hostility toward me had in fact started at the inn, the first day. Of this I was sure. That meant it had nothing to do with either man.

My troubled thoughts were interrupted by a timid knock at the door. Susanna McArthur entered when I invited her to do so, looking very pretty in a muslin dress with tiny bows. From its fit, I guessed it had belonged to my godmother and they had simply pulled the sash very tight at the waist to fit the girl's slim figure.

"Are you leaving?" she asked, seeing the luggage.

I nodded, only hesitating because now I was not so sure I should leave the Manor before unraveling the entire mystery surrounding Claire Lewis and her reasons for trying to murder me.

"I need your help, once again," she said, twisting her hands and appearing distraught. "It's my aunt."

"Has she been scolding you? She hasn't the right anymore, you know, now that you are a married woman."

"She's gone! I went into the room across the hall, where we were staying, planning to make sure I had not left anything behind. You see, the McArthurs are anxious to leave tomorrow. Mr. Goodwin's party was only a stopover on their way to Clacton on Sea in East Anglia."

"Yes, you mentioned they are going to visit your father-in-law's family in that area."

"They would never have traveled all the way from Torpoint just for Mr. Goodwin's birthday, but instead combined the two trips."

"I understand. Please go on. About your aunt?"

"So when I went in my old room, Aunt Louise was not there."

"That doesn't mean she has left—"

"All of her clothes are gone. She cleared out. Even things I remember seeing on the bureau and dressing table, pretty things of your godmother's, are gone now."

"Was there a note for you?"

Susanna shook her head. "I cannot understand her leaving so abruptly, without telling me. Mrs. Goodwin had assured my aunt she was welcome to stay on a few days longer if she wished. I know my aunt loved it here. Who wouldn't? She enjoyed the delicious food, and having so many servants at her beck and call."

"So something must have happened. But what?"

We shared an uncertain look.

Then all at once I realized why her aunt had abruptly departed. Just before leaving for Ellen's funeral, when I had exchanged a few words with Miss Rogers, I told her she would not get away with it. Staying my thoughts from leaping to a conclusion, I knew now that I had been thinking of my wagonette's destruction, but had I mentioned that specifically to her at the time? I could not recall. So why had Miss Rogers hastily left the Manor? Unless… a horrified thought came to me: what if Louise Rogers had killed Ellen, and she had thought I meant I knew she was guilty of murder and would not get away with the crime?

Pieces fell into place, and I felt proud of my deduction. However, I decided not to shock Susanna with this news until I was certain of it.

"Do you want me to ask my godfather to send a servant after her?" I asked.

"I am not sure what to do," she confessed. "It is so odd that she would simply vanish."

"You don't suppose there was mischief against her, do you?" I asked suddenly, but it seemed unlikely. Apparently, Miss Rogers had heard of the rainstorm predicted for today, and had decided to go. "Not leaving a note for you was just her spiteful way of saying she is angry about your marriage," I suggested, and Susanna nodded in agreement. No other explanation came to mind.

She spent a few moments longer with me. I did not know what to say about Samuel's engagement to Claire Lewis, but I felt the subject was a wall between us, and I finally put her mind to rest by saying that it was a situation she should be happy for, and I wished her all the best with her new sister-in-law.

We hugged, and she kissed my cheek before leaving.

I knew that I would probably not see Susanna McArthur again, unless at some future event here at Kenwick Manor.

Regarding the prospect for my own future, however, I quickly slammed the door upon any speculation.

CHAPTER 35

After I made certain that Susanna McArthur had gone downstairs to join the others, I slipped into Claire Lewis's room, intent on searching it.

Without a sound, I closed Claire's bedroom door behind me. I hesitated in the untidy room. She was apparently still in the midst of packing, but it seemed there was an extraordinary amount of mess, as if a child had run through the room, tossing clothes and ribbons in the air, letting them drift down to land haphazardly. I knew one of the housemaids would have periodically tidied the room for Claire during her stay here, so it must be that she had been looking for something at some time today after the room was cleaned.

Outside, storm clouds gathered, and yet I feared to light a lamp in the room to make my search easier in case someone on the grounds might see me in here, where I did not belong.

Hoping that no one would surprise me and question what I was doing, I hurried to the Regency wardrobe where I felt into pockets and poked my fingers into corners, uncertain what I was seeking, knowing only that I did not want to waste this opportunity to find out more about Claire Lewis. Perhaps I would find a letter which would explain some of her behavior. Maybe even a weapon, or the cloak I had seen the rose-scented attacker wear in my room. Having decided that Claire might be a morphine user, I thought I might find evidence of that, but my search turned up only a note from Mrs. Harmon asking Claire to see her before dinner. The note was undated, and innocuous. It proved nothing. I already knew the two had whispered secrets they did not want me to hear, and at times had seemed in collusion against me.

I moved over to the mussed-up bed and its night-table. Again my hunt was fruitless. The same result awaited me when I rummaged through the meager contents of the Wellington chest with its secretaire drawer dropped down, and the single drawer of a gilt-trimmed washstand. Only the dressing table remained, but I had searched the top thoroughly.

I was so involved in my search that I lost concept of time. It seemed I had been in her room no more than a quarter of an hour, but I had no way of knowing Claire's whereabouts, or when she might decide to return to her room. However, unless their plans had changed, the McArthurs were not leaving until tomorrow morning, and there was still time for her to enjoy the party and put off packing until tonight.

I had looked through all but a few bottles and boxes on the dressing table when I suddenly became aware of voices approaching in the hallway. I froze, my hand arrested on a drawer pull. Words were indistinct, but two women were speaking, apparently coming from the staircase. Rather than passing, and fading away, the voices grew louder, coming closer.

There was no point in hiding. The only places were in the wardrobe or under the bed. My crinoline skirt would not allow me to slip into small spaces where I would otherwise fit. My thoughts whirling with what I would say to explain my presence, I decided to claim I was looking for hair pins.

But suddenly, the voices moved on. I recognized Serena Harmon's distinctive voice, and imagined she was continuing on to her own room.

Relief rushed through me like waves of cool water, and I realized all at once that the second voice had been the elder Mrs. McArthur's. However, since they had come upstairs, that might mean Claire Lewis was on the way as well, so I hastily raided the dressing table drawers, not caring anymore whether my search left a tell-tale path. With so much disorder, a little more would probably not be noticeable.

In one of the drawers, I came across a fluted bottle, tightly capped and hidden beneath stockings. Suddenly certain of what I would smell, I opened the bottle, and was not surprised that it contained Serena's rose cologne.

So Charles Weatherby's question about who had been wearing the cologne was now answered: Claire Lewis was the one who had attacked me the night before. I quickly put the bottle back and continued searching.

The final drawer would not open. I yanked, but it was not merely stuck, it was locked. I hurried to the secretaire and returned with a letter knife. With this, I pried open the drawer and found a long narrow box in the back. With trembling fingers, I tried the lid but it, too, was locked.

Something about the wooden box was vaguely familiar. Of a sudden, I recalled the day of my riding accident, when I had come in to accost Claire and saw her sweep something shiny into the box. I had assumed it was a sewing needle, and taunted her about darning her stockings.

Now I knew that had been a hypodermic needle not a sewing needle, and without caring if I made noise, I applied the letter knife to the box and pried it open.

I was shocked, but not surprised, to see my surmise confirmed. She was a morphia user, and here were both the morphine she had used and more of the headache powder she had given me, although I was now uncertain whether it was really for headaches or some kind of poison she had brought with her to give me.

Remarkable by its absence: there was no hypodermic. I knew that I had it in my own room, along with the one Dr. Harris had left. Claire must be frantic to get hold of one or both of the hypodermics she had tried to use on me, so that she could inject in herself the drug that she had become accustomed to using.

I felt overcome with sadness. Taken singly, there was little significance in the things I had noted about her, the flushed and itchy face, her alternating moods of sadness and euphoria, her finicky appetite, nausea and pinpointed eyes.

If I had not experienced these symptoms from the morphine Dr. Harris gave to me, I would never have suspected Claire's addiction.

It seemed so obvious now. She had used her own hypodermic on me, filled with morphine from her own supply, and in her other hand or pocket she'd had the one she had taken from my bedside table the night before when I felt someone had come in my room but had quickly left. That one was the hypodermic Dr. Harris had left behind and I had been accused of hiding for my own use.

I had been afraid of Claire Lewis, angry and mistrustful of her, but now I pitied her.

A sharp peal of thunder broke into my musings and I hastily took up the box and left the room. I had to find Charles Weatherby. He would know what to do.

After stopping in my own room to wrap Claire's box in a shawl and take it with me thus concealed, I flew down the stairs and headed toward the rear of the house, planning to seek Charles in my godfather's study or library. If that failed, I would ask a servant where I might find him.

By happy chance, before getting to the study, I encountered Mr. McArthur, who had done a *volte-face* about Gordon's marriage after seeing how much he and Susanna loved each other. Now that he did not share his wife's upset over the marriage of their younger son, he greeted me warmly, and politely told me in response to my query that Charles Weatherby was at the stables. It seems that one of the McArthur horses was off its feed, and my godfather had told the man of Mr. Weatherby's expertise with animals, so Charles had gone to see if he could be of assistance.

I thanked him and hurried away, passing a few of the other guests who were playing cards and talking about the coming storm. I heard Claire's voice, and then Samuel's, and surmised that she would be there with him, smarter than I had been. She was not leaving him alone for a moment, for fear, no doubt, that I would manage to wrench him away from her, as if we were two fishwives squabbling in the market over a fine catch.

From what I could gather in the snatches of conversation I overheard as I quietly sped past, fearful of discovery, some of the travelers were deciding whether to stay longer at the Manor than planned, and wait out the storm, or leave now, and try to beat it. Since no one was leaping to his feet during this, it appeared to be idle chatter and I assumed no one would be leaving today. Even I had decided to stay til morning. I couldn't leave without solving the mysteries surrounding me here at Kenwick Manor.

But shortly after reaching the safety of an empty room, the sound of another burst of thunder, seeming closer than before, made my steps slow. Why venture outside and chance being rained upon, I reflected, when I could as easily wait for Charles to return to the house?

Seeking a place where I could watch the gardens for his approach, I paced by the french doors, impatient to tell him about Louise Rogers, and more importantly about the box I had discovered in Claire's room.

I hugged the shawl to me, careful to prevent the box from slipping out and falling to the marble floor.

The rain began, heavy drops that hit against the ground like they had been flung with an angry hand from above.

At least a half hour passed, and I grew impatient for Charles, wondering how much longer I should wait for him. After a moment, I admitted to myself that he might have already finished in the stable while I was talking to Mr. McArthur earlier, or have returned to the house from a different direction and even now be upstairs in his room, washing up and changing his clothes if he'd been caught in the rain.

Hesitation kept me a prisoner there, as I fretted over what I should do.

The rain pelted down in earnest now, in long sheets of water. Trees bent under the assault, and I would be a fool to go out. But then, a movement outside caught my attention. I saw a woman running out of one of the sheds and darting in the direction of the bridge. The glass on the door fogged from my breath as I strained to see who the woman was. Impatiently, I flung open the door and stepped out onto the terrace to identify her.

Too late, for she was hidden by trees now, and all I could see was a figure in a cloak dashing from one shelter to the next, clutching something in her arms and glancing back now and then. But something about her movements and her size, made me think it was Louise Rogers, Susanna's missing aunt.

CHAPTER 36

Holding Claire's box tightly in one hand, I raised the shawl over my head and ran out into the storm. I gasped, and was quickly soaked, and the weight of my gown impeded my progress. But I had to see who it was, to find if I was right about Miss Rogers, and so I kept running as fast as I could in hoop skirts and flimsy shoes not meant for inclement weather.

Beneath a tree, I paused for breath and tried to see which way the woman had gone, but she was out of sight. Disappointed, I set down the box and began wringing out the shawl, deciding I would return to the house, change out of my wet clothes and ask a servant to locate Charles Weatherby for me, as I should have done before if I had been thinking more logically.

All at once there was a small sound behind me and I glanced around just as the flat broad side of a small spade struck my left shoulder, having missed my head because of my movement.

I staggered, stunned by the pain, dropping my shawl in the mud, heedless of anything but the pain. Then the spade came down again hard on its original target, and I sank to the ground.

I do not know how long I was unconscious, but probably not long, as the sensation of being dragged along the ground brought me to awareness and I opened my eyes. Rain spattered my face.

My view was of the swaying trees and dark clouds. It took a moment to comprehend that I was being pulled by my arms, with my feet trailing over the ground. The shoulder which had been struck by the spade ached with each movement and I longed to have the person stop.

Trying to lean my head back to see who it was did nothing but make me feel dizzy. The person's back was to me, but appeared to be a woman. Could Louise Rogers be strong enough to pull me? I could hear her harsh breathing, and knew that pulling me was hard work. Hopefully, she would grow tired soon and stop. I hastily formed the plan to feign a stupor and then when she was not vigilant, I would leap to my feet and run to safety.

The ground changed, becoming softer as she pulled me across grass, and I realized we were approaching the stone bridge. My heart leapt in fear. I could tell from the tight grip she had on my arms that it would be useless to struggle, and would only alert her that I had come back to consciousness. I tried to make a plan, but my mind was confused from the blow to my head.

If it weren't for the rain, the lad I'd seen with the kittens would probably be out playing, or other servants and tenants would be passing and someone would surely come to my aid. But I was alone in a rainstorm with this crazed woman. I did not know if Louise Rogers had the strength to pull me like this, but who else could it be? I had seen her running outside, and the others were in the house, playing cards, idly waiting for the rain to stop.

Abruptly, my arms were released and my upper body dropped to the ground. I kept my head from hitting the ground too hard. To my dismay, I was too stunned to sit up at once. It took a struggle, but I managed to prop myself on my elbows, gathering my strength to get up. I shivered, thoroughly miserable, wet, in pain and deeply afraid. At least, I reasoned, she could not still have the garden spade as it would have been impossible to carry it while pulling me.

I struggled to my feet, and turned to see not Louise Rogers, but Claire Lewis glaring at me with murderous intent.

I gasped for air. "But… you were in the house with the others," I began, feeling tricked, but knowing at once that I had spent so long at the french doors, looking out, that she could have easily seen me there and gone outside by another exit.

We were close to the middle of the bridge, and I gave a short laugh of disdain. "You plan to throw me off the bridge?" I asked her, incredulously. "Why are you doing this to me?"

"So I can marry Samuel McArthur."

"But he already announced your engagement. I do not stand in your way."

"I've seen how he looks at you! I have to be sure he will marry me."

"What happened to marrying Charles Weatherby?"

"The McArthurs build boats," she said simply. "I like boats."

I looked at Claire and saw that her eyes kept darting about, as if she feared someone would come upon us here, and prevent her from carrying out her plan.

"You don't deserve two husbands," she said, following her own path of mental logic, "when I never had even one!"

I thought I might distract her. "Did you see Susanna's aunt out here a little while ago?" I could tell at once from Claire's dress that she was not the cloaked woman I had seen running off.

She looked at me in confusion. "Miss Rogers? Out in the rain? No."

While she was thinking, I slowly backed away from her, intending to put a distance between us and then turn and run, but she dashed forward and grabbed my arm with unexpected strength. I pulled back from her. The rain had eased, but we were both soaked. She had to be as uncomfortable as I was.

"Go back in the house, Claire," I said, "and I will not mention this to the others. Proceed with your plan to kill me, however, and you will hang for it."

"No I won't. Everyone knows you have brain-fever. They will not be surprised that the legend came true, and in despair over not marrying Samuel McArthur, you threw yourself from the bridge. Just like Ellen."

"What do you know about Ellen's death? Did you see Miss Rogers?" I could tell from her baffled expression that I had missed the mark. And all at once, I realized the truth. "You killed her. And you killed my cat."

She shrugged, and did not deny either accusation.

"But why?" I cried out.

She explained patiently, "So they would believe the legend when they found you here."

"Clever girl," I said, feigning admiration, knowing now that she had gone mad, and there was no use in reasoning with her. "I thought Miss Rogers had killed Ellen out of spite, annoyed that I had helped Susanna and Gordon form a match."

"I did it," Claire said proudly. "I had to. She should never have tried to keep me away from you. Ellen saw me come out of your room last night. She had come up to check on you. I could not take the chance that she would be believed." She paused to gloat. "I had already made sure that you would not be."

"Yes, you did that so well," I said. "Very smart planning, Claire."

She eyed me narrowly.

I quickly went on, wanting to keep her talking in the hope that I could either convince her to not harm me, or allow time for someone to see us out here and come in hailing distance. "Ellen's body was found here, under the bridge. But how did you manage that? Did you carry her all the way from the house?"

"I am not that strong. Or that stupid. I told her that I could show her where I buried your emerald necklace, and that once she had it, I would go with her to your godparents and confess that I had been in your room."

"And she believed you," I murmured to myself. Poor Ellen! Wanting to help me, her good nature had led her into a trap. Out loud, I said, keeping my voice calm so as not to alarm Claire and put her on guard against me, "So you brought her to the bridge and then…."

"I hit her over the head with the spade, and shoved her over, onto the rocks."

"And left her for dead."

Claire shrugged heedlessly, clearly considering Ellen's death of no more importance than that of the kitten she'd drowned.

Remembering how Charles had taken Samuel McArthur by surprise despite the latter's greater size and strength, I suddenly lunged and slammed my right fist into Claire's stomach.

She cried out, but at once her arms locked around me in a powerful vise.

The rain came down hard again, pummeling us with cold drops, making our footing slippery and our grips as well. The stones on the bridge ran with eddies of water.

I pushed into her, and she skidded away from me, towards the low wall of the bridge railing.

I was too exhausted to run. My left arm ached terribly from the blow she had given it with the spade and all the pulling she had done on it. I knew if she thought to grab it again, I would be at her mercy.

She stalked me. I backed up as she advanced, but to my dismay found myself leaning against the wall at the other side of the bridge. One mighty push is all she would need to send me over, and onto the treacherous rocks below.

Lightning flashed, charging the air with an eerie light.

Her malicious face loomed over me and her pinpointed eyes gleamed with a new lust for killing. The madness had overtaken her and the lackluster young woman I had known before was now replaced by this monster, intent only on murdering me.

I screamed suddenly, as loudly as I could, yelling out 'Help!' over and again, in the desperate hope that someone might have come out of doors to see the lightning, or be near a window and possibly hear me. There was slight chance of this, but I had to try something more than letting myself be Claire's next hapless victim.

Leaning against the low wall to brace myself, I quickly kicked out at her, or at least I tried to do so. The damnable hoop skirt was in my way, impeding my movement, effectively caging my legs so that I only kicked air. I had remembered how sensitive her stomach seemed to be, with frequent upsets and nausea. That region was her Achilles' heel, but I had lost my only advantage in this strange combat she had initiated.

If only I wore breeches like a man! Amelia Bloomer had the right idea about dressing women in ankle-length trousers beneath a knee-length dress. I wish I had trousers on now. Then I could fight Claire Lewis with some advantage on my side. She had the upper hand because she wore a simple gown and no crinolines, having apparently taken off her hoop skirt before coming outside, and leaving it hidden away somewhere so she could get it later and pretend to have run out in the rain to help me, looking the same as when she had left the party except for being wet. She had tied up the extra length of her gown by belting the fabric at her waist. Perhaps if I could grab at her skirt and loosen it to its fullness, she would trip over the fabric. But as I tried to get closer to her, she danced just out of reach.

I tried again to kick at her by pulling at my skirts to give my legs freedom. Seeing the dilemma caused by my hoop skirt, she laughed almost gaily. But then she lunged toward me, sliding on the wet stones, finally going on all fours to stop from skidding further.

As she struggled to her feet, I glanced toward the Manor, and thought that I saw someone come out of one of the doors. I screamed again for help. If no one else heard me, perhaps my godmother's dogs would, and their barking might alert others as to my peril. I yelled again.

With a cry of rage, Claire shrieked at me, "Stop doing that!"

She lurched towards me and our dangerous dance resumed, as each of us tried to move into a more favorable position. Each time I tried to go toward either end of the bridge, so I could escape her, she blocked me as if we were playing a child's game of some kind.

"Why are you doing this, Claire?" I called to her, wishing she would finally explain.

"You know the reason!"

"No, I don't. Won't you tell me why you have done so many things to hurt me?"

"I've given you enough time to figure it out. It is not my fault you are stupid! Look at my eyes and tell me you do not understand!"

I couldn't think what she meant. Desperate, I asked another question, wanting to know how she had broken my engagement to Samuel McArthur and quickly taken my place in his affection.

She laughed. "It worked with Charles Weatherby, so I told him the same thing! That you don't have money! But I know it's a lie, and now I'll get it all!"

Then several things happened all at once, in a blur. She barreled toward me, her head aimed at my chest like a battering ram. I twisted away at the last moment, and so her momentum propelled her past me, and she flew over the low wall to the rocks below.

A familiar male voice shouted out from a distance, "Loretta! Are you alright?"

In the flash of lightning, I saw Charles Weatherby race towards me and take me into his arms. I winced, and he saw at once that I was injured.

"Claire…" I cried breathlessly, pointing with my good arm toward the water.

He understood my meaning at once, and quickly ran down to the edge of the stream, went in, and dragged Claire to safety.

I walked more slowly down to join him, holding my sore arm against my side, exhausted and overwhelmed by all that had happened.

There was blood on Claire's head where she had hit the rocks. She was still breathing, but not conscious.

He picked her up and took her to the shelter of a tree where he laid her on the ground.

"I'll go for help," I offered.

"We'll both go," he corrected. "This is one time you are not going to run from me."

CHAPTER 37

It seemed impossible to me that it was only Wednesday evening. I had arrived with Ellen Armstrong and Claire Lewis on last Friday, and now both of them were dead, Claire having succumbed to her injuries an hour after she was carried into the Manor.

Unbidden came the memory of her telling me when we arrived at Kenwick that she never wanted to leave. Now, she had her wish. Also, she had been frightened when realizing she was the thirteenth house guest, having been the last to be invited after twelve other people. Strange how her superstitions and fears had come true in a roundabout yet eerie way.

She had regained her senses only briefly. Dr. Harris is the one who told me about her death while checking over my injured shoulder and pronouncing it a strained muscle that would heal with… what else? Bed rest.

So I had been unable to quiz Claire any further about her motives for all she had done, and now, with her passing, I lost all hope of finding out where she had buried the emeralds she had promised to show Ellen. The necklace was gone to me, and perhaps one of the estate workers would one day find it. Too late, no doubt, to help my diminished station in life.

Earlier, while waiting to hear Claire's prognosis, I had told Charles Weatherby the reason I had gone outside was to find him, and then I told him my suspicions about Louise Rogers, who had vanished from the Manor with no explanation. He had listened thoughtfully, and then gone back into the room where Claire Lewis had been brought, and was still alive.

Now that she was gone, I realized that although Claire Lewis had tried to kill me, she had been unbalanced, and so I felt sorry for her rather than vindictive.

The painful duty fell to me to notify her stepfather, and find out what he wanted to do about a burial. I sat at the desk in my room, and penned a letter that would be delivered by messenger, with a return reply requested.

Looking in my purse, I saw that the money this would cost would deplete my funds almost completely. A harsh laugh escaped my lips and I realized I had better get used to the sight of an empty purse from now on.

I stood, and looked out the window a moment. The rain had stopped. Tomorrow a new day would dawn, and I would embark on a whole new kind of life. So be it.

I turned away, briskly took the letter, and left the room.

Downstairs, after arranging for the letter to be delivered to Claire's stepfather and a reply brought back to us, I was greeted by many abashed faces. Apologies began to land at my feet one by one like flowers, as each person who had blamed me for making unfounded accusations against Claire Lewis now admitted I had been right all along. It was small comfort, but I thanked them all as graciously as I could, knowing Ellen would want it thus.

My vindication seemed complete when Serena Harmon approached me in private and said stiffly, "I am sorry, Loretta, for the things I said, and for the help I gave Claire Lewis."

"Did you know she was trying to kill me?"

"Of course not! All I knew is that she had formed a grudge against you, and it suited me to aid in her little schemes to annoy you."

We walked together into a small room that was seldom used, and sat by the window, facing each other in plump satin chairs.

"She told me that you killed my kitten," I said, "and she tried to stop you from doing it."

Serena shook her head. "You must believe me. I did see the cat, but too late to save it. I was afraid to take it out of the water. I guess I'm squeamish, but I could see it was dead."

"But how did you happen to go into my room?"

"Claire had left the ball for a time, and then suddenly reappeared, looking flushed and overly excited. She gloated to herself, saying something to herself such as, 'I did it! I did it!' when she thought I did not hear."

"What did you think she meant by that?"

"I confronted her. She merely shrugged and said she had done nothing. I suspected that was not altogether true and at the first opportunity, I hurried upstairs and went into your room to see what she might have done."

"I saw you coming out."

"And so you thought I was the guilty one."

"Don't forget all the threats you made," I reminded her.

"I know my position is not a strong one, but I hope you understand I say things sometimes, in passion, that I would never do, in fact."

"Claire told me she knew a secret about you. That is how she lured me on the horseback ride where she tried to kill me. Is there really a secret? Or did she make that up?"

The redhead blushed, telltale admission to there actually being a secret. "I am *enceinte*," she said, smiling.

So I had been right about her thickening waistline! Serena Harmon was expecting a baby. No wonder she had been even more vicious in her jealousy of me, thinking I might steal her husband at a time in her life when she needed him most, with a child on the way.

I congratulated her, and started to leave, but then I remembered something else that had been troubling me.

"Did you know that the gypsy fortune teller warned me that my life was in danger, and that I needed to be wary of a hidden enemy, a ruthless and treacherous woman?"

"Are you making that up?"

"No. Actually, she gave me two fortunes," I added.

"Why two?"

"Let me explain. The first time the gypsy read the cards, she said I would not get married and to forget the idea."

Serena seemed to nod, as if already knowing this, but caught herself. "Go on."

I continued hastily, knowing Mrs. Harmon might grow impatient at any moment and simply leave the room before all my questions were answered. "I was so upset, I gave her another coin and she read my cards again. I couldn't help wondering later if Claire said something to the gypsy in advance. Claire broke into the queue and pushed in ahead of me, and then insisted that I go next after she came out, practically knocking Susanna Rogers down in her haste to make sure I went in to the gypsy right on her heels."

Serena made a small *moue*. "I got the idea about bribing the gypsy when you said there would be a fortune teller at the ball. I gave Claire some money and she took care of the rest, making sure the gypsy would give you an unwelcome prophecy, and spoil the party for you."

"So the first deck of cards she handed me, the blue deck, was one she had arranged in advance, in case I knew something of the tarot from other gypsies. Then when I pleaded with her, she gave me a deck of black cards to handle, and that was my true fortune, the one saying I was in danger."

We shared a look.

"But then again, it was just a parlor game for entertainment," I said drily, remembering how skeptical I had been before going into the gypsy's lair, and then how startled I had felt on my way out a short time later.

Thinking of this reminded me of the gypsy talisman that I had been carrying around. When I had come back in the house, soaking wet from the rainstorm, I had changed to dry clothes and carefully transferred the medallion to the pocket of the gown I wore now.

I pulled it out to show Serena.

"What is this old thing?" she asked, taking a look.

"The gypsy gave it to me, for luck, to protect me."

"I never realized you were superstitious, although I had hoped a bad 'fortune' would startle you and make you feel uneasy." She gave it back to me.

"I'm not superstitious, not really. But it worked. I stayed safe, again and again. I wish it had worked to get back my emerald necklace," I added morosely.

She was suddenly alert. "What! Didn't Claire give it back to you?"

"What do you know about the emeralds? Did you tell her to steal the jewel case from me? The same way you told her to bribe the gypsy?"

"No. You must believe me," Serena pleaded. "I had nothing to do with it."

"Then why did you look so strange when I said she did not give it back?"

"Because I told her to give it to you," she said.

"How did you know she had it in the first place?"

Serena quickly explained that on Sunday, when everyone was in the dining room gabbing about the runaways, wondering if they had eloped, Claire told Serena that she had begun getting even with me.

"For what?" I asked, still not understanding why Claire Lewis had formed a vengeance against me.

"She never said. And I did not ask. It was all very general in nature until she said it was a good thing you had not taken her up on the offer to search her room for the necklace."

"I realized later it was stupid of me."

"I assumed she had the emeralds you were so anxious to find," Serena said, "otherwise why would she feel lucky you had not looked for them. I asked her if she had the necklace, and advised that the joke had worn thin and she should return the jewels before the situation became more serious. She told me she had hidden the case in her room."

"Then why didn't I find it there? I looked, twice." I wisely left Charles Weatherby's name out of this, not wanting to admit he had helped me search Claire's room the first time. "She gave me the jewel case, and pretended surprise that the necklace was not in it."

We looked at each other, and another puzzle piece fell into place. "She thought it was there," I said. "She lied when she said it must never have been in the box. When she saw it was gone, she knew I would not believe her about it. So she did not dare claim someone else stole it after she herself had stolen it, and hid it in her own wardrobe." I pressed a hand to my brow. "I don't understand."

"Isn't it clear?" Serena asked, some of her old asperity returning, "Someone knew she had your jewel case, knew about the necklace, and took it for their own reasons."

"Why would she tell my maid that she buried it by the bridge…." My brow cleared. "It was a lie, a ruse to get Ellen outside, that is all. The necklace isn't buried anywhere. Someone has it. But who?"

Serena stood up and smiled languidly. "That is your problem to solve. I have told you everything I know." She left the room.

CHAPTER 38

I finished packing all but the few items I would need in the morning, so that I would be able to make an early start back to London. I did not want to be around when the McArthur party left. It would be difficult enough to say goodbye to everyone tonight and know that so much had happened since the party began Friday, and now my whole life was about to change.

Before coming to the Manor, I had considered the option of asking to live here, help with the household in some fashion, but seeing my godfather's health deteriorating, noticing how quickly my godmother's nerves became overwrought, and also knowing of his own monetary problems, I could not bring myself to ask them for assistance.

I came to the decision that I would stay in my Hyde Park house as long as I could manage to do so by selling more of the paintings and antiques I had clung to. Perhaps I would write novels and make some money in that way, or bring in students and start a classroom for young ladies in my own home. If the neighbors did not prevent me from doing so, I might even turn my town house into a boarding house where I would take discreet lodgers and make ends meet in that way.

Countless other women had been through this dilemma before me, and somehow I too would survive, and keep my head above water... hopefully, without having to lose everything I knew and loved. I had already lost so much. And in my correspondence with Mrs. Goodwin I would simply continue to paint a rosy picture of my gay life in London, and she would be none the wiser even if I ended on poor relief and lost everything.

Thinking of Samuel McArthur and his hasty engagement with Miss Lewis, I wrote him a brief sympathy note, barely knowing what to say and falling back on *clichés* about being sorry for his loss, and taking comfort that she was with the angels now, and at peace.

Going out in the hall to slip the note under his door, wryly recalling the love note I had written during my campaign to marry him, I recalled in passing Claire's door that I had offered to pack her room so her personal items would be ready to go when the coffin was transported to her stepfather's home, which had been Mr. Lewis's request in his reply to the messenger.

Inside Claire's room, I felt the sadness and futility of her young death wash over me. I cringed from touching her things, but forced myself to neatly pack everything she had brought. During this, I found the small bottle I had seen her corking the day of our arrival and hiding in a shoe. Curious, I looked at it, and discovered it was laudanum. I knew from my extensive reading that this was considered the drug of the working class, since it was cheaper than a bottle of gin. Nurses gave it to babies to keep them quiet, and many children died of an overdose. Sadly, I suspected that she had perhaps first filched a bottle of laudanum at the sanitarium where she read to patients, liked the effect and gradually wanted something stronger, hence becoming habituated to the use of morphine by injection.

I sighed to myself. Rather than letting her stepfather find these things about Claire, I put aside all the implements of her drug use and decided I would dispose of them discreetly. No one ever needed to know this about her.

To make sure I did not overlook anything, I stood on a chair and peered about the room in case she had tossed something on top of the wardrobe. Nothing was there, but I spied a small notebook on top of the canopy over the bed. Moments later, the notebook was in my hands, and I realized at once it was Claire's diary.

Sinking to a chair, I hastily skimmed the pages. To my disappointment, it was an annual book and not much had happened to her in the past few months since the new year had begun.

Two pages stuck together. I pried them apart, not expecting to see much more than I had already, namely a sporadic account of her dreams and wishes to marry well and leave her stepfather's farm. I glanced at the words on the new pages, and was startled to see my name. Reading more slowly, I realized I had discovered her motive. I knew why Claire Lewis thought she would benefit by killing me.

Sadly, I closed the book, hesitated a moment, and then placed it with the items I would destroy. All of her secrets would go with her to the grave.

I took a final glance around and left, closing the door tightly behind me with a sense of finality, and of forgiveness.

When I went downstairs to say goodbye to everyone, I walked with a lighter step, not having to fear someone would rush up from behind and try to shove me down the stairs, or be lying in wait for me just around a corner.

I had been here barely a week, and it seemed I had aged a year, learning so much about how each of us is motivated by fears and dreams that cannot always be seen on the outside or detected in our everyday conversation.

Passing my godfather's library, I glanced in, sobered by the memory of my arrival Friday and my gay optimism that I would find a husband at the ball, and all I needed for distraction were a few modish magazines. But then Serena Harmon had come in, with jealous threats, and after that, nothing had been easy for me.

To my surprise, when I reached the front parlor, Miss Louise Rogers was the first person I saw. I must have gasped, because several people looked up. Susanna hurried to me and drew me aside.

"Charles Weatherby found her!" she told me.

"Where?" I demanded.

"She was in the village, having taken a cart and pony from outside one of the tenant's cottages, but Mr. Weatherby forced her to come back."

"Did you find out why she left in such a hurry, without leaving a note for you?"

Susanna frowned. "I am not certain about all the details as he was not forthcoming, but...." She trailed off, and looked around uneasily, realizing we might be overheard although the others were sitting on couches, engaged in conversation and tea.

I took her to a small sitting room nearby where we could sit alone. It seemed to me that I had been having more than my share of private dialogue in secret rooms, but I wanted to know what she had discovered about her aunt.

"I have known for a year or more that my parents left money for my support," Susanna began, "and that after their death my aunt took me in, not for the pure charity of heart that she had always claimed to me, but because she received an annuity for doing so."

"And those terms would end with your marriage?"

Susanna nodded.

"But she agreed to let you come to the ball and find a husband? Wait," I said, thinking it all out, "she agreed so you would not complain to anyone about mistreatment at her hands, and perhaps cause the lawyer or banker to investigate her methods, but then she tried to make sure you would not look attractive enough to appeal to any of the bachelors."

"I assured her, after I married Gordon, that she would have a stipend from us."

"Maybe she was angry over the elopement because she thought you could have done better than the second son."

Even though we smiled about it now, something didn't quite make sense about Louise Rogers. I dismissed my nagging thoughts. I was happy for Susanna that her aunt was safe, and now she could go off with the McArthurs and enjoy married life without needless worry over what had happened to her spinster aunt.

When I returned with Susanna to the parlor, several people had left, including Charles Weatherby. My heart sank, but I knew it was better this way. I did not relish the prospect of saying goodbye to him, and now I did not have to. I could quietly depart and he would find out about it after I had already gone.

CHAPTER 39

I needed Ellen's advice, and she was no longer there to give it. The secret I knew about Claire Lewis weighed heavily on me, and I was not sure it was right to keep it to myself. It explained so many of her actions, and so I could not help wondering if I should put the diary with her clothing after all.

Earlier I had separated the diary from the things I was going to burn: the morphine supply, the wooden box wherein she'd kept her hypodermic. The diary I had decided to keep until I came to a final decision of whether to show it to Mr. Lewis. I did not know if it would come as a shock to him, or if he was already aware of what she had written.

My sense of loss regarding Ellen had been delayed by Claire's attack on me and her subsequent death, but now I gave myself over to the grief over losing the one person who knew me well. She had known my brother, my mother, my father. All gone now. She was the only one who was able to stop my headlong chatter and bring me back to a logical viewpoint when impetuous thoughts took hold.

But even as the thought formed, I knew it was not quite true that she was the only one I knew like that. Charles Weatherby was the same. He was fair and direct, quick to ignore extraneous ideas and home in on the truth.

He despised deceit, and yet I had deceived him from the start. Hadn't he told me upon our first meeting that he demanded honesty from all his friends? He had given me ample opportunity from the start to confide in him, and I had consistently lied. Lies and half-truths were strewn over the path of our short relationship like brambles and thorns.

And if I were to suddenly approach him, admit to the dishonesty, throw myself at his mercy, what then? Hadn't he asked me if I had need of advice and help, and hadn't I claimed again and again that I had nothing to tell him? I had played the part of the carefree widow, and now I had to pay the consequence.

I had chosen my course on the first day of meeting him, and must stick to it. Either way, my future did not hold Charles Weatherby in it, so why humiliate myself by telling him I could not pay his dowry? I knew that he was probably like so many young men I had met the past several years. They knew their way around society, they were charming and gay, but they were weighted by heavy debts or obligations to parents and property and they could not simply say to a girl, *Oh you are charming but poor, let's live on our happiness and forget the dowry!*

Shaking my head, knowing my thoughts would only go in circles if I did not put an end to them, I moved away from the window overlooking the entrance to the Manor, waiting for two servants to finish taking out my valises and trunk.

Then I steeled myself for a final look at my *boudoir*, the room that had been the source of both joy and sorrow in this visit and many others over the years since childhood. Perhaps I would be able to come to Kenwick Manor again, I reminded myself and then hastened to leave before I was overcome with sentiment and began to cry.

At the carriage house, I found my wagonette loaded and ready for departure but my groom was not in sight. Looking at the ripped seats, I couldn't help thinking bitterly of Louise Rogers and the damage she had caused out of spite. She had admitted to it earlier, saying she had been angered at my part in her niece's engagement, but then had refused to give me any recompense, saying loudly that I could afford another carriage any time I wanted, unlike herself with her new state of poverty due to an ungrateful niece.

Finding that line of speech unbearable, I had given up and walked away, but now I half-wished I had grabbed her by the scrawny neck and forced her to pay an honest remuneration.

A little earlier, I had made a hasty farewell to my godparents, promising to write often, and giving the darling little terriers a final pat. I was glad now that no one in the house party was outside to see me go. I turned to climb up into the back of the wagonette, taking a seat on the bench that faced backward so I could have a final look at Kenwick Manor as we drove off.

I felt the springs move as the driver took his seat behind me, and I called out an order to go. He clucked to the horses, and soon we were moving away from the stables and passing the bridge where I had nearly come to my death.

Thinking of Ellen, I closed my eyes and murmured a quiet prayer for her soul, and then another prayer, this time for my own.

My high flying plans had sunk without a trace, and now I would return to London, resigned to my fate and the public humiliation that doubtless awaited.

As we rolled down the long driveway toward the entry gates, I looked at the Manor and tried to recall happier times, from my childhood, but all I could think of was that I was leaving Charles Weatherby behind, and with him, my heart. I found myself scanning each window, searching for his dear face, hoping that he had somehow sensed I was leaving, running away from him yet again… so that I did not have to tell him the truth.

The wagonette turned onto the road that led to London, and I could not help thinking of the empty house which awaited me there. It would be even emptier than before, since I was not returning with Ellen Armstrong. I did not look forward to having to tell Dora what had happened, as she would blame me for it. Not out loud of course, but I knew her thoughts would be the same as mine: that Ellen would be alive if I had not been too proud to tell Claire Lewis about my debts.

We had only gone a few miles and were just passing a wooded area when the driver suddenly pulled to the side of the road and stopped. Worried, I called out, "Is there a problem?"

There was no response, but I felt the wagon rock as the driver climbed down, and then he was at the side, looking at me, and took off his hat. He hadn't needed that gesture, I recognized Charles Weatherby right away, but I was speechless.

"Running away from me again, eh?" he drawled, taking a picnic hamper from the driver's seat where it had been hidden from my view.

"No, I wasn't running, I just—"

"Tell the truth, Loretta dear," he scolded cheerfully. "You hoped never to have to talk to me again, didn't you?"

He tethered the horse, then held out a hand to assist me to the ground. Taking up the basket, he led me to a small clearing in the wood not far from the road.

I looked around, almost expecting to see a swing made out of vines hanging from tall branches, and for foxes to appear and join us for the picnic Charles was spreading out on a blanket he had brought.

A wild fox darted across the edge of the glen, and I gasped out loud.

Charles saw the fox, too. He looked at me, frowning. "Haven't you ever seen a fox before?"

He gestured to the lunch, and invited me to sit with him.

Still feeling as if I were walking in a dream, I complied.

"Go ahead," he said, "fire away. What do you want to know first?"

"I'm not sure what you—"

"Because if there is one thing I've learned about you," he said, "you always have questions."

"Is it really you?" I whispered, and to my embarrassment my eyes filled with tears.

CHAPTER 40

Lunch was delicious, but I think sawdust would have tasted wonderful to me, with my beloved looking at me the way he was. I kept smiling foolishly, and shaking my head, refusing to answer when he asked what was funny. Finally I said, "Everything."

But then, I thought at once of Ellen, and of Claire, and even my little marmalade kitten.

"Do not blame yourself," Charles said, reading my thoughts as he so often did. "You tried to tell everyone you were in danger—"

"How did you know what I was thinking?"

"I can usually tell," he replied smugly.

I threw an apple at him, and it hit him on the chest. He snatched it up and took a quick bite of it. Chewing, he said happily, "It tastes all the more ambrosial because you touched it."

"Why are we here?" I asked him, finally putting my deepest question into words.

He dug around in the bottom of the picnic hamper and withdrew a napkin. "Close your eyes," he said. And almost as soon as I had done so, he said, "You can look now."

I opened my eyes, to see my emerald necklace dangling from his fingers. "Where was it!"

"Louise Rogers had it. That is why she left in such a rush, and why she was so furious when I found her."

"You suspected her? But why?"

"A lucky guess," he said modestly.

I took the necklace and looked at it, thinking of how much energy I had spent trying to figure out where it was, whether I had indeed left it at home and been wrong about its being in the jewel case. So much trouble, over bits of green stone. No wonder Louise Rogers had blanched when I told her that I knew what she had done and she would not get away with it. She had thought I found out she stole my emeralds from Claire's hiding place, and so she had fled before I could tell anyone about her.

He told me that he found her luggage hidden in a shed, and I realized that the cloaked woman I saw running had indeed been Louise Rogers, clutching what clothes she could manage to carry as she ran toward the tenants' farms, seeking quick transport. She had not dared to drive back with the pony cart to get her other luggage, but the necklace was with her at all times.

This explained why Charles was here. His flair for the dramatic had prompted him to kidnap me and present the missing necklace. Now what? Would he drive me back to the Manor so the hired groom could take me home to London?

Smiling sadly to myself, I put the necklace in my reticule, and took out the gypsy talisman. "This has proven to be of more worth to me," I commented, showing it to him and explaining why the fortune teller had given it to me, for protection from danger.

"And good luck, as well," he said, giving it back.

With a shrug, I laid it on the blanket next to me. "My luck has remained poor." I bit my lip, wincing at my unwitting choice of words and hoping he would not notice anything. Hastily, I put in, "It is my fault that Ellen died. I argued with her like a child, told her to leave me alone and go sleep upstairs when she wanted to stay in my room and guard me."

"But you did not kill her. Miss Lewis did, and that fact does not change. As for Claire herself, you know that she would've hung for Ellen's murder, so her accidental ending spared both her and her father much agony of trial, imprisonment, notoriety, execution."

I looked at him as he said that, and came to a decision. Reaching in my reticule again, I pulled out Claire's diary and opened it to a certain passage. "When you say 'her father,' as it turns out, you actually mean Edward Whitney, my husband. She even hinted at it, saying on the bridge that I should know her motive by her eyes. I had taken the comment to mean I should look into her eyes and search her soul, but I realized after reading this that the reason she always seemed so familiar to me is she shared her father's hazel eyes. They both had a similar look about them, but not so remarkable as to notice it when the relationship was neither known nor suspected."

Taking the notebook from me, he quickly read the portion where Claire wrote of a plan to become close to me so that she would inherit her rightful fortune as her father's heir.

"If only I had told her—" I stopped, terrified that I might have been indiscreet and told him the rest.

Charles did not seem to notice anything amiss. He turned away to pack the picnic hamper, and I breathed more easily. Whereas Claire's secret, that she was the illegitimate child of a man her mother had an affair with years ago, was now known to him, I could not divulge my own secret. I simply could not bear the humiliation of having Charles Weatherby find out what a sham my life had become and how many times my pride had induced me to lie to him.

He glanced up and calmly said, "You mean that if Claire knew about the debts, she would have understood no inheritance remained for her, and she would not have tried to kill you so she could get it."

My face drained. I tried to think of what to say, but I had no quick riposte this time.

"How long have you known?" I asked, trying hard not to cry.

He got up and moved around to my side of the blanket, then sat and took me in his arms. "Want to know your one mistake?"

I shook my head.

"You forgot that your godfather hired me for certain skills. I am the type of man who cannot bear to come across a mystery and leave it unsolved."

"You mean the mystery of the emeralds?"

"Mystery upon mystery, my dear. The most remarkable to me was why would a lovely young woman like you throw herself at that boorish Samuel McArthur? There had to be a reason, and so I sought to find it."

Shamed, I ducked my head and gathered my things. "I'm ready to go now. Take me back so my groom can drive me home. I will wait outside by the stables. Please... don't tell the others."

He gently tilted my chin until our eyes met. "I once told you that we are two of a kind. Remember?"

All I could do was nod, recalling how I had tossed off a sarcastic rejoinder that we were nothing alike.

"You denied it," he went on politely, "and I chose not to explain myself at that time. I knew you would not be easily convinced since you had already made up your mind about me."

"No I hadn't!" I hotly denied.

Laughing, he waited until I slowly smiled, grudgingly admitting the truth of what he'd said. "What I meant by it was this: we both are determined to accomplish what we set out to achieve, no matter the obstacles. We both are stubborn—"

"I am not!"

"And unwilling to admit defeat. We don't mind a lie or two, when it is necessary. And even if no one else is aware of our goal, we strive mightily toward its fulfillment, no matter what the personal cost. Am I right so far?"

I looked away. "You are mocking me, sir."

Gently, he said, stroking my hand, "The drawback is that we also hate to admit when we make a mistake or misjudge someone, and instead rush ahead willy-nilly until we make a total mess of things."

"Now you are kind by continuing to say 'we' when you mean 'you.' I am guilty of all you said, and I will carry the shame of it."

I could not bear to stay another moment. Quickly standing, I snatched up the gypsy talisman I had left on the blanket, shoved the picnic hamper into his lap, then looked around for the path we had taken so I could run back to the horse and make my escape.

He sensed my plan at once, knocked the hamper aside and leapt to his feet. He lunged to grab my arm as I moved off but I evaded his touch and began running, heedless of my direction, only wanting to escape him and further humiliation as he recounted all my faults, one by one.

"Loretta!" he called out behind me. "Don't run away from me again!"

I heard the unspoken threat behind his words, that if I left this time, there would be no other chance.

But just because he knew Edward had left debts did not mean he fully appreciated the extent of my ruin, and there was no point explaining it.

My heart betrayed me, however, and I could not help turning to look back at him a final time, and thus memorize his face. But suddenly, as I looked at him, my feet seemed glued to the ground and I could not move, even as he approached and then stood in front of me, taking my hands in his.

"Thank you for holding still," he said. "I have grown weary of chasing you. After we are married, I hope our little children do not entreat me to play games of hide-and-seek because I will have to beat them instead, just for reminding me of all it took to finally catch you."

"If I become your legal property," I said, "as any wife is, then you must know this property includes heavy liens against it and you may wish to reconsider the offer."

"A woman should be nobody's property but her own."

I looked him over carefully. "What say you to slavery?" I asked.

"Against."

"And women's suffrage?"

"For," he said firmly.

"Do you despise bluestockings?"

"I am pleased to know you are one."

"Do you approve of the telegraph or think it is a foolhardy idea?"

"We need the telegraph and other inventions even more thrilling!" he cried delightedly.

We smiled at each other.

But reality intruded, and I blurted out, "I cannot pay you a dowry of twenty thousand pounds."

The way he stared at me, with a gaping mouth, I realized all at once that Serena Harmon had lied to me, simply to be spiteful. Claire had overheard and had believed it, as had I.

"You don't want…" I began, then stopped when I saw that he was baffled, and shaking his head.

"And I never have…" he started to reply, only to trail off, with a gleam in his eye. "Someone has misled you, and perhaps even implied that I was a fortune hunter?"

I nodded miserably, knowing that if only I had told him the truth early on when he'd inquired about my finances, that I would have had my fears about him put to rest on the spot. Instead, I had needlessly fretted, denied us the happiness we both wanted so much, and inadvertently caused one episode of tragedy after another, like a train wreck.

"We will happily uncover and discuss all the details together," he said, "at my country estate in Sussex, or my London town house, or my apartment in Paris. Or… what say you to traveling to America? Maybe we should not wait until their war ends but go quickly, to help in the abolition movement."

"What about your mother's Shakespearean herb garden? Aren't you a clerk with a small cottage…?" I trailed off as I saw amusement fill his eyes and knew that I had leapt to far too many conclusions over the past week.

We talked about the future we would have together, the family we would raise and the causes we would support. Tears filled my eyes as I realized how much he understood me and my dreams. He gently brushed the tears away, and then he kissed me.

The gypsy talisman dropped from my fingers as I flung my arms around Charles's neck, and kissed him back, knowing in my heart that I had truly found my perfect match, and he had found me.

THE END

978-0-595-40279-3
0-595-40279-8

CPSIA information can be obtained
at www.ICGtesting.com
Printed in the USA
LVOW08s1056281216
518964LV00001B/56/P